W9-BDA-545

SECRETS AND SHAMROCKS

A JORDAN MAYFAIR MYSTERY

SECRETS AND SHAMROCKS

PHYLLIS GOBBELL

FIVE STAR
A part of Gale, Cengage Learning

 GALE
CENGAGE Learning·

Farmington Hills, Mich • San Francisco • New York • Waterville, Maine
Meriden, Conn • Mason, Ohio • Chicago

GALE
CENGAGE Learning·

LIBRARY OF CONGRESS CATALOGING-IN-PUBLICATION DATA

Names: Gobbell, Phyllis C., author.
Title: Secrets and shamrocks / Phyllis Gobbell.
Description: First edition. | Waterville, Maine : Five Star Publishing, 2016. | Series: A Jordan Mayfair mystery
Identifiers: LCCN 2016024178| ISBN 9781432832346 (hardcover) | ISBN 1432832344 (hardcover) | ISBN 9781432832391 (ebook) | ISBN 1432832395 (ebook) | ISBN 9781432834975 (ebook) | ISBN 1432834975 (ebook)
Subjects: LCSH: Women private investigators—Fiction. | Women detectives—Fiction. | BISAC: FICTION / Mystery & Detective / General. | GSAFD: Mystery fiction.
Classification: LCC PS3557.O17 S43 2016 | DDC 813/.54—dc23
LC record available at https://lccn.loc.gov/2016024178

First Edition. First Printing: November 2016
Find us on Facebook– https://www.facebook.com/FiveStarCengage
Visit our website– http://www.gale.cengage.com/fivestar/
Contact Five Star™ Publishing at FiveStar@cengage.com

Printed in the United States of America
1 2 3 4 5 6 7 20 19 18 17 16

SECRETS AND SHAMROCKS

CHAPTER 1

Green, green, everywhere, green. Meadows, hedgerows, tree-lined lanes. Every shade of green in the artist's imagination. I had left the M8 to drive on narrow, winding roads, edged in rock walls, that took us through one pastoral vista after another. My uncle Alex, who had arranged the trip, would be so sorry he'd dozed off some distance out of Dublin, but I had a feeling we'd be seeing more of these *green* picture-postcard scenes during our two weeks in the Emerald Isle. On the flight over, Alex had read to me from one of Colin's e-mails, and I could almost hear the lilt of his words: "Ireland is the most beautiful place in the world. You'll be over the moon when you see it!" I believed it already.

I steered our rental car down a hill and around a curve, still getting used to driving on the wrong side of the road, and suddenly we were right upon a flock of sheep. I hit the brakes and shrieked as the car lurched to a stop a few yards from the bleating animals. The herder, trudging along in boots and carrying a staff, made no effort to move the sheep out of the road. He didn't even glance toward us or gesture *Sorry—please wait for my wooly creatures to cross.* His shoulders drooped. His shaggy hair was the color of the sheep's coats. I wondered how many years he'd been herding sheep in the green pastures along these roads.

Alex woke with a jolt, mumbling, "What? What is it?"

"Sheep in our path," I said. "Can you get a photo?"

Alex rubbed his eyes, took in the sight, and began to rummage in the red duffle at his feet. He came out with his camera and started clicking, making noises of approval: "Ah, yes. Good one. Look at that frisky lamb!" As the last of the flock crossed the road, the sheepherder raised his hand and inclined his head toward us, and I could almost swear he winked, as if he and his sheep had arranged this photo op just for us.

Back on the motorway, we left the emerald countryside behind. A few kilometers more, signs that we were coming into a town began to crop up—houses built close together, tall, narrow buildings with storefronts. We were on the outskirts of Thurles (pronounced "Tur-lis"), where our friends Colin and Grace O'Toole ran a bed and breakfast. Alex checked our map and directed me to turn before we reached the town proper. I hadn't set the GPS. Alex preferred a good map to fold and unfold, and he was an excellent navigator.

"Colin said the B&B was a short walk from the town square," he said.

"We'll be there in time for tea," I said, but I wondered about that *short* walk. It looked as if we were heading back into the country, the dwellings more sparse now.

Alex straightened himself and ran his hand through his gray hair, still thick for a man about to turn seventy-three. "It will be so good to see Colin and Grace," he said, adding, "after all these years."

I darted a glance at my uncle, who was so rarely sentimental. "Colin was a fine student, a good friend," he mused. "And Grace—delightful girl."

I was about to mention Patrick, born while Colin and Grace were in Georgia, now a married man, Alex had said, but the rustic sign with Old English script caught my eye. "Is this it?" I read, "Shepherds Guesthouse Bed and Breakfast." I thought of the sheep back there.

Alex confirmed that this was the place. I maneuvered the car through the opening in the rock wall that ran along the property, glad yet again that we'd chosen the little Ford Focus instead of the full-size Saab we had considered. What was originally a country house—dating to the 1800s would be my guess—was set back on a patch of lawn as lush as a golf green. Green, green, everything green, except for a few bursts of pink blossoms on the shrubs near the house. We followed a gravel driveway to a parking area and pulled in next to another car that looked to be a rental. Some tiles were missing from the high-pitched roof, near a chimney, I noted on our approach. Close-up, I saw that the high-level window moldings could use fresh paint.

"What do you see?" Alex said as I stared up, and I felt a stab of shame that the need for repair was the first thing to grab my attention. I was wired to notice details like that. I could see Drew, my brother and business partner, shaking his head, saying, "Only an architect."

"Nothing," I said. "Let's go in." I needn't have added that we could come back for our luggage. Alex was already on his way.

A few stepping-stones led us to the entrance. The heavy wooden door was wide open, and the modern storm door was unlocked. It seemed we were supposed to go in, and we did. The room was furnished with dark furniture upholstered in faded red brocade. A Reception desk, like one you'd see in a hotel, had been added in the corner. Behind it, a door, leading to—an office? The wood was dark, a good match with the furniture, but the straight lines were a little too contemporary for the room that came off as an old-fashioned parlor. *Only an architect.*

"Hello?" I called. No answer. "I guess we should announce ourselves," I suggested, looking for a bell to tap, but there wasn't one.

Alex, still standing at the door, turned his attention to something outside. "That's odd," he said. "There seems to be something going on, maybe something wrong out there."

I joined him and peered at two women and a man, conferring at the far end of the parking lot, pointing this way and that. Even as Alex cracked the storm door to listen, we couldn't make out what they were saying, but the tenor of their voices and their excited gestures indicated, as he had said, that something was wrong.

"Good afternoon. May I help you?" someone said.

I turned with a smile, expecting Grace, but I should have known better. This tall, slender woman's accent was King's English. Grace was born and raised in Atlanta. I remembered her honey-sweet drawl, not an easy thing to lose, even after all this time. Plus Grace was a smallish woman, maybe five-foot-two, and this woman was at least my height, which was five-ten.

"We're friends of Colin and Grace. We're checking in," Alex said.

"I'm afraid Colin and Grace had to leave." The woman stood straight as a wooden beam, a model of good posture, with her hands clasped. "It's rather an emergency. I'm a guest here myself. I can't check you in, of course, but I can offer you tea."

"What's the emergency?" I asked.

"It's the child," she said. "The little boy is missing."

Thirty years ago, Colin O'Toole from Dublin had been a student at the University of Georgia, where Alex taught history. I could say this for Alex: he had a way with his students. He connected with them, befriended them, forged relationships with them that often continued long after they graduated. I knew it for a fact. Stuart, my husband, who did not live to see our five children grow up, once had been Alex's student for a single semester, and they'd hit it off. Later, when Stuart was a med student at Emory, Alex invited him to his home in Buckhead—the Carlyle family home—for a Christmas party. I was invited to that party, too. Alex was not beyond playing Cupid if the occasion called for it.

Stuart had left UGA before I arrived as a freshman, but Colin and I were there at the same time, and we knew each other through Alex. Time and again he took Colin and me out for pizza or burgers or meat and three, Alex's least favorite, but there was a nearby diner-type eatery that Colin especially liked. Sometimes other students joined us, a study group from Alex's undergraduate class or one of his dissertation students. And there were those wonderful little dinner parties for his colleagues at his comfy faculty apartment. Even as a self-absorbed architecture student, I realized how fortunate I was that Alex was my uncle. There I was, accustomed to living on Ramen noodles, and Alex would call. A few nights later I'd be dining with a select few of Alex's faculty friends, enjoying tenderloin medallions, asparagus, and crème brulee, and drinking excellent wine. Good times.

I remember Colin at a couple of those dinner parties, but he was usually at work. He bartended at an establishment just off campus with the likely name, The Irish Pub. With his pixie face and red hair so wild that the thought of a leprechaun always skittered through my mind when I saw him, Colin was the only thing *Irish* about the place, other than the name. But it was a fun spot. Sometimes my friends and I wound up at the pub after a late night in the architecture studio, and Colin was always there, working long hours, laughing, charming the ladies with his accent, which he could exaggerate or downplay at will.

Colin never had the money to return to Dublin for the holidays or breaks, so he often stayed in Alex's apartment while Alex went home to Buckhead. To say Alex was generous was an understatement. After Colin met Grace, an Atlanta debutante, she and I became fast friends, too. More good times. Then I graduated. For Colin and Grace, there was a hurry-up wedding and a baby on the way, and the next thing I knew, they had left with their baby son for Ireland.

Alex and his former student had stayed in contact for a while. "Christmas greetings mostly," Alex had told me, "but you know how it is. After a while, one or the other misses his turn. A couple of Christmases pass, and there you go." I would bet it wasn't Alex who had missed his turn. "Imagine my surprise a year or so ago when I received an e-mail from Colin," Alex had said. "Somehow he'd found out about my travel series. I think there was an announcement about the book deal on the *Publisher's Weekly* website. Isn't technology a wonderful thing?" Time came to make arrangements for this trip to Ireland. Alex was working on his second travel guide. The purpose of his books was to steer tourists away from the touristy spots, to tell them how to experience the authentic culture of a region. No wonder he'd made our reservations at the Shepherds Guesthouse Bed and Breakfast.

When Alex was writing his first travel guide, he had hoodwinked me into accompanying him to Provence, making me believe there was some issue with his health and his doctor insisted that he travel with a companion. This time, I was genuinely worried about my uncle's health. When he'd announced that his second book would be taking him to Ireland, I made my position clear: "I'm not about to let you travel alone."

"A child, missing?" I heard in my voice every mother's great fear.

"Apparently so," said the woman, pushing back a strand of bottle-blonde hair that had slipped from behind her ear. "Little Jimmie. He must be about two years old."

"*Two!*" I whispered. A flash of memory, Michael as a toddler, disappearing from the backyard for the longest, most horrifying fifteen minutes of my life.

"Whose child?" Alex asked.

"Colin and Grace's grandchild," the woman said, taking a step away from us. "Please, let me make you a spot of tea. We can talk in the kitchen." Alex and I followed her through what looked like a breakfast room. Like lambs, I thought, because we didn't know what else to do.

"Please make yourselves comfortable." She gestured to the square table with high-backed chairs in the center of the kitchen. "Forgive me for not introducing myself. I'm Helen Prescott," she said as she began to fill a tea kettle with water. "My husband and I are on holiday. We live in London. You may have heard of Charles Prescott. He played on the Tour."

"The Tour?" I said.

"The European Tour. Do you follow golf?"

"I'm afraid not." I glanced at Alex. He looked so distracted, I wasn't sure he'd heard her.

Helen gave a wave of dismissal. "Yes, well, he retired from the Tour some years ago."

"I'm Jordan Mayfair," I said, "and this is my uncle, Alex Carlyle. We're from Georgia."

The kitchen smelled like a bakery, the aromas that seep into the walls in a kitchen where bread, cakes, and pastries are baked day after day, year after year.

"How long has the child been missing?" Alex asked in that tone I recognized as professorial, down to business, no more small talk.

"Half an hour, perhaps?" Helen was assembling cups and saucers, crème pitcher, and sugar bowl on a tray to transport half a dozen steps to the table. Leave it to the English.

"That's a long time for a two-year-old to be missing," I said.

"The authorities have been notified, no doubt," Alex said,

more question than statement.

"I would think so." Helen seemed to be trying to decide how much to say. A quick glance our way, and she said, "Actually, it's all somewhat strange."

I waited for more, but she continued to busy herself with preparations for tea.

"We should *do* something," I said after a minute.

"Quite right, but what?" Helen finally turned toward us and leaned against the counter while the water was heating. "I heard the disturbance and came running downstairs. Enya and Grace sounded so—upset. They *flew* out the back door. Enya rang up someone, Patrick, I suppose—the girl is never without her phone!—and Grace came back inside looking—I have to say, not as *worried* as one would expect, but *bothered*. That's the word, I think. I asked her what had happened. Because I knew it was something more than a family row, though—well, never mind that. Something was wrong, clearly." The tea kettle began to whistle. Helen paused in her story to pour boiling water into a decorative teapot, over the tea leaves she had measured.

"Who's Enya?" I asked.

"Enya is Patrick's wife. I get the impression that she's quite unhappy here."

So the child must belong to Patrick and Enya, I reasoned, wondering why Helen hadn't just said so instead of saying he was Colin and Grace's grandchild.

"Grace told me Little Jimmie had disappeared while Enya was supposed to be watching him and asked if I would look after things while they went out, and I said certainly I could do that, and that's really all I know." She opened one of the cabinets. "Ah, here're the biscuits."

I hadn't expected tea time to be exactly like this. A child was missing, a toddler, and here we sat, sipping tea and munching on the best shortbread cookies—biscuits—I'd ever tasted.

Maybe Helen was trying to distract us from worrying. According to her, she was taking charge at Grace's request. I wondered if Grace would be pleased that she was so gossipy about the other guests at the B&B.

Ian Haverty, Helen said, was a charming young schoolmaster from Dublin, with black curls and "dreamy" eyes. Two ladies had arrived just that morning, one of them "rather *loud* in her pronouncements." The man Helen knew only as Mr. Sweeney was unfriendly, aloof, "*rude,* actually," she said, "except to Enya. He was trying to chat her up this morning when she was putting out the sausages. But Enya is rather standoffish herself, and Mr. Sweeney is old enough to be her father! I could tell the girl was embarrassed that this man, who hasn't spoken a complete sentence to anyone else, was so eager to have a conversation with her."

On and on Helen continued until her voice became like the sound of a TV blaring in another room, something I was aware of, but mostly tuning out.

Alex interrupted her monologue. "I expect Colin is out looking for the child, too?"

"Colin?" Helen blinked, as if she'd lost her bearings for a minute. "He wasn't here when it happened. I believe he'd gone into town, but they may have been able to reach him."

"I should get our luggage," Alex said, rising from his chair.

"I'll go with you." I stood up, too.

"You can't check into your rooms yet, not until Colin and Grace come back, or Patrick," Helen said. "I'm sorry I can't give you your keys. I'm just—you know—helping out in a pinch."

"We appreciate your hospitality, Helen. Really we do," I said. "And probably there's nothing we can do to help find the child, but—it feels *wrong* to be enjoying tea and biscuits when a toddler has been missing for—it's been close to an hour now, hasn't it?"

Helen stood, and we were eye to eye. "Jordan, please don't think I'm—*unconcerned*. I *am* concerned, but Grace seemed— well, she didn't act as if she thought Little Jimmie was actually in danger."

"How could he not be in danger?" I said.

She waited a moment before saying, "It happened before, just like this."

Alex had already left the kitchen. Noises were coming from the front of the house. Voices. The storm door banging once, twice, needing a new spring, I noted.

I caught sight of a little red-headed boy in his grandmother's arms. Yes, it had to be Grace carrying Little Jimmie, though they were headed up the stairs, out of my view after just a glimpse. I breathed a silent thank you. Behind them was Enya, no doubt, a dark-haired beauty, her full mouth set in a rigid line, followed by a young man so resembling young Colin O'Toole that I knew it had to be Patrick. The man and two women we'd seen at the end of the parking lot made the storm door bang again and again. I suspected the handsome young fellow was Ian Haverty, judging from Helen's report.

And then a cheery, boisterous "Alexander Carlyle! Sure 'tis my old friend or a ghost of himself!"

I didn't hear Alex say a word, but I heard his hearty laughter, blending with Colin's.

I waited to join the reunion until the bear hugs and back-slapping were over.

Colin squeezed me, too, until I gasped for breath. "Ah, you've not lost your beauty, girl," he said, touching my hair, a darker auburn than his fiery red.

"Colin, what a scare! Is the little boy all right? Where did you find him?" I asked.

"He's a wee bit frightened, but no harm done. Ah, Jordan, Alex, how good it is to have you in our home. Grace will be down as soon as she gets the boy settled."

"We should get our luggage from the car," Alex said.

"Sweet Mother! You don't have your room keys, do you? What a fine welcome for our friends! Would you like to go to your rooms first or maybe you'd like a nice cup of tea?"

"We had tea and cookies—*biscuits*. Helen took good care of us," I said, looking around for Helen, but she must have been in the kitchen, cleaning up our dishes.

"Let's go get your bags then," Colin said, heading to the door. He shook his head and said in a sing-song of apology. "All this commotion, Sweet Mother of God."

"All that matters is that you found Little Jimmie and he's all right," I said.

"Right you are, Jordan. That's what matters," and then with a smile that made his blue eyes light up, he said, "Little Jimmie is safe and sound. All is well."

CHAPTER 2

The only meal Shepherds Guesthouse provided was breakfast, and Alex had made Colin promise they would treat us like the paying guests that we were. Even so, I was not surprised that Colin went back on his promise first thing, pleading with us to join them for the evening meal.

Grace had come downstairs looking flustered, but seeing Alex and me, she'd managed to put on a happier face. Time melted away as we embraced. I knew we'd take up where we left off, all those years ago. Grace insisted, "I'll be cooking for our family. Setting two more places won't make any difference." But Alex stood firm, and Colin finally gave in. He called a friend of his who was the proprietor of Mitchel House to reserve a table for us.

"It won't be crowded on a Wednesday night," he said, "but they'll make no mistake about who you are." He added with a wink, "Now you'll be wanting to stop by Finnegan's Pub on your way home."

Though the sun had made for a pleasant day, the evening had turned chilly and the night promised to be downright cold. That, we'd heard, was typical May in Ireland. "We could walk. It would be good for us," Alex said when we'd left Colin and headed up to our rooms to get ready for dinner. Probably, but I convinced him to wait until we could make that *short* walk—if, indeed, it was short—in the warmth of the sun.

Alex was waiting when I came downstairs, and he'd made

friends with the two women we'd seen earlier that day. "Doreen and Molly Quinn. They're going into town, too," he said.

The one he'd indicated as Doreen took over. "Your uncle offered us a ride. I hope you don't mind. Molly and I fancy the buffet at the Hayes Hotel. It's a wee bit out of your way."

"Not at all," I said. It was the first time I'd seen them close-up. They were both petite and fair-skinned, with reddish-gold hair that they wore in a similar style—a kind of page-boy look that flattered Doreen more than Molly—but the age difference was now apparent. As it registered with me that they must be mother and daughter, Doreen said to Molly, "How's your headache, love? Feeling better?" The young woman might have replied, but I was preoccupied finding the car keys. Doreen said, "Molly plays the violin. She'll be performing with her ensemble at The Source this weekend. You know The Source Arts Centre?"

"I read something about it. Sounds like I need to check it out for my book," Alex began. Chivalrous as always, he opened the passenger door and gestured for Doreen to sit in the front. He must have expected that she'd ask questions as people were apt to do when he revealed that he was writing a book—but it was as if she hadn't heard.

"I'll just sit in the back with Molly," she said. "We don't mean to trouble you."

"It's no trouble," I said. "You can give directions. We haven't been into town yet."

Molly had not said a word. I caught a glimpse of her as I adjusted my mirror. She was looking down at her hands, folded in her lap. I thought of my own Catherine, nineteen. Probably Molly was a little older, or maybe the pants and tailored jacket she wore, much like her mother's outfit, made her seem older. But her shyness made it hard to tell her age. I could not imagine my daughter remaining silent for more than a minute in a similar setting.

Doreen was an effective navigator. She pointed out The Source Arts Centre and when we crossed an old bridge, she identified the River Suir. The Hayes Hotel was right in the middle of what appeared to be a lively town center. When we let Doreen and Molly out in front of the hotel, Doreen gave further directions to Mitchel House. She thanked us, and then, from behind me, I heard a timid, "Thank you."

I turned to Molly. "I want to hear more about your performance when we get a chance to talk. Maybe at breakfast."

I was rewarded with a smile and a nod.

At the Mitchel House restaurant, I sipped from my wine glass, nearly empty. "I'm beginning to relax for the first time since we arrived in Thurles," I said.

"Seems we arrived at a bad time," Alex said. "But, as they say, all's well that ends well."

I was reminded of Colin's words: *"All is well."* I didn't believe it. Something seemed *off.* The whole episode surrounding Little Jimmie's disappearance left me wondering about so many things. I was anxious for the time we could have a real conversation with Colin and Grace.

"Alex, did Colin ever tell you Patrick had a little boy?"

I shifted in my seat, a high-backed booth, as I saw our waiter approaching with a tray. I might have had a big smile plastered on my face. Since our late breakfast in Dublin, shortbread cookies, delicious though they were, had been our only food all day.

"Colin never mentioned the child, but our e-mails were not what you could call chatty," Alex said. "I remember when he first told me Patrick and his wife had come from Dublin to help out, and Patrick had been hired at Tipperary Institute. He does something with computers."

The waiter delivered our first course—roasted field mushrooms with sweet red peppers and red onion marmalade, topped with gorgonzola cheese. I was glad to see the generous portion. Alex and I had opted to share the starter. We'd both ordered shank of lamb for our entrees, the waiter's recommendation. He'd said, " 'Tis our most popular item."

"Do y'need anything else?" he asked. We thanked him, but no, we needed nothing but to take up our forks.

Typical of Alex's compulsion to keep accurate notes, he retrieved from the inside pocket of his jacket the small notebook he carried everywhere. "What do you think of Mitchel House?" he asked.

"It's more contemporary than I expected." I noted the modern décor, simple lines, lack of clutter. Upscale, but not pricey. Families with children appeared to be welcome.

"It's the twenty-first century *everywhere,* my dear," Alex said.

I raised my eyebrows. I would have imagined that Alex was hoping for a more traditional *Irish* eatery, but he often surprised me.

From all indications, he would give Mitchel House high marks. So would I. I'd never cared too much for lamb, but this dish was extraordinary, and I wouldn't have imagined creamed potatoes could be so tasty.

Alex ordered dessert, a kind of fruit tart that had to be healthy because it was *fruit,* he insisted. I was pleasantly full, so I settled for a cup of tea.

"How about a stop at the pub Colin suggested? Finnegan's. I saw it, near the Hayes Hotel," Alex said. I agreed. The scrumptious meal had given me a second wind.

The waiter came with the check. Alex and I reached for our credit cards and asked him to split. That's how we always did it. When the young man returned for our signatures, he said, "I hope the O'Tooles are well."

"Yes, I think so," I said, on a note of surprise that he knew who we were.

"We just arrived today," Alex said.

"They're good people," the young man said. "I used to do odd jobs for Colin at Shepherds. I refinished a crib and a rocking chair when the little one was born. I like to work with wood. But that was before Patrick and Enya came down from Dublin."

"Oh." The word slipped out. I tried to cover up. "We haven't really met Patrick and Enya yet. We arrived so late this afternoon. And we've barely seen Colin and Grace."

Something in my voice must have alerted the waiter. He picked up his copy of the receipts, gave a wide smile, and said, "Tell them hello from Davin Callahan, and you come back now. I hope you enjoy your stay in Thurles."

We thanked him and said goodnight, but we sat there a minute longer.

"What did you make of that?" I said.

"Maybe Colin and Grace were getting ready for Patrick and Enya and the baby to move in." Alex drained the last drop of wine from his glass. "But that wasn't how it sounded, was it?"

"No, it wasn't," I said. "Let's go to the pub."

The pleasure that spread across Alex's face when we entered Finnegan's Pub made me smile, too. *This* was what I—and Alex, apparently—had expected of an authentic Irish pub.

The bar was tended by an old fellow who laughed as he poured drinks, his eyes twinkling in slits above his pink cheeks. A couple of craggy-faced men at the bar, dressed in working clothes, their gray hair tousled, sat hunched over their substantial glasses of beer, looking like they'd been there a while and didn't plan to leave anytime soon. A few younger patrons sat at the bar, smiling at the jolly bartender who may have been telling a story as he worked. I took in the scene—small tables, upholstered banquette seating, wainscoting on the walls, sconces giving out gentle light, fireplace not in use in May, but what a treat it would be on a snowy night. A mix of age groups, no one dressed up, as in "going out." A table of student types wore jeans. The cozy room, long and narrow, was reasonably full but not packed. The noise level was low, a blend of quiet conversation and laughter.

"Shall we grab those?" Alex said, indicating two barstools. There appeared to be no empty tables. The bartender took note of us and by the time we were settled at the dark polished bar, he was welcoming us to Thurles.

"Colin O'Toole told me to be looking for you."

I wondered how Colin had described us.

"Now you must have a Guinness. First is on me. I'm Finn. This is my pub—me and my boy's. Brendan still lets me behind the bar some nights if I promise to behave meself."

His laugh was deep and musical. Some chuckling came from others at the bar. The matter settled that we were having beer, Finn went about his business before we could say anything except to thank him. He bantered with someone a few barstools away, mixed a drink for someone else, and then returned with glasses of dark beer.

A man and woman entered the bar. The woman, whose only outer garment was a sweater, was shaking off the chill. I said to Alex, "Maybe we should have made arrangements to meet Doreen and Molly and give them a lift back to Shepherds."

"Doreen won't mind asking for a ride if someone's going that way," Alex said. "I wouldn't worry. I expect they're used to walking—it's what people *do* here."

"They're not wearing very warm clothing." I thought of their lightweight tailored jackets.

"Jordan, it's May, not January," Alex said.

The road out that way was dark, no moon tonight. How safe could that be? But my frame of reference was dark country roads in Georgia. I let it drop with Alex.

"Look. I think that's one of the guests at the B&B," he said.

The nice-looking young man we'd seen that afternoon was motioning for us to come to his table. We picked up our drinks and joined him.

He introduced himself as Ian Haverty. "We haven't met, but I'm a guest at Shepherds. I know you arrived today," he said with an outstretched hand. "And this is Dr. Malone, a physician here in Thurles." Alex and I introduced ourselves and we shook hands all around.

Dr. Malone, dressed in collared shirt and tweed jacket, looked to be forty-something, somewhat younger than myself, I'd judge. His close-cropped hair suggested it might have been brighter at one time, but as he had aged, it had lost its sheen. Still, he was a redhead, as were so many of the Irish, though the shades varied.

"I'm just leaving," he said, "but it's a pleasure to make your acquaintance. Welcome to our little town."

"We'll be in Thurles for more than a week. Maybe we'll see you again," Alex said.

I added, "Though not professionally, I hope."

The men laughed. "Give my best to the O'Tooles," Dr. Malone said, and he bid us goodnight. Ian, Alex, and I fit into the banquette seating without having to squeeze, as the doctor and Ian had taken up more than their share of space.

"Everyone knows Colin and Grace," Alex remarked.

"It does seem that way," said Ian. "I've been in Thurles since Friday, and everywhere I've been, people know the O'Tooles and they seem to know I'm a guest at Shepherds."

Alex explained that he was from Atlanta, Georgia, and I was his niece from Savannah, that he was working on a book, and Colin had once been his student.

"What a coincidence! I'm working on a book myself," Ian said.

"You don't say! What are you writing?" Alex asked. I had to hand it to him. I knew he wanted to talk about *his* book, but I expected he'd get his opportunity.

"A book of Irish tales," Ian said.

I raised my glass. "To men of letters."

Alex gave me an appreciative smile, and Ian, who couldn't have been older than my oldest daughter, added, "And to the lovely American woman who, from the looks of her beautiful hair, must have a few drops of Irish blood somewhere in her veins."

I nodded. "My great-grandmother on my father's side." We clinked our glasses.

I sipped at my Guinness as Ian and Alex finished theirs and ordered another round. "Jordan's the designated driver," Alex explained to Ian, and I didn't have to say that beer wasn't my drink, not even a Guinness, so highly regarded in the Emerald Isle.

"Now, you were saying about your book," Ian said, starting in on the refill. Not just a young man with black curls and "dreamy eyes," as Helen had put it, but one with good manners as well, willing to let a much older man go first. I took the opportunity to visit the restroom. I had heard Alex's spiel once or twice.

"Just in time," Alex said when I returned. "Ian was just about to tell me about the book of Irish stories he's writing."

"Let me back up a wee bit," Ian said. "As I told your uncle, I'm a schoolmaster at The Kerrigan School for Boys. I teach English Lit 9. Try to get the boys interested in Joyce and Yeats and Heaney, the great Irish writers—but you know what boys at that age, thirteen or fourteen, have on their minds." He took a drink and licked the foam from his lips. "From time to time I try to come up with a new approach. A couple of years ago I had them do a research project on Irish tales. Some of the boys took to it all right. It wasn't the success I'd hoped for the class. But the fascinating thing that happened was the wealth of stories *I* discovered. So I began to write, and I guess you could say it got in my blood. I've got a dozen stories so far."

Alex asked, "Do you have a publisher?"

Ian gave a shrug. "One publisher I've contacted likes the idea but he says I need twice that number of stories for a collection. They're none of them lengthy. So that's why I'm in Thurles, hoping to gather more legends and tales. My family's from Tipperary, and all the stories I have so far take place in this county."

"What's your title?" I asked.

"Tales My Grandda Told," he said, his eyes alight with pride. "Some did come from Grandda. I won't swear all of them did."

"I'm impressed, Ian," I said.

"Have you come up with any new stories since you arrived in Thurles?" Alex asked.

Ian laughed. "Finn has stories to fill a book, himself, though I'm not certain he doesn't spin them out of thin air on the spot."

"And you'd want authenticity?" Alex was sounding like a professor, but if Ian minded all the questions, he didn't show it.

"It's not that, exactly. Leprechauns might be part of the legend—often they are, and who's to say, y'know? But I'm not writing fairy tales."

The conversations around us that had hummed like soft music in the background seemed louder. Ian leaned in toward us. "The *history's* the thing that I'm passionate about. One of the legends—if you care to hear—goes back to the 1650s."

"Certainly we care to hear!" I said. Alex nodded his agreement.

"I'm not sure how much you know about Irish history, but that was the year Oliver Cromwell's forces invaded Ireland."

"I know a little about Cromwell," Alex said. I had to suppress a smile, thinking about Alex's professional career of more than forty years, teaching history at the university level.

"It was a brutal period in our country's history. Catholics were forbidden to practice our religion in public. If priests were discovered conducting mass, they could be expelled from the country or executed." As Ian found his storyteller's voice, his words became more lyrical. "There was a man, a devout Catholic, who lived on a remote farm with his daughter. He had a spotted cow and a white one, and his neighbors knew that if only the white cow was grazing in the morning and the spotted cow was in the barn, the priest would be coming at noon to conduct secret mass."

His attention shifted as a voice sounded: "Ah, will you look who's here, Molly!"

Doreen, *loud* in her pronouncement, as Helen had said, stood beside Molly at our table. Ian stood and met them with a hearty greeting, somewhat more enthusiastic than the occasion seemed to warrant, but it made sense when I saw the shine in Molly's eyes. Looked like her headache was much better. Looked like Ian was finished with his story for now.

Alex gave up his seat, darting a glance at me that I'd learned to read as *Ready to go?*

"We thought we'd have ourselves a drink before the walk home," Doreen said.

"You'd be welcome to ride with us," I said, standing, "but we're going on now."

Doreen gave a gesture of dismissal. "Thanks all the same. We'll be fine."

"I'll see that the ladies get home safe and sound," Ian said, sliding into the seat beside Molly.

We gave Finn a wave on our way out, and he called back,

"Come again!" We said we would.

"Delightful!" Alex said as we stepped into the chilly night.

CHAPTER 3

The morning was gray, with a fine mist in the air that looked cold. Not a pleasant day for sightseeing. I wondered what Alex had in mind for our itinerary.

Molly was standing at the sideboard, stirring her tea, when I went down to breakfast—early, because I was hoping for this very opportunity, a chance to talk with her without Doreen's overbearing presence. She greeted me with a bright "Good morning!" A different young woman from the one we'd dropped off at the Hayes Hotel last night, but not so different from the one at Finnegan's, smiling at Ian Haverty. "Would you like tea?" she asked, the longest string of words I'd heard her speak.

"Ah, this is what I need." I indicated the large coffee urn beside the samovar. "I do like tea, but I just have to have my coffee first thing in the morning," I said, picking up a mug.

From the breakfast room, I could see Grace, Enya, and the baby in the kitchen. Little Jimmie sat in a high chair, focusing on his finger foods and sippie cup. Grace stood over the stove. Enya was loading up a rolling cart with platters.

Molly sat at one of the three four-top tables in the small breakfast room, and I joined her. "I was hoping to see you this morning," I said. "I want to hear about your performance. You must be excited."

"Are you coming to see us?" she asked with child-like eagerness.

"I'd love to," I said. "How can I get tickets?"

"I can get tickets for you and your uncle," she said.

"Please do. I know Alex would want to go, too. It's this weekend?"

"Friday night, Saturday night, and Sunday matinee," she said. "We have two other performances Monday and Tuesday for schoolchildren, but I'm sure you'd be welcome to come to one of those."

I thought I should check with Alex, but I said, "Saturday."

Enya appeared with the rolling cart. We hadn't been introduced, so I said, "I'm Jordan Mayfair. My uncle and I knew Colin and Grace a long time ago in Georgia."

She nodded. "I've heard about you," and proceeded to unload the trays.

The aromas made my stomach growl: bacon, eggs—the food smelled like breakfast everywhere, but I didn't recognize a couple of the dishes she lined up on the buffet.

"You're Enya," I said.

"I am," she said. I heard a crash and a couple of thumps from the kitchen and Grace's voice, gently scolding. Little Jimmie had dropped his sippie cup on the floor. Enya pushed back a strand of her dark hair and sighed, as if her task was overwhelming. "I'll bring more soda bread, but this will get you started," she said, and rolled her empty cart back into the kitchen.

How could I be so hungry after last night's meal? But I was.

Molly identified the dishes I didn't know. Blood pudding, a type of sausage made with congealed pig's blood and oatmeal. Mushrooms and tomatoes fried with bacon and butter. I recognized baked beans but had never had baked beans for breakfast. I tried a little bit of everything, even a few bites of the blood pudding. Not bad.

Molly and I had about ten minutes before the other guests came to breakfast. I learned that she was about to graduate from the UCD School of Music—University College of Dublin. She'd started playing the violin at age five. Her father taught music and played "every instrument you might think of," Molly said, "or so they tell me. I don't remember much about him."

I thought of Stuart and the car wreck on a rainy night that took his life. I had tried to keep his memory alive for the children with photographs and stories—but it didn't seem appropriate to bring up our family history at the moment. Nor did I feel I should ask more about Molly's father. I said, "You must be incredibly talented to play in an ensemble for the college."

A shy smile made its way across her face. "It's my third year with the ensemble."

"What are you going to do when you graduate?" I asked.

She gave a little shrug. "I'd like to teach music to children, but I don't know."

Her vague answer left me wondering if she really hadn't made plans—surely she'd taken the required music education courses—or if she was waiting on some particular development that she wasn't ready to talk about. Maybe it just wasn't my business. Another topic I'd let go.

We heard voices, and Molly's demeanor changed. She cut off a bite of sausage—blood pudding—and looked down at her plate as she chewed. Helen Prescott arrived with a younger-looking man whom she introduced as her husband, Charles. He had an annoying habit of jerking his head to get his hair out of his eyes. She'd said he was a golfer. I wondered how he managed his hair when he was making a shot on the golf course. They stood at our table for a minute, Helen doing most of the talking, until Charles said, with wry humor, "You need to let these ladies get on with their breakfast, Helen," and excused himself, making a little bow.

"I suppose we should fill our plates as well," Helen said.

Molly, who had looked up only once when Helen was making introductions, now turned her gaze to the doorway as Ian Haverty entered. He smiled our way—mostly Molly's way—and said, "Good morning," but went straight to the buffet. Molly kept darting nervous glances his way as he filled his plate. Oh, if she only knew how transparent she was. I could almost hear her school-girl heart beating, *"Sit here, sit here, sit here."*

But the next person to come to breakfast was Doreen, and she came straight to our table, marking her spot with a brochure. "I thought we'd go to Kilkenny today," she said. "You'll be having rehearsal tomorrow, won't you, love?"

Molly's nod was almost imperceptible. Doreen continued with her cheery chatter. "Where's your uncle this morning?" she asked me.

"Sleeping in, maybe," I said. "Or sometimes he gets up early to work on his book."

"A good morning for sleeping," she said, eyeing the square window. What had been a mist, I'd now call drizzle. "But you know what they say. The only thing predictable about the weather in Ireland is that it's unpredictable. By noon, the sun could be shining bright."

Helen Prescott, who was setting her plate at the table next to us, chimed in. "I do hope the sun comes out. Charles gets very grumpy when he doesn't get to play golf."

Charles and Ian chuckled as they joined Helen at the table. Molly's disappointment was hard to miss. Her shoulders drooped. She looked down at her plate, toying with the eggs.

Grace brought more bread. "How do you like our Irish breakfast?" she asked me.

I said I'd have to watch myself or I wouldn't fit into my clothes by the end of the trip.

In the kitchen, Enya removed the baby from his high chair and disappeared.

"Could I help you clean up the kitchen?" I asked Grace.

"Certainly not! But let's have tea later and talk." She touched my shoulder.

I caught snatches of conversation from the other table, Charles saying that he finished thirteenth in the Open in 2006, that he used to party with Lucas Riordan, and Helen adding that the Riordans were a *very* important family in Thurles.

Alex finally arrived. "I confess, I overslept!" he said.

"No need to confess. It's not a sin," Doreen said.

And then came the man who had to be Mr. Sweeney, I judged from what Helen had said on the previous afternoon. Thin hair slicked across his head. Sagging jowls. Distracted expression. He headed for the food, not bothering to glance our way. Our table was full, but he could have joined the Prescotts and Ian. Instead, he took a seat at the empty table, without a word or gesture of greeting. He wolfed down his breakfast and was the first to leave the room.

When everyone had cleared out except Alex and me, Grace did allow me to help her take away the last of the dishes. Alex followed us into the kitchen. "Where's Colin?" he asked.

"The bank, or maybe the *big house*," Grace said, making quotation marks in the air around *big house*. "He's been trying to see Mr. Riordan for a month now, but they say he's not well. I don't know if it's true. He hasn't been to the bank. Colin wants to talk to *him*, not Lucas."

The three of us sat around the small table where Helen had served tea the day before. Grace had made herself a cup of tea. Alex and I had our coffee.

"Riordan," I repeated. "I heard the Prescotts say that name at breakfast."

"The Riordans are a prominent family in the community. Liam Riordan, the old man, is not only rich, but he's generous. He's done a lot for the town, for the whole county. He helped

33

Colin and me get our loan seven years ago, to buy this place. He's a good man. The son, Lucas—let's just say he's nothing like his father." Grace sipped her tea, and her tone was lighter as she said, "We have so much catching up to do. I know you've retired from the university, Alex."

"Oh my goodness, yes," he said. "More than a decade ago."

"And you decided to become a world traveler," Grace said.

"Alex was *always* a world traveler," I said, remembering the tales about his adventures in his younger days. Berlin before the wall came down. Iran when the Shah was in power.

"I started writing for travel magazines after I retired, short pieces often with a food focus, and one thing led to another. Suddenly, I had a deal for a series of book-length travel guides." He told about the first book, a guide to Provence, due to come out in the summer. "I try to get away from big hotels and 'touristy' spots, to play up the more intimate venues."

"I hope you'll be kind to Shepherds," Grace said with that beguiling smile I remembered from so long ago, when Colin was first smitten. Her hair that used to be the color of cornsilk was a darker blonde, but she still wore it shoulder-length. She was still a pretty woman.

"You can count on it, my dear," Alex said.

Grace asked about my family, and I tried to make it as brief as I could, with five children. "Holly, the oldest, lives in Nashville. She's engaged, but they don't seem to be planning the wedding yet," I began. "Claire is a jewelry designer in Santa Fe, and she doesn't tell me *anything* about her plans about *anything*. Julie is still trying to find herself, so to speak. She's in Savannah, taking care of my dog, Winston Churchill, while I'm gone. And the twins, Michael and Catherine, are finishing their first year in college. Michael at Georgia Tech and Catherine at Emory," I added because Grace was an Atlanta girl.

"Good for them!" she said. "You know, I go back to Atlanta

every few years now. Colin hasn't made the trip because we can't both be away at once, but my parents have mellowed. They visited us once in Dublin. We're finally on good terms. We Skype just about every week."

I remembered how distraught her parents were when their debutante daughter, pregnant with Colin O'Toole's child, married him.

"Skype." Alex pursed his lips and nodded. "Ah, the wonders of technology."

"I have to give it to Patrick. He told us Shepherds just *had* to have a presence on the Web, more than just a mention, if we were to make a go of it. We weren't getting the business we needed to stay afloat, but Patrick developed our website. Much more attractive and user-friendly, and this season looks promising. We're already filling up." Grace looked into her cup, swirled the tea, and I thought she was about to say more, but she didn't. I suspected there was something about their finances that was troublesome, from what she'd said about the Riordans.

"It must be wonderful for your parents to Skype with you," I said, picking up that thread. "Especially with Little Jimmie. They can watch him grow."

"Yes," she said.

In that awkward moment, I realized that Grace was struggling with how much to tell us, or maybe she was trying to figure out *how* to tell us something. I didn't want to appear nosy, but it seemed to me that Grace wanted—needed—to unburden herself. I was trying to think of a tactful opening when Alex said, "Grace, please tell me if I'm being meddlesome." His voice was full of kindness, his eyes, too. He leaned slightly forward. "Yesterday—you must have had a good reason not to notify the authorities about Little Jimmie's disappearance."

Her eyes began to glisten, but she blinked a few times and

went on, with a forced smile. "You must have thought we were all crazy! A baby kidnapped, and then we came home with him and everybody went on as if nothing had happened."

That said it all, I thought, but I tried to dismiss the idea. "Just so glad he was all right."

A long moment passed before Grace said, "I hate to draw you into our troubles."

"You can tell us anything," I said, "or *not*."

She nodded, stirred her tea, and said, "There's an old woman named Magdala who has a cottage in Red Stag Crossing, not too far from here. Hunters have tramped down some of the underbrush, but you still can't get to Magdala's cottage by car. Magdala looks like something out of an old folktale, bent over, missing teeth, dressed in rags, and she goes on about fairies and leprechauns. I don't know how she lives out there, no electricity, no bathroom. The cottage must be same as it was two hundred years ago, maybe three hundred or more." Grace paused to sip her tea. "It's heartbreaking to think of the baby in that place, even for a little while."

"Was that where you found him? In the old woman's cottage?" Alex asked.

Grace nodded. "I know everyone thought the sensible thing to do was call the Guard, but we knew where he was." She hesitated. I wasn't sure she'd go on, but she did. "You see—that wasn't the first time. It's always the same. We knew Little Jimmie was all right. He's a baby and won't remember any of it, thank God."

"How many times has this happened?" Alex asked. I thought this *might* be straying into meddlesome territory, but Grace gave no indication that she minded.

"The first time was a couple of months ago. It's happened twice in the last week."

"Are you saying it's the old woman who takes the baby?" My

voice was incredulous, and, I feared, judgmental, but Grace spoke before I could amend my question.

"Not Magdala," she said. "Bridget. When she's in one of her dark spells, she goes to Magdala's cottage and won't come home. The old woman gives her food and shelter, such as it is. Then Bridget gets it in her head that she wants the baby, that's he's in trouble, and she must save him"—Grace blinked hard a few times—"and she takes him."

Neither Alex nor I asked who Bridget was.

"She's our daughter," Grace said. "She's Little Jimmie's mother."

CHAPTER 4

The wind kicked up all at once. A branch scraped against the kitchen window. I jumped. I think we all jumped. Grace gave a little "Oh!" and went to the window. "What a nasty morning, for your first day here." Turning back to us, she said, "But this will all blow over soon. That's how the weather is here in Ireland." Doreen had made a similar comment.

I hoped Grace would finish telling us about Bridget, but she seemed to need a moment. She made herself another cup of tea and asked us if we'd like more coffee. We said no. When she returned to the table, there was a distinct shift in her mood, no holding back now. A note of relief, I thought, sounded as she said, "Bridget is twenty. Colin and I thought Patrick would be our only child. We tried and hoped, and then, when we were resigned to having just one, we were blessed with Bridget. Such a happy child. A sweet girl, as she was growing up."

A shadow of sadness crossed her face, but she seemed willing—even anxious—to go on. I was sure now that Grace *wanted* to unburden herself.

"Bridget was thirteen when we came out here from Dublin. Patrick had trained in computers. He was on his own, with a good job. Bridget hadn't started high school yet. It seemed like a good time to make the change." Grace hunched her shoulders. "I don't know if it would have been different for Bridget if we'd stayed in Dublin. She was fine, here in Thurles. She made good grades, had friends, thought she wanted to be a nurse, and she had the right temperament for it. But things changed. When she was seventeen, she got pregnant."

Grace gave a brittle laugh. "Now I know I'm not one to judge a girl for *that*. But when I found out I was pregnant, I *knew* Colin and I were going to be together. I had no doubt, and we married right away. With Bridget—no one ever came forward and took responsibility. To this day, she refuses to say who the father is."

I couldn't help wondering what I would have done if one of my daughters had been pregnant at seventeen. A child having a child. It happened—but I knew there was more to this story than a pregnant teenager.

"Was there a boyfriend?" Alex asked, and then amended the question, "One that you knew about?"

"She'd been going around with Davin Callahan, but she denied they were anything but friends. And we know Davin." Grace shook her head. "If Jimmie was his child—if he thought it was possible—he's not the kind to turn his back on something like that."

Davin Callahan, the waiter at Mitchel House. It was not the time to deliver his greeting.

"Colin and I told Bridget we'd help her out as long as she needed us, and she seemed to take to becoming a mother. But after the baby was born, a terrible change came over her. She's never been able to take care of her child. He'd cry, and she'd start crying, too. She just wanted to stay in bed." Voices sounded in the front room. We were going to be interrupted. Grace lowered her voice. "We thought it was post-partum depression, but now we don't know. Her doctor—a good family doctor who delivered Little Jimmie, but he's not a psychiatrist—he can't say much to Colin and me. Confidentiality, you know. He just says she must take her medications."

"Can you see the difference when she takes her meds

regularly?" I asked.

"We don't know if she's taking them or not. She's twenty and headstrong." A note of frustration had crept into Grace's voice. "Colin's cousin is a surgeon in Dublin. He could set her up with a good psychiatrist, but she won't hear of it. She—she runs away if we bring it up."

I couldn't help the "Oh, Grace" that escaped from me.

"We'll talk again later," she said, rising from her chair as Helen appeared in the doorway.

"Sorry to bother," Helen said. "Do you happen to have a map that will get us to Cork?"

"I'm sure we do," Grace said, following Helen. At the doorway, she turned to Alex and me. "I'll need to check on Enya and Little Jimmie, and do some housekeeping."

"Don't worry about us," I said.

"Charles and I decided we'd take a drive to Cork since he can't play golf this morning," Helen was saying as they went through the breakfast room. "My great-grandfather was a British soldier. They sent him to Cork sometime around 1920, to help keep the peace."

Under his breath, Alex said, "A black and tan? She might not want to publicize that fact here in Ireland."

I took our cups and put them in the sink.

"What are your plans this morning?" Alex asked as I stared out at the rain.

"I haven't really unpacked. I guess that's a good thing to do on a day like this. You?"

"I think I'll do some serious organizing," he said. "I need to go through all my materials and make my list of must-see and must-do items."

I had to smile. For his first book, Alex had his list long before we boarded the plane for France. He seemed much less stressed on this trip, which was nice, but he seemed less energetic, as well.

"Maybe the weather will improve, and we can get out this afternoon," I said. "Or—we could go in the rain. I doubt we'd melt."

He chuckled as he left the kitchen. "Yes, that is an option, isn't it?"

I remained at the window for another minute. I was picturing a young woman huddled in a small, shabby dwelling far off the beaten path, wondering if she was staying dry. Not likely. How did Colin and Grace bear it?

By the time I'd finished unpacking, the rain had passed over. By noon, the sun was out.

Alex knocked on my door. "Amazing weather! Would you like to go to Kilkenny?"

"Kilkenny Castle?"

"The castle and the town, and I understand there's a walking trail in a nearby village that takes you by a megalithic tomb—if we have time." Alex's puppy-like eagerness made me laugh.

"Sure. How far is it from here?"

"Doreen said it's about an hour."

I gave him a mock scowl. He looked a little sheepish. "Doreen and Molly were planning to walk into town and catch a bus to Kilkenny, but it seemed like a good idea to let them ride with us. Doreen will be a good guide, I think."

I didn't mind, but I was amused, and I had to bet that the suggestion came from Doreen. She just made Alex *think* it was his idea. "I can be ready in—shall we say half an hour?" I said.

"Half an hour? Will it take you that long?"

"Is that a problem?"

"No. Take your time, Jordan," he said in a placating voice. "I'll tell Doreen and Molly that it's going to be a few minutes."

"They're waiting, aren't they?" I said.

He nodded.

"I think you'll find the castle fascinating, Jordan, from an architect's perspective," Alex said. He began to read from a brochure: "*Over the past eight hundred years, the additions to the original Norman fortress have represented a diversity of architectural styles, making Kilkenny Castle a very complex structure.*" He held the brochure between us, showing a photo. I had to remind him I was driving.

"The gardens are grand," Doreen said from the back seat. "I've been there, y'know."

"Three times, I believe," Alex said.

"This is my third. Molly's been once before. Sure, the castle's fine, but it's just so peaceful-like strolling about the grounds."

Alex read on. "*Originally, the castle was a square structure built with towers at each corner. Three of the original towers remain today. The North-Eastern tower was destroyed during Oliver Cromwell's siege in 1650.* Cromwell's name does come up, doesn't it?"

"You know the River Nore meanders through the town," Doreen said. "You can walk along the river and see swans and herons and the like. And y'know what would be grand? If we could make a wee side trip, out to Tullahought."

"Tullahought?" I said.

"The little village. Kilmacoliver Walk. The tomb they say is five thousand years old."

"I remember something about that," Alex mumbled. He wasn't fooling me. He'd already talked with Doreen about it. "I suppose we can see how much time we have," he said, and continued reading, "*Many of the beautiful stones are quarried locally, limestone, old red sandstone, and black marble.*"

The trip went on like that, until at last Kilkenny Castle loomed before us, dominating the town that had grown up around it. Alex began to scribble in his little notebook, recording his first impressions, no doubt.

"There's a parking area along Castle Road. The Parade, they call it," Doreen said. She directed me to the very heart of the small city, overshadowed by the castle. The buildings were tall and narrow, painted a variety of lively colors. A space opened up for us, as if on cue, and Alex cut his eyes at me. I returned a smile, acknowledging that Doreen was, indeed, helpful.

She pointed out an upscale complex across the street from the castle. "They call that the Design Centre. It used to be the castle stables. If you fancy a bite to eat, there's a nice place up on the second floor. Salads and sandwiches, light fare. Tourists seem to like it. Myself, I'm not a bit hungry. How about you, love?" Molly's answer was inaudible. Alex said the Irish breakfast at Shepherds would keep him going for a while longer, and I was ashamed to admit I had room for a salad, but I could wait. We headed to the castle, across spacious grounds, past a few picnics.

"You'll be wanting the guided tour," Doreen said at the entrance. "It takes about an hour, as I recall. We've done the tour, Molly and me, so we'll go off on our own. We won't get lost."

"I think the tour will be an hour well spent, don't you?" Alex said, when mother and daughter were out of earshot.

I was more the *self*-guided tour type, as Alex knew, but I said, "Maybe we can learn something that Doreen doesn't know."

"Do I detect a note of sarcasm, Jordan?"

We paid for the tour and waited for our group to assemble.

"Doreen is all right—in small doses—but I do feel sorry for Molly. Has she said one word since we left Thurles?"

"I'm not sure I've heard the child speak at all," Alex said.

"You should've heard her at breakfast, before Doreen arrived." I remembered to tell Alex about the concert Saturday night. He was delighted that Molly was getting tickets for us.

A young woman about Molly's age took charge, and our tour began. A short video presented an overview of the castle's history. So much to see—I couldn't imagine we'd accomplish the tour in an hour. Our young guide was a fountain of facts and stories about the furnishings and paintings, as she led us through, room by room. As Alex had predicted, I found the architecture fascinating, the styles that represented numerous time periods, from the Classical arched gateway to the modern conference center housed within one of the towers. I would have stayed longer in the long, narrow Picture Gallery, a nineteenth-century addition with its high-pitched roof and its gilded animal and bird motifs on the crossbeams, but our guide wasted no time. Another reason I liked *self-guided* tours. The formidable corner towers were reminders of the structure's medieval beginnings. Much was made of the tower that had been destroyed during the Cromwellian siege. I thought of Ian Haverty's words: "It was a brutal period in our history."

Doreen and Molly were waiting for us at the end of the tour. One hour on the dot.

"Molly and I could do with a cup of tea," Doreen said. "Did you see the Castle Kitchen?"

Our guide had pointed out the small eatery, and I'd been tempted to run in and grab one of the "lovely scones" she'd promoted. This time I thought Doreen's suggestion was just fine.

The daily special was soup and a veggie wrap, and we ordered four specials and two pots of tea. "You'll not be wanting to miss the gardens," Doreen said, with a glance at her watch that seemed a little regretful. It was getting on toward three o'clock.

"How far is the little village—what was the name?" Alex said.

"Tullahought," Doreen replied. "About twenty kilometers, I'd say. And the trail—it could take two to three hours, I've heard, depending on how fast you can walk."

"I'd like to spend some time just browsing in the little town," I said, trying for extra kindness in my voice and expression. "And of course the gardens—as you've said—it would be a shame to hurry on and not stroll through the gardens. There's so much to see, and we got a late start. Maybe we can come back to Tullahought another day."

"I was thinking the same," said Doreen. "Only this may be the last day Molly has to see the sights. She'll be rehearsing and performing into next week. Isn't that right, love? We'd planned to leave after her final performance, but I suppose we could extend our stay, if the O'Tooles can keep us on."

"I don't have to go to Tullahought." Molly's voice—a surprise—was cross at first, but then she seemed to reconsider. A certain sparkle came into her eyes. "I wouldn't mind staying on, though—if you want to, Mam."

I went back to the counter and ordered a plate of the lovely scones. Alex was relating the high points of our tour when I returned to the table with four scones to share.

"I suppose they told you all about the Butler family," Doreen said.

"Kilkenny was their principal Irish residence for most of six hundred years," Alex said, "until the family presented the castle to the town for a token payment. I think it was 1967."

"Y'know the Butlers were Protestant," Doreen said, taking a dainty bite of her scone. "But it was all a long time ago."

It was dark when we pulled up at Shepherds. Sightseeing in Kilkenny, the town, with its winding streets, its air of history, turned out to take the rest of the afternoon. Molly seemed to cheer up after lunch. In one of the stores in the Kilkenny Design Centre, she bought a silver bracelet. She had her own money—I wouldn't have guessed—and when Doreen told her she could buy a bracelet elsewhere for much less, Molly just smiled and said, "I like this one."

"You know these Irish-designed gifts are mostly for tourists," Doreen said. I took her advice and bought bracelets for my daughters at a tiny store on Abbey Street, where I also snapped a picture of the only remaining gate to what was once a walled city.

Coming into Thurles, we'd discussed dinner. No one was really hungry, but we thought we should get a bite to eat. Doreen suggested the café at The Source Arts Centre. Light entrees, inexpensive, a view of the River Suir—it was just right. The prospect of Molly's performances over the next few days dominated the conversation. Doreen's suggestion that they stay on in Thurles for a while longer than they'd planned had done wonders for Molly's demeanor.

Back at Shepherds, we talked with Patrick O'Toole for the first time. He was behind the Reception desk, speaking with Mr. Sweeney, who brushed past us with a gruff sound—neither a greeting nor an apology—when he was finished. Patrick shrugged, as if to say he couldn't figure out the man either, and then his eyes widened. "You're Alex and Jordan!"

I resisted the temptation to say that when I'd last seen him, he was about *so* long—and make a measurement of about twenty-two inches with my hands.

We spoke for a moment before the phone rang. Patrick raised his finger, indicating that we should wait. "Yes, it's very bad," he said to the caller. "I think you're right. No one will want to meet tomorrow. Better to reschedule." He thanked the caller and promised to let Colin know.

"Sorry," he said. "The business owners in town have a lunch meeting on the second Friday of the month, but it's postponed. There's been a tragedy."

Before he could elaborate, Grace appeared in the doorway

between Reception and the breakfast room. She was holding the hand of a bouncy red-haired toddler. "I thought I heard your voices," she said. Motioning for us to join her, she said, "I've made a pot of tea."

It was our first chance to see Little Jimmie up close. He was blue-eyed, with fine, wispy red lashes, chubby hands, and plump cheeks. He babbled something, and Grace put him in his high chair, where she had cut up a banana for him. "He's already had his dinner. Nothing wrong with this child's appetite," she said.

Dinner for the adults must have still been cooking— something delicious, from the aroma.

"A fine-looking young man," Alex said.

The little boy gave one of those heart-wrenching smiles that you can't help but return. He showed a mouthful of tiny white teeth. I asked his age. Grace said he was twenty-two months.

She produced the tin that Helen had found in the cabinet and put out several shortbread cookies. Little Jimmie reached out and whined when she set the plate on the table. "You can have *one*," she said. She brought cups and a teapot to the table and sat down at last, with a long sigh that revealed much about how her day had been. "I heard Patrick tell you what happened."

"He didn't say what happened, just that it was a tragedy of some kind," I said.

She stirred her tea, waited a beat before she said, "Dr. Malone is dead. He was stabbed."

I caught my breath. "We met him last night at the pub. Ian introduced us."

"I'm not sure he ever made it home." Grace put both of her hands around her cup and looked down. "I can't believe it. He's so well respected in the town. *Was.*" She reached over to wipe Little Jimmie's mouth. "He was Bridget's doctor. I don't know what we'll do now."

"Are you saying he died last night, after he left the pub?" Alex asked.

"He didn't show up at his office this morning." Grace crumpled the napkin. She stared into her cup again, her voice a kind of sing-song. "Colin came back from town around noon saying that Dr. Malone was missing. Word gets around in Thurles. This afternoon we heard he'd been found. His body had been found. Soaked from the rain, so it might have happened last night or maybe this morning early. What he was doing out there, I can't imagine."

"Where?" I asked.

Grace looked up, meeting my eyes, communicating her worry. A shiver ran down my spine as she said, "Red Stag Crossing. Not far from Magdala's cottage."

CHAPTER 5

Once again, our conversation with Grace was interrupted, this time by Enya. Her bobbing walk made her look like a prissy teenager. No one had actually said how old she was, but I'd assumed she was close to Patrick's age, which was twenty-eight. The impression she gave was one of perpetual dissatisfaction, but she was a natural beauty, dark-haired and dark-eyed.

"What's cooking?" she asked, crossing over to the stove.

"Stew," Grace said. "It needs another half hour."

With a pot holder, Enya raised the lid off the stew and sniffed. One would expect a comment—I had never imagined Irish stew would smell so wonderful!—but she simply said, "I'll go on and bathe Jimmie," to which Grace agreed. I supposed that was something.

"You've met Jordan and Alex, haven't you?" Grace said.

"We met this morning," Enya said with a glance my way, in a manner that was neither cross nor friendly, just matter of fact.

"I haven't had the pleasure," Alex said, standing, the perfect gentleman.

He must have impressed Enya. Her expression altered. She didn't smile exactly, but she was more pleasant as she took a step closer, studying him. "I'm Enya." She added, "Patrick's wife," with a kind of bite that left no doubt there was some resentment there. Did she feel no one valued her, except in her role as Patrick's wife? She didn't stick around for conversation. She whisked Little Jimmie out of his high chair and they left through the back of the kitchen, where a staircase must have led to the family's rooms. It was reassuring to hear her speak to the baby in a kind voice—"Play with your boats, sure"—when he said something I couldn't understand.

Grace started to speak but instead she got up and went to the stove.

I said, "We'll get out of your way now," darting a look at Alex, who added that our trip to Kilkenny had been enjoyable but also tiring. "We had a light supper at The Source, the little café—Doreen is quite the tour guide," I said, trying to lighten the mood.

Grace stirred with a ladle. "Colin hates that he hasn't spent any time with you," she said, looking at the stew, not at us. "If you feel like it, come down later tonight after everything settles down, and we'll open a bottle of wine."

We said we would, but she might not have heard us. She continued to stare into the pot.

In the large front room they called Reception, which was the sitting room of the original house, Charles Prescott and Ian Haverty were playing chess. Helen was lounging on the Victorian-style sofa, reading a paperback. It was the first time I'd seen the guests gather in the room, but then we had arrived only yesterday. Was that possible, that we'd been in Thurles just a little over twenty-four hours? So much had happened. It was incredible that of all the citizens of Thurles, the man who was murdered—stabbed!—was someone we had met just last night. More significantly, he was someone with a connection to the O'Tooles. Grace had been visibly shaken by the news of his murder, and especially by the fact that he'd been found near the cottage where she believed their daughter to be. What a time for Alex and me to be visiting!

Alex went on upstairs to work on his notes, while I spoke

with Helen. "We spent the day in Cork. Lovely day, though Charles was not at all happy after the sun came out," she said with a glance his way. Charles didn't look up from the chess board. I had the urge to brush back the hair that was hanging in front of his eyes—how could he see?—but then he shook his head and pushed the strands behind his ear.

"He wanted to come back and play golf, of course," Helen said. "We had quite a row."

"We did not have a row, Helen," Charles said, still not looking up. "Simply a discussion."

"We most certainly did, but it's of no importance now." She patted the seat beside her. "Please, Jordan, won't you join me? Let me tell you about Cork. You should go. It's a beautiful city, and small enough that you can see a lot in a little time."

I sat beside her and listened to her travelogue. She made a point of mentioning the influence of the English. They'd had lunch at the Ballymaloe Cookery School and perused the English Market. "I purchased some delightful chocolates," she said. "And the architecture! Someone said you're an architect. You should *definitely* go. I went on a walking tour—very nice. Oh, the churches—I don't remember all the names." She raised her voice, as if to be sure her husband heard. "I'm sure the pub was nice, too, wasn't it, Charles?"

"Quite," he said.

"Did you kiss the Blarney Stone, Helen?" Ian asked, his voice playful.

"Kiss the Blarney Stone?" she said.

"Blarney Castle is one of the sights in County Cork. I'm surprised you don't know of it. According to the legend, if you kiss the Blarney Stone, you'll always have the gift of gab, of eloquence. But you have to hang upside down from the tower to do it." Ian's attention turned back to the chess board, where

Charles had made a big move. "Oh, you're a dirty dog, you are."

"You see what can happen when one concentrates on the game," Charles said.

"We did not go to any castles today," Helen said, "or kiss any stones." She turned back to me. "I wish we could have taken a tour of the Big Houses, the homes of the Anglo-Irish gentry before the Irish Civil War. Splendid country houses. Many were burned, but a few still exist."

I nodded. "I read Elizabeth Bowen's *Last September.*"

"My great-grandfather was sent to Ireland, to keep the peace," Helen said, repeating the announcement she'd made earlier that day. "My grandmother died last year, and we found letters from her father to her mother that none of us had ever read. He told about his duties in Cork. In one of the letters he wrote about the burning of one of the Big Houses by the rebels and what a shame it was. Though the family made it out alive, they could not rescue the wolfhounds."

Ian, who had hunched over the chess board, straightened his shoulders and turned his gaze on Helen. "He was a tan? Your great grandda was?"

I remembered that Alex had said Helen might not want to broadcast that fact. Now she bristled, too. "He was a British soldier, sent by the Crown to keep the peace because the Irish were fighting among themselves. He was a man of honor."

The fire in Ian's black eyes did not match his soft voice. "I won't say anything against your family, but there's a whole story there that you might not know. The tactics they used, the black-and-tans, how they terrorized whole villages. And if you'd dug into Cork's history a little deeper, you might have come upon the story of how the tans burned down the center of the town." Ian's voice rose a notch. "I don't expect you to know all of Ireland's sorrows, but be careful talking about honor among the tans. We don't see it that way."

Helen's natural gift of gab seemed to momentarily fail her. Charles chimed in. "Look, old boy, all of that happened a long time ago. Some tensions between England and Ireland may exist, but not the violence, not anymore. Even the Queen has visited Ireland. Isn't that something?"

"It's something," Ian said. "One goodwill gesture for all that England's done to us for centuries."

Charles stood up, reaching over to clap Ian on the shoulder. "What say we go to the pub and cool off. Our game can wait."

Ian drew a long breath and stood as well. "I don't like losing my temper like that, but it's a touchy subject, the long, tortured history of Ireland."

Charles took care as he lifted the chess board, with the game unfinished, and transported it to a spot behind the Reception counter for safekeeping. Notwithstanding the English–Irish differences, the Prescotts seemed quite at home here at Shepherds.

Helen assumed the tone of one who, in the face of victory, chose to be charitable. "Charles is right, Ian. We should not dwell on the things that happened a long time ago. We should put the past behind us. We should try to forget."

I caught a flash in Ian's eyes that might have been renewed anger, but it passed quickly. His words actually seemed to hold compassion, as he looked hard into her face. "Ah, you don't know us, Helen," he said. "The Irish don't forget."

In my room, I sent texts to my daughters and my brother, Drew, who was also my business partner. Since it was afternoon in the States, I managed to connect with all of them except Claire in Santa Fe, the only one who would go for hours without checking her phone. Alex would find it amusing that all but one of my family members had their phones in hand and replied to me within minutes—even Michael, who said he was in class. Alex had only recently bought a cell phone and hadn't brought it on our trip. "Why *should* I?" he'd said. "You have yours if we need instant communication."

Sometime after nine, I went down to see Colin and Grace, as she had suggested. No one was in the kitchen, but I heard voices and saw that a door I'd earlier wondered about was partially open, revealing a small sitting room. Alex was already settled in a comfy-looking chair with a glass of wine. "Jordan!" Colin said, popping up from the loveseat he shared with Grace.

"I just this minute said I should go knock on your door," Grace said. Her cheeks were a little flushed, her glass nearly empty, and she was smiling. It was not a joyful smile but, rather, one that masked unease. I could only imagine her thoughts, with Bridget at the center.

Colin hugged me. "Ah, Jordan, I can't tell you how good it is to have you and Alex with us. It's been far too long. Come. You sit with Grace. Sweet Mother, you don't look a day older than the girl we knew in college." He reached for the wine bottle on the low glass-topped table, poured my drink, and topped off his own glass and Grace's. The bottle was nearly empty, but another one, yet uncorked, awaited our next round.

"And *you*, Colin, are just as full of blarney as you always were," I said. Everyone laughed, Colin included. I had a memory of something I'd heard about the Black Irish, brooding, given to anger or passion, like Ian, and the Red Irish, like Colin, fun-loving and charming.

Colin took a seat in the chair next to Alex, one with arms but not overstuffed. The cozy sitting area was configured around a fireplace that I suspected got plenty of use throughout the year. Dark-paneled walls and bookshelves filled with books, beige tones with coral accents, warm lighting—it was a most inviting room. I told Colin and Grace that I had been speculating on the floor plan, trying to figure out where all the rooms were, but this room came as a surprise.

"You know how it is with these old, old houses," Colin said. "So many additions and renovations, what you get is a hodge-podge."

"Like Kilkenny Castle," Alex said.

"Right you are," Colin said. "Now that's a muddle, if ever there was one."

"Disjointed, but fascinating," I said.

"I like *disjointed*. That's a good word for this place, too," Grace said.

I couldn't keep from asking questions about the house. "How old is it? Do you know?"

"We know it was built before 1800," Colin said. "There are records of the family ownership through the years. Around 1960 the house sold to a man named Riley who made some renovations and opened an inn. He had a good business head and his family kept it going for about thirty-five years. Called it the Dark Horse Inn."

"I like Shepherds," I said.

"That's *our* contribution," Grace said. "Dark Horse sounded too ominous. And by the time we bought it, the inn was needing a whole new personality."

"The people who came after Riley—two brothers—just about ran it into the ground," Colin went on. "Maybe it was greediness, maybe just poor business sense. They cut up some of the bedrooms to accommodate more guests. What's that saying in the movie: *Build it and they will come?* Well, they didn't come." Colin reached for his glass.

Though I hadn't been in any of the bedrooms but my own, I'd noticed that some doors had been added later than others. An effort was made to match the style, but it didn't quite work.

"In all fairness," Grace said, "Thurles was growing, and this place had competition, and all the hotels and inns and B&Bs

were advertising on the Internet. The Dark Horse Inn just couldn't keep up."

"What made you decide to buy it?" Alex asked. "You owned a pub in Dublin, I believe."

"Running a pub is hard work, let me tell you. Finding staff you can trust, keeping the late hours. I had no life besides the pub. An opportunity came our way—it was like a sign from God." Colin looked at Grace as if signaling her to take up the story.

"I had a clerical job at a real estate firm," she said, "and Mr. Riordan from Thurles—Mr. Liam, the old man—had holdings in Dublin. I got to know him. He'd call from Thurles and I'd take care of things for him. *We* got to know him, Colin and I."

Colin chuckled. "He spent a good bit of time at the pub when he was in Dublin. Like my own da, bless his soul, Mr. Riordan liked his Guinness a bit too much. Sometimes I'd help him to his hotel after closing. He had to give up the drink after he had a bad heart attack, but he'd still come by the pub to chat. He's the one told us about the Dark Horse Inn for sale. The owner was deep in debt, letting it go for a song. Mr. Riordan considered buying it for Lucas to run, but he backed off. Though he didn't say it, he had to know his son was good for nothing but partying, playing golf, and spending the Riordan money."

"Colin and I wound up making an offer on the inn, and Mr. Riordan helped us with the financing, and here we are." Grace reached for the corkscrew and the second bottle of wine.

I was still interested in the layout of the first floor. Colin confirmed that the once-spacious dining room was now the breakfast room and an office with a door that opened behind the Reception counter. I'd noticed that door, too. "Patrick must have been working in the office earlier tonight," I said. I didn't mention that he'd cracked the door and looked out when Ian and the Prescotts were having their heated discussion about England and Ireland.

"Patrick's in there every night, on the computer. God bless the boy. I don't know what we'd have done if he hadn't come to help us—Enya, too." Colin and Grace exchanged a private glance, and he said, "Ah, Grace, don't be so hard on her. You can believe Enya didn't imagine she'd be working in a country inn when she was flittin' all about Dublin."

"That much is true," Grace said, rising. "I think I'll get us some cheese."

Colin continued to answer my questions about the house. I had figured out that Helen and Charles, Doreen and Molly had rooms in a first-floor adjoining wing. Colin and Grace, Patrick and Enya had rooms in one wing of the second floor that they could enter from the stairs in Reception or from a separate staircase behind the kitchen. My room and Alex's were on the second floor at the top of the main staircase. There were two others in the main wing. "One is Bridget's. Used to be hers and Little Jimmie's, but now the boy's with Grace and me. Bridget comes and goes, but it's her room. She'll be back. We don't rent it." Colin looked to me and then to Alex. "Grace said she told you about our Bridget."

I nodded. Alex, who had been less talkative than usual, surprised me by saying, "She told us about Dr. Malone, too. His death, tragic as it is, may be the thing that leads Bridget to another doctor, one more capable of dealing with her needs. A specialist."

"A psychiatrist, you mean. I pray you're right." Colin took a long drink of wine. Grace returned with a plate of cheese and crackers, and Colin continued as if he'd never left off. "The other room on the second floor, down from yours, Alex, is Ian Haverty's."

"What about Mr. Sweeney?" I said.

"On the third floor that's mostly attic space, there's a room with a toilet, sink, and bed, not luxurious, to be sure," Colin said. "Mr. Sweeney called just last week for a reservation. We told him we were full, but he was so insistent, we finally agreed to give him the room on the top floor. We told him what to expect. He didn't seem to care and he hasn't complained."

"Why didn't he just call another B&B in Thurles?" I said.

"I suggested that he do just that, but he said something about—someone had posted a blog about us—I don't remember exactly. I guess I was seeing a few more Euros in our pockets."

"A blog?" Alex raised his palm to me. "I know what a blog is. Isn't that a picture, though, Mr. Sweeney following blogs? Makes me feel I'm *far* behind when it comes to technology."

"Ah, Alex, you'll be posting blogs, I'll wager. Promoting your books," Colin said.

We stayed with our friends until it was close to midnight. Alex did talk about his books, but mostly we reminisced about good times at UGA. We didn't discuss the murder.

"One more question about the house," I said as we were all saying goodnight. "Did you redecorate this room yourselves? It's so tasteful, so welcoming."

"The keeping room was one of Mr. Riley's additions," Colin said. "A nice room, but, oh, it was in dire need of redecoration when we moved in. You're so right. All of this is Grace's touch. We didn't have the money to spend on other upgrades, but it was important to Grace to have a pleasant keeping room. She's in the kitchen so much."

She beamed at her husband. It was good to see such affection between them, good to see that, for a moment, the worry lines had eased from around Grace's eyes.

The smells of coffee and bacon were evidence that Grace had already been working in the kitchen. I hadn't slept well. Ian had come in at about two a.m., making too much noise on the stairs and in the hall. Calling down to Charles, something about making sure the front door was locked. After that, my sleep was fitful. Too much swirling in my mind.

Halfway down the stairs, I saw Colin open the door for two men. I stopped. The burly man with a deep voice made no effort to keep the noise down, though it was barely seven o'clock. He had to know that in a B&B, with guests on holiday, some might still be sleeping. Flashing identification, the visitor announced, "I'm Inspector Tom Perone, and this is Garda Mallory. Is Bridget O'Toole here?"

"And what might you be wanting with my daughter?" Colin asked.

"We have some questions for her," Perone said. "You've heard about Dr. Malone?"

"For God's sake, what does that have to do with Bridget?" Colin said, his voice rising.

"We'll not know for sure till we get some answers." There was no sympathy in the inspector's voice as he said, "Your daughter may have been the last one to see the doctor alive."

CHAPTER 6

"That's ridiculous!" Grace came in from the breakfast room. "Dr. Malone was at Finnegan's that night. I'm sure Finn and a dozen others can swear to it. Bridget wouldn't have seen him after that." As she said it, her gaze turned up to the stairs. "Jordan! You saw the doctor. You told me."

I could no longer remain unobtrusive. I came downstairs and joined the little knot. "Yes, my uncle and I were at the pub, and we were introduced to Dr. Malone."

"What time was that?" the inspector asked.

"Ten o'clock, maybe. It could have been earlier. But Grace is right. The pub was full. There may be others who know exactly when he left."

"Your name?"

I gave my name, and he eyed the other officer who was already writing it down.

Colin ran his fingers through his wild red hair. I had never seen Colin O'Toole quite so undone. But he gathered his wits—you could see the change come over him—and he said, "My daughter is not here, Inspector. I'm sure she knows nothing that can help your investigation, but I'll bring her to the Guards station so you can question her. Will you let me do that, sir? Will you give me a chance to go after her and bring her to you?"

It was arranged. The officials departed, and then Colin left for the old woman's cottage where he presumed he would find his daughter.

"Bring her home," Grace said. "Please, Colin, bring her home."

In the States, I'd be saying, *Get a lawyer.* But this was Ireland. Colin would surely know what to do. I followed Grace back to the kitchen. "What can I do to help?" I asked.

Grace buried her face in her hands, but then, like Colin, she pulled herself together.

"I don't want our guests to know about all of this, not yet anyway," she said. "You can tell Alex, of course, but not the others."

"I wouldn't," I said. "Can I help with breakfast?"

Grace began to fill trays with breakfast foods. "You're a *guest,* Jordan."

"Right now, I'm an old friend. Give me a job."

She sighed. "You can take these trays to the breakfast room. My God, is Enya still asleep? Now, the time I need her most!"

All morning, we waited for Colin. Grace asked me to come with her and Little Jimmie to the keeping room, where he played with wooden stacking blocks. Adorable child, sweet-tempered. He called Grace *Ma.* Twice he crawled into her lap, sucked his fingers for a moment, and then went back to his play. Grace warmed up leftover stew for us. I wanted to keep her company, so I accepted her invitation to lunch. Waiting had to be so hard.

Enya had made a brief appearance to help with breakfast, but now she'd gone out. "Seems she's made a few friends in town," Grace said. "I suppose she needs a social life. She was quite the social butterfly in Dublin."

"How long have Patrick and Enya been in Thurles?" I asked.

"About a year and a half. Little Jimmie was just an infant, and Bridget was getting worse by the day. Patrick started looking for a position at Tipperary Institute—now it's LIT Tipperary, since they joined the Limerick Institute of Techology. He got a job, beginning winter term. We didn't *ask* Patrick to come, but he has that sense of responsibility that Irish boys seem to have. Just like Colin brought his family to Ireland when his father was dying. I know Enya resents us because Patrick moved her out here." Grace put a few more crackers on Little Jimmie's tray. "I suppose I should give Enya credit. She helps out, but her heart's not in it. Sometimes I could shake her! I want to say, *Do you think it's easy for any of us? For Patrick, your husband? Be a grown-up, Enya! Your days of partying are over!*"

"Do you think she wants children?" I laughed. "I don't know where I got that idea."

"You know, she might," Grace said. "You'd think caring for children would be the last thing on her mind, the way she acts, but she may just think there's no chance for her and Patrick to have their own family as long as they're so involved with us— and our problems."

Grace was a little more settled now, discussing Enya instead of Bridget. Little Jimmie finished his lunch and Grace took him upstairs for his nap. Ian and Charles were playing chess in Reception, maybe winding up last night's game. Alex and Doreen had gone to the little village called Tullahought to take the nature walk Doreen had so promoted. Alex drove. I was a little nervous about his driving, but Doreen had proven to be an excellent guide. Molly was going to her rehearsal today, and I was in no mood for sightseeing.

It was a sunny day, cool but pleasant. I went for a walk around the grounds. On the back of the property, a rock wall lined the perimeter of the lawn. Mr. Sweeney was sitting on the rock wall, not far from a swing set. I was curious about the man and took this as a good opportunity to make his acquaintance.

"Good morning!" I said. "Or maybe it's good afternoon."

He grunted.

"Today is much nicer than yesterday," I said. I took a seat on the rock wall, a reasonable distance from him. "I'm Jordan Mayfair, from the States. Savannah, Georgia. We haven't really met, but you're Mr. Sweeney, aren't you?"

"Seamus Sweeney." He took a long drag on his cigarette and exhaled.

I waited, hoping he might ask *me* a question or show some interest in engaging me in conversation, but when he didn't, I asked, "Where are you from?"

"Dublin." Now he darted me a glance that seemed to ask why I was being so inquisitive.

I took his reticence as a challenge. "Shepherds is nice, isn't it?"

"Nice enough." He flicked the ashes onto the ground and looked away.

"My uncle and I knew Colin and Grace a long time ago, when they were in school," I said. "That's why we're here. Alex is working on a travel guide."

He nodded. Whether signaling that he approved, I couldn't tell.

"We went to Kilkenny yesterday," I said.

"The castle," he said. "I've been to it. Don't expect I'll go again."

"What are you planning to see while you're here?" I asked.

He dropped his cigarette butt and gave it a tap with the toe of his boot. "Don't know," he said. "I didn't come here to see any sights."

"Oh?" I didn't ask *Then why?* but it was surely implied.

He blinked. A moment passed, an awkward silence that I thought I could wait out, but I couldn't. "I've asked too many questions," I said finally, standing up. "I just wanted to meet you and introduce myself, since we're both guests here. Have a nice rest of the day."

When my back was to him, he said, "My wife died last

month." I turned around to face him. He said, "I needed to get away from home for a while."

"I'm sorry," I said, and before I could help myself I was asking another question. "Had you been married a long time?"

No hesitation this time. "Twenty-one years if she'd lived till July."

"I'm so sorry," I said again.

I felt foolish for thinking so poorly of him. He was just grieving. But I wondered why he'd wanted to come to this place, in particular. According to Colin, Mr. Sweeney had been insistent. Maybe he and his wife had once visited the Dark Horse Inn. I wouldn't ask.

He turned his eyes up to mine for the first time, and I saw the pain in his expression, but it was replaced quickly by indignation. "Any more questions? I'm not all that interesting."

"No more questions," I said. It seemed like a good time to walk away.

Colin returned shortly after that. Grace had finished her housekeeping chores and Little Jimmie was still napping. We were having tea at the kitchen table. Grace's breath caught when she saw Colin without their daughter, but she didn't ask what had happened. She had to know her husband would tell her everything. She simply began preparing tea for him.

Scooting my chair back, I told them I'd be in my room, but Colin stopped me. "Don't go, Jordan. Maybe we could use your clear head. Mine's a muddle, and Grace must feel the same."

It was then that I said what I'd been thinking: "Maybe you need legal advice. Do you know a lawyer you could contact?"

"I could find one. I'm hoping we won't have to do that, but—we would manage." He took a seat at the table. A look passed between him and Grace. Were they thinking of attorney's fees? Money they didn't have, and where would they get it?

Grace poured his tea. He added a few drops of cream and stirred. Grace did not hurry him. He sipped his tea, part of the ritual, it seemed they both understood, before he could launch into his story. "I think our girl is in the clear. The coroner says the doctor died early yesterday morning, and Magdala, bless the old crone's heart, she swears Bridget slept in the cottage that night and didn't leave in the morning."

"Did Magdala go to the Guards station, too?" It was the first question Grace had asked.

"It wasn't quite like that." Colin drew a long breath. "I had a wee bit 'o trouble with Bridget. I couldn't make her go with me, short of throwing her over my shoulder like a sack of flour, which I didn't think would look right at the Guards station. So I went back to the road where I could get phone service and called for Inspector Perone. He was at the Riordans' house, thank God. I explained the situation to Garda Mallory the best I could. Told him Bridget was not well. I confess, I didn't try to explain exactly why she was at Magdala's cottage."

"I don't know how you could have explained," Grace said. "It doesn't make any sense, does it? I'm sure he thought it was peculiar."

"Mallory spoke with a Sergeant Casey, and they came to us," Colin said. "I don't know what they thought or didn't think, but both of them are good men just doing their job. The sergeant talked nice to Bridget, and she answered their questions the best she could, I think."

Colin finally got around to saying why the police had believed Bridget was the last person to see Dr. Malone. The doctor and his wife, who was Liam Riordan's daughter, were separated. Norah Malone was living at the Riordan house. She'd been on the phone with the doctor after he came in from the pub, and he'd told her someone was at the door.

"Mallory probably wasn't supposed to tell me, but the

sergeant didn't object. Norah Malone heard a woman shouting, the doctor trying to calm her, and then he came back on the line saying it was Bridget O'Toole, she was hysterical, and he had to take her home."

I wondered if a doctor would use those words—"she's hysterical"—about his patient, but maybe to his wife, his estranged wife, he would.

"Was this at the doctor's office?" I asked.

"He lives above his office," Grace said.

"Bridget didn't deny going to see him, but she didn't remember much about it. You know how she was when we left her that afternoon, when we brought Jimmie back home." Colin regarded Grace with that look, that acknowledgment of what they'd both experienced.

"Did she tell the reason she went to see Dr. Malone," Grace said, "why she was out in the dark night, walking through the woods and into town?" It was a chilly night, too, I remembered.

"I don't think she knows why," Colin said. "She began to get all—anxious—with the questions and said she didn't remember. But it seems the doctor did take her back to the cottage. Magdala couldn't say what time Bridget returned—they don't have any timepiece out there—but she said the moon was high, and Bridget just came in and went to sleep after that."

"It's a bit of a flimsy story," Grace said. "A girl who doesn't remember and a woman who's not right in the head. I'll be surprised if the Guards really believe it."

"Maybe they do and maybe they don't, but unless they get something else on Bridget, I don't see how they can—blame her."

A moment passed. It was clear he'd meant *arrest* her.

"Do you think she's taking her medications?" Grace asked.

"Maybe. She wasn't like we've seen her, the awful ups and downs." He gave a weak smile. "Sure, she refused to go to the

Guards station, but she's a willful girl, our Bridget."

"And she refused to come home," Grace added.

I excused myself. Grace said she needed to get Little Jimmie up, or he'd never go to sleep tonight. Colin said he had work to do, phone messages and e-mails from that morning when no one was in the office. "Inquiries about reservations, we can hope," he said. I took my teacup to the sink.

Another question occurred to me. "How did Bridget come to know Magdala?"

"Bridget was doing volunteer work for Dr. Malone when she was in high school," Grace said. "I think I told you she wanted to be a nurse at one time. Someone—one of Magdala's neighbors, I imagine—contacted the doctor and said Magdala was very sick, and he went out to see her. She had a bad case of flu, I think it was, and he treated her."

"Bridget went with him to the cottage?" I asked.

"Maybe not that first time," Grace said, "but Dr. Malone was good to Magdala. He kept going out there, probably has continued up till now, taking her vitamins and cough syrup and sometimes prescription medicine when she was sick. Bridget would go with him, as long as she was volunteering in his office. That's how she met Magdala."

"Something about the old woman," Colin said. "Bridget kept on taking her food and warm sweaters and such."

"After Jimmie was born, you mean," I said.

"After she left school, and was no longer volunteering with Dr. Malone," Colin said.

"After she got pregnant," Grace amended.

So Bridget had befriended Magdala, and now Magdala was befriending her. I didn't know what to make of it, but maybe it shed some light on why Bridget retreated to the cottage in her dark times.

"Bridget has a kind heart," Colin said. "Always has."

"I wish she'd share some of that goodness with her baby," Grace said, flaring suddenly. "I can only hope the effects of all of this on Little Jimmie won't be too bad."

Colin reached for her hand and squeezed it. "Hope, ah yes," he said. "We must hang on to hope."

CHAPTER 7

Finnegan's Pub was even livelier tonight than it had been two nights ago. Not just crowded, with more customers standing than seated at the bar, but spirits were brighter tonight, as strains of Irish music filled the air.

"On Friday nights the local musicians come in and play in the back room," Finn said, serving up a Guinness for Alex and an Irish coffee for me. We'd managed to squeeze in at the bar to order. "Go on back," Finn urged. "People come and go."

The room at the back of the pub was full, and even the doorway was jammed, but, as Finn had promised, people came and went, so we made our way to where we could see the musicians, and finally a couple of seats opened up. Wall sconces provided dim lighting in the small, intimate room. No more than twenty people at a time could squeeze in at the tables. One could imagine a parlor gathering. Five men and a woman sat in straight-backed chairs in a semi-circle. As we edged in at one of the tables, they were playing an Irish jig. The fiddler was the obvious leader of the band. The other musicians played the mandolin, guitar, wooden flute, a whistle, and a drum-type instrument called a bodhran, I learned when the fiddler announced, "Kevin Conner on the bodhran has a fine new baby boy. How 'bout that?"

On the next tune, everyone joined in, singing, *"In Dublin's fair city, where the girls are so pretty, I first set my eyes on sweet Molly Malone."* I remembered the statue of Molly with her cart in Dublin. "A street-hawker she was," the tour guide had said. "A woman of the streets who died young, and Dubliners have made her a legend. 'Molly Malone' is a favorite drinking song, sung with the fervor of a national anthem." We'd heard the song several times in the pubs of Temple Bar, the cobbled-street area of Dublin. I joined in on the chorus, and the last time around even Alex sang: *"Alive, alive, oh, Alive, alive, oh, Cockles and mussels, alive, alive, oh!"*

After a while, I said, "We should give up our seats." Alex frowned, but when he glanced at the doorway, packed with onlookers, he nodded.

Back at the bar, we found Helen and Charles engaged in conversation with Finn. Another bartender seemed to be doing most of the work tonight. "Me boy, Brendan," Finn explained. "Takes both of us on nights we have the music." He winked.

"Finn was telling us that he also operates a tour service," Helen said.

"What I said was, if you're wanting to go some place in the area, I can provide you with transportation," Finn said. "I have no papers as a tour guide, but I've been living in County Tipperary all my life. My minivan seats seven."

"We should get a group together from Shepherds," Helen said. "Where should we go?"

Finn leaned on the bar. "I can take you to the Cliffs of Moher—a sight to behold! The way the cliffs just drop off to the crashing sea. On a clear day, you can see all the way to the Aran Islands. Or Kilkenny if it's a castle you fancy, and not far from Kilkenny is a village called Tullahought, where you can start the Kilmacoliver loop if you fancy a nature walk."

"We went to Kilkenny yesterday, and Alex went back to Tullahought today," I said.

It was the prompt Alex needed to tell Helen and Charles about the Kilmacoliver Walk. "It's a two-and-a-half-hour walk, maybe closer to three if you take your time, and there's much to see, so why hurry. The view from the summit of Kilmacoliver Hill is simply spectacular."

"You can see five counties," Finn added. "A spectacular view, it is."

Alex raised his finger to call attention to something important. "At the summit there's a circle of standing stones called the Burial Ground, believed to be a prehistoric tomb."

"Dates back five thousand years, they say, and the stones aligned with the setting sun at the time of the Winter Solstice," Finn said.

"Exactly," Alex said. Helen's eyes were fixed on him, expectant. He took a sip of his Guinness, and then it seemed he'd delivered most of the information he could come up with, regarding the Kilmacoliver Walk. "Interesting wildlife and woodlands, all very pleasant to see, especially on a nice day," he said, without his initial enthusiasm.

"I'd like to do that. Wouldn't you, Charles?" Helen said.

Charles gave a faint nod, one of those polite gestures that communicate more than words, and then he perked up. "Is that Lucas? I can't say I expected to see him out tonight." He craned his neck to look down the bar, to the far end, where a man sat drinking alone.

"Oh! Wasn't that his brother-in-law found dead just yesterday? The doctor?" Helen said.

"Stabbed, I heard. Several times," Finn said.

Helen made a face at the gruesome thought. "Lucas Riordan," she said, turning to me. "His father is Liam Riordan. They're a very prominent family in Thurles." Helen had the gift of gab but not the gift of remembering. I nodded and didn't mention she'd told us already, at breakfast on our first morning. I expected to hear the rest, that Charles used to party with Lucas Riordan. I caught a look in Finn's eyes—not disapproval, exactly. More like skepticism.

"I should speak to him. Extend my condolences." Charles threw back the last of his drink and excused himself.

Lucas Riordan, with his sharp nose and sloping forehead, brought to mind a rodent. I couldn't help it. That was my first impression. And yet he was surely the kind of man who believed he was handsome. I could tell from a distance that his immaculately-cut jacket was expensive. He had dark, wavy hair that he might have used to disguise the severe slope of his forehead, but he wore it combed back, emphasizing the waves. The way he carried himself, leaning into the bar, not slumping, like the working men near him who kept their distance from him, the confident air that the well-to-do possess—he was easy to pick out as the son of the "very prominent family" that Helen kept mentioning.

Charles spoke to him and he seemed startled, as if he'd been in a daze. I wondered if they knew each other as well as Helen had suggested, but then Lucas clasped Charles's shoulder and called on the bartender—Brendan—for drinks. Apparently, he was glad to see Charles. Sad that he seemed so alone, I thought, if he'd come to the pub to find comfort among friends. But from what Grace had said about him, maybe it was no surprise that people didn't flock to him.

"Seems they found the body of poor Dr. Malone out in the Red Stag Crossing," Finn said, startling me out of my own daze. "I can't imagine what he was doing out that way, though I've heard he took medicines and such to the old woman out there, name of Magdala." He began to wipe the bar. "I liked Dr. Malone. Can't say much for his wife. I'm no seer of the future, but when the doctor married Norah Riordan, I never thought it would last. Coming from that posh Riordan house to live in rooms above a doctor's office—not a promising move!"

"How long were they married?" I asked.

Finn paused to run his fingers through his thick white hair. "Five, six years, I'd say. Not long. She'd left him in recent months. Gone back to her father, who's not well, I've heard. Someone said Parkinson's disease, and someone else said it's a heart problem, so what do you believe?"

His son motioned to him, and Finn's eyes twinkled. "Guess my break's over."

"We'll let you know if we can get a group together for some sightseeing," I said.

"You do that now!" he said.

Alex gave me a curious look. I shrugged. Something about Finn. He had his finger on the pulse of Thurles. He was someone we needed to know.

Helen set down her glass. "Lucas Riordan is not exactly what I expected." I wondered if she had the same *rodent* thought I'd had.

"You haven't met him?" I said.

"No." She gave a little laugh. "Charles and Lucas knew each other in their youth, long before I met Charles. They were all about partying and golfing, that sort of thing, but then Charles's career took off. Lucas didn't have what it took to be a professional golfer. Oh, he wanted it! But he didn't have the discipline."

"They've remained friends, it seems," Alex said.

"They hadn't seen each other in years until last month when they were both—quite coincidentally—playing at Turnberry. We invited Lucas to our wedding—that was seventeen years ago—but his mother died and her funeral was the day of our wedding. The very day! Isn't that a remarkable coincidence?" Helen paused to sip her drink but before I could manage a comment she took up her story again. "So there we were at Turnberry, and Lucas invited us to Thurles. Oh, I don't know that you'd call it an *invitation* exactly, but he said Charles might be interested in a development he's planning. Something that's not public knowledge, but a golf course will be part of it. So that's why we're here. Charles is hoping Lucas will bring him in to consult on the golf course. He would be a great asset! He's done that sort of consultation from time to time. Not recently." She began to toy with her necklace. "Oh, I'm afraid I've said too much! Charles would be furious with me!"

Alex and I exchanged a glance. "We won't mention it," I said.

We had walked into town. Not my idea. Given that Alex had made the Kilmacoliver Walk today—more than two hours of walking, he'd said—I worried that this would be overdoing it. But he'd insisted, and it was a mild night. Colin had said, "You'll need a torch," and had given us his.

I was glad we had the flashlight as we left the lights of town and turned onto the dark road that led to Shepherds. I was thinking of Bridget O'Toole, out alone and cold on the night she went to see Dr. Malone, when someone called from behind us: "Alex! Jordan! Wait up!"

It took a moment to identify Ian Haverty, running to catch up with us.

"We didn't see you at Finnegan's," Alex said.

"No, I was at The Monks Pub tonight." Ian took a few deep breaths. "Listening to Celtic music."

"That's what we've been doing. Friday night must be the night for music," I said.

"That it is. I was at Finnegan's last Friday night, my first night in town. Good band. So it was tonight at The Monks. The one at Finnegan's might play a little more in a traditional style, but both grand." Ian was setting the pace now, and I had to ask him to slow down a bit. He laughed. "Sorry. You know we walk everywhere so we think nothing of it."

"*Age* comes into play, too," I said.

"Speak for yourself, Jordan," Alex said.

"I was!" I said.

Now the lights of town were some distance behind us. The flashlight was of some use, illuminating the ground in front. I would not have wanted to be out here alone. No cars passed.

"This is early for you to be turning in, isn't it, Ian?" Alex said.

"Ah, maybe so, but I was out much too late last night," Ian said with a chuckle. "Charles Prescott can hold his drink. I'll say that for him!"

We walked a little while in silence, except for the gentle tramping sound our footsteps made on the roadside. As we passed a stand of trees, an owl hooted and Ian jumped. "Mother of God!" he said. "Sounds like the bird is right on us!" I was surprised by his skittishness.

A little farther on, Alex said, "You didn't finish the story you started when we were at Finnegan's—Wednesday night, was it?"

"I remember. The Quinn ladies came over. I suppose they were there tonight, too?"

"No, Molly's performing at The Source tonight," I said. "I'm sure that's where Doreen is. Alex and I are going to the performance tomorrow night."

Before Ian could indicate whether that was of any interest to him, Alex put in. "What about the man with the cows, the priest who performed secret mass—the story you were telling us?"

"I can give you the short version, but you know, I have it on my blog," Ian said.

"Your blog?" Alex said.

"That's what they call it. You post a blog about—well, about whatever you fancy."

"I know what a blog is," Alex said with a trace of irritation. "It's just—*everyone* seems to be posting blogs these days."

75

"Or reading what someone else posted." I was remembering what Colin had said about Mr. Sweeney. He'd read someone's blog about Shepherds.

"Tell us the rest of the story, Ian," Alex urged.

He began, and as before, his voice took on the lilt of a storyteller. "In the days of Cromwell's siege, a man lived with his daughter in some remote part of County Tipperary. He had a spotted cow and a white one. His neighbors knew, if he took only the white cow from the barn in the morning, it meant the priest was coming to his cottage to say mass in secret. Catholics were forbidden to practice our religion, but they couldn't be stopped." Ian paused and looked around him, as if he might have heard something.

"What is it? Is this story too scary to be telling out here on this lonely road, on a dark night?" I was only half-serious, but Ian seemed uneasy, and that made *me* uneasy.

"It's not so scary as it is sad," he said. "The story goes that one day some of Cromwell's men intercepted the priest as he was leaving after he'd said the mass, and they went back and dragged the man from his cottage because he'd been hiding the priest. The daughter rushed after her father, screaming and crying. One of the soldiers raised his weapon and shot her. She fell, clutching her breast, and there she died, under an alder tree. Legend has it a patch of shamrock plants sprang up from the ground where her blood soaked into the earth."

It was a long moment before Alex spoke. "A powerful story."

" 'Tis that," Ian said. "I hope my telling of it, the writing of it, I mean, does it justice. You should go to my blog."

A distant light came into view. Shepherds. I was glad to be this close.

And then a shot rang out.

Instinct took over. We all crouched on the ground, shouting, shrieking—that was *me*, actually. Alex pushed me down, leaning

over me, whispering, "What in damnation was that?"
Ian groaned.

"Ian? Are you all right?" I said, getting my bearings.

"Holy Mother. I think I've been shot," he said.

CHAPTER 8

"What's the emergency number?" I said as we tended to Ian, there on the roadside. Alex tied his handkerchief around Ian's upper arm. I was still crouching beside them, afraid to stand up.

"It's 999, isn't it?" Alex asked Ian. "We need your phone."

Alex was clear-headed enough to realize that it would be an international call on my phone, country code and other numbers, but it should be easy enough with Ian's phone.

"No doctor, no Guard. I don't think it's too bad." Ian touched his arm and made a face, but he was insistent. "Just get me to Shepherds."

There hadn't been a lot of blood. That seemed promising, but I didn't know much about gunshot wounds. "You don't want to risk an infection," I said.

"We *must* call the police—the Guard," Alex said. "Someone may still be out there."

Ian might have relented, but the first car lights we'd seen since leaving town came into sight. Not an ambulance, but it was better than nothing. Alex stood and waved. I hoped he was wrong about someone lurking in the dark hedgerows. The car slowed down and pulled over.

"What happened?" a young man called, standing at his car door.

"He's been shot." Alex said. "Those lights. That's where we're going. Can you give us a ride?"

"Of course! That's Shepherds."

"Who shot him?" asked the young woman in the passenger seat who had opened her door to get a better look.

"We don't know," I said, looking around, wondering that myself.

"Someone must be half-cracked to discharge a weapon out here by the road," she said.

"If it's a hunter—I'm not one myself, but I do know those who go hunting for foxes and rabbits at night. But I expect you would've heard dogs," the young man said.

He started the motor. We huddled in the back seat. Ian was able to sit up between Alex and me, but his expression, a brave grimace, showed that he was in pain.

Overly-friendly, as Alex often alleged, I asked, "Do you know the O'Tooles? Colin and Grace?"

"Of course!" said the young man.

The young woman said, "I went to school with Bridget."

Alex darted a look at me. He must have thought I was going to ask a lot of questions about Bridget. Really! I had better judgment than that, under these circumstances. I said, "Thank you so much for stopping to help us." We could have been carjackers. On the other hand, they could have seen us as easy prey to rob. Sometimes you just had to trust.

"We're coming home from a concert," the young woman said. "It must have been divine intervention that made us stop by the pub—or we would have been along this way an hour ago."

Divine intervention or coincidence—whatever it was, I was happy and thankful for the safe conveyance to Shepherds. The color had drained from Ian's face as the car turned into the driveway and pulled as close to the door as possible.

Alex reached over the driver's shoulder with some bills. "You have done a good thing," he said, giving the shoulder a pat. I didn't know the denomination of the Euros, but the young man drew in a quick breath before voicing his gratitude, and the look he gave the young woman indicated that Alex must have been generous.

I helped Ian out of the car. He managed to say "bless you" in a weak voice.

I was prepared to rouse Grace and Colin if necessary, but Colin was working in the office. "I'll get Grace," he said. "She's not been upstairs ten minutes. Go to the keeping room."

Ian walked, propped up by Alex and me. I thought he was about to faint before we reached the keeping room and helped him to lie down on the daybed. I brought him a glass of water and braced his head with my hand while he took a sip. Colin came back with some towels and blankets. "What in bloody hell happened?" he asked.

We told him what we knew, which was not much. "You didn't see anyone? You have no idea what it's all about?" No, we insisted. With a swipe at his face, Colin said, "Good God. What's happening in Thurles? It's always been such a peaceful place."

By the time Grace arrived, some color had returned to Ian's cheeks. Grace was wearing a robe. She'd had time to remove her makeup. She might have even been asleep already. Colin had said ten minutes, but he hadn't actually timed it. My bet was, if Grace's head had touched the pillow, she'd slept. With infinite calmness, she examined Ian's arm. "It's a superficial wound. You'll be fine," she said.

"I knew it. Though my arm feels like it's burning off," Ian said, his voice a little stronger now.

"Just because the shot grazed your arm, it's doesn't mean you won't hurt like hell," Grace said. "It just means I can fix you up right here with peroxide and bandages, and you won't need to go to the A&E tonight. There's nothing to dig out." Ian scowled. I think I did, too.

"*Now* we should call the police," Alex said.

"I'm not keen on going to the Guards station to make a statement," Ian protested. "Not tonight."

"I'll call. Maybe someone at the station can come out," Colin said without great enthusiasm. I imagined he was ready to be finished with the Guard.

No more than ten minutes later, the police arrived. Colin gave a sigh when the uniformed officers, male and female, flashed their badges and introduced themselves. If they knew anything about the investigation that morning by Inspector Perone, Sergeant Casey, and Garda Mallory, they gave no indication. They took the information from Alex and me and the female officer said, "We'll be letting you know what we find."

"Not likely they'll find anything," Alex said after they were gone. "But we had to report it." I agreed that it was the right thing to do. Was there a chance the shooting was somehow connected to Dr. Malone's murder? I couldn't see how, but at least the police had the report.

A moment later we heard voices in the front room, Helen's, in particular, her shrill question: "What on earth were the bobbies doing *here*?"

Colin said, "Better that I explain to them so they won't worry. Or speculate." He left us in the keeping room.

"You should sleep here," Grace said to Ian. "I'll get you something for the pain."

"Thank you," he said. "Don't know that I'm up to climbing the stairs."

"You will be tomorrow," she said.

The Prescotts and Quinns had come in all at once. Even Mr. Sweeney had returned, it seemed, while Colin was telling the guests what happened, trying to ease any fears they might've had about Thurles. Everyone in but Patrick and Enya. "Friday nights they usually go to Dublin," Grace said. "To dinner or a club, and then overnight with Enya's parents.'"

"It's the compromise Patrick makes," Colin said, closing the door of the keeping room, leaving Ian to sleep after the other guests had gone to their rooms.

"Maybe he enjoys it," Grace said, hooking her arm in Colin's. "You may not remember, Colin O'Toole, but it's good to have a night out sometimes."

"I remember," he said, "and I swear we'll be having one ourselves, girl. Just as soon as we can get all this other business settled."

In my room, I checked my phone. I had a text from Catherine, saying she was leaving Emory, on her way to Savannah. "Relief, a 4.0!" she wrote. "Have fun! Stay out of trouble!"

I hadn't planned on trouble, but I had to wonder: Was the shot *meant* for Ian? Or for Alex? Or for me?

"Lovely! It was simply lovely!" Doreen was saying as I came into the breakfast room. "I must say Molly outdid herself. She wouldn't like me to boast, but it's true."

Grace was unloading the breakfast cart. I saw that Colin was in the kitchen with Little Jimmie and remembered that Patrick and Enya were in Dublin.

"Looks and smells scrumptious, as always," I said. "Did you get any sleep?"

"Oh, yes. Running a B&B, you have to learn how to get by on a few hours. Last night was better than some. How about you? You're up early," she said.

"I've been waking at the crack of dawn, eager to get on with my day, I guess."

"I heard you had some excitement last night," Doreen said as she made her tea. "Any idea what that was all about?"

"Not a clue," I said. "Did you and Molly walk home?"

"We started out to walk, but Helen and Charles stopped for us."

Probably a good thing, I thought, though I couldn't shake the notion that the shooting was not a random thing.

"How is our patient?" I asked Grace.

"He's up. Colin went with him to his room but he said Ian was surprisingly strong on his feet." Grace pushed the empty cart away from the buffet. "Go ahead. Enjoy your breakfast."

Doreen and I filled our plates and sat talking mostly about Molly's performance. Alex joined us, and then Molly. The Prescotts arrived as we were finishing. "I guess Ian isn't going to make it down to breakfast," Molly said. "What a terrible thing that happened to him."

"Not as bad as it could've been," Doreen said.

Mr. Sweeney didn't come to breakfast, but if he was missed, no one said so.

I excused myself, leaving Alex and the Quinn ladies at the table. As I went into the kitchen, I heard Doreen say, "So, Alex, what's on the schedule today?"

Little Jimmie was having his breakfast, and his grandparents were busy cleaning pots and pans. "Maybe I should take Ian some toast and tea," I said, after I'd stopped to say good morning to the little boy, whose smiling face was smeared with jam.

"Good idea," Colin said. "I'll make the tray."

I took the tray up and knocked on Ian's door. "It's Jordan," I said, "with breakfast."

Ian answered without delay. "Good morning. Ah, now that's what I need."

"You look much better than the last time I saw you," I said.

"I just finished cleaning up a bit. I'm feeling like I might live now," he said. "Please come in if you don't mind the mess."

I saw the desk was cluttered and looked for somewhere else

to set the tray, but Ian went to the desk and moved the books, papers, and laptop onto the foot of his unmade bed to make a space. "This is grand, right here," he said.

"I see you're not using your left arm," I said.

"Better that it wasn't my right."

I put down the tray. "I don't suppose you have any idea who shot at us—at you."

"Do you think someone was aiming at me? I thought I was just the unlucky one."

"I can't imagine why Alex or I would've been the target. We're not from around here."

"I'm not from around here either," he said, pouring tea from the pot. "Sure, I've been asking questions, trying to gather more legends and tales for my book. You don't think there's a connection with my book, do you?"

"I have no reason to think so, but I don't think the shot was fired by a hunter," I said.

"Who then? And why? I have no enemies that I know of." He finished with the cream and sugar and stirred. "Sweet Mother, I don't want to spend the rest of my holiday jumping at shadows, thinking someone's going to shoot me."

I didn't mention that he *had* jumped at shadows a couple of times last night. We'd probably all seemed a bit jittery out on the lonely, dark road, with the owl hooting.

Ian raised the cup to his lips. His expression showed that the tea hit the spot. "You look pensive, Jordan. Tell me if you have some theory."

"I don't have a theory," I said. I was back to the question: Was Ian the target, or Alex, or me? I turned toward the door. "Enjoy your breakfast. I guess you'll be staying in today, resting."

"I probably should," he said, "but a man at Monks last night told me I should try to find an old woman who lives out in Red

Stag Crossing. He said she's probably ninety, and she's lived there all her life, plus she's a little—you know." He made the whirly sign for crazy.

I tried not to show any reaction, but I wondered what Grace and Colin would say if they knew he was going to seek out Magdala. "You should give yourself a little more time to get stronger." Before he could answer, I added, "Why don't you go to The Source with Alex and me tonight. Assuming you're feeling up to it. It shouldn't tire you too much, just to sit in a comfortable seat and listen to a concert."

"That's Molly's performance," he said.

I gave a coy little smile. "Bet she'd be happy to get you a ticket."

"I'll go then," he said. "Would you mind asking her about the ticket?" I couldn't tell if he was playing innocent, showing no particular interest in Molly, nor acknowledging her interest in him. If he was, he was good at it.

The door was open. I was about to enter the hall when he said, "There is one thing."

I turned around. He made a motion for me to close the door. He set his cup on the desk, asking, "Did you hear anything before it happened?"

"Before the shot?"

He nodded. "A rustling sound? I don't know—maybe it was just—a feeling, something you sense when someone is near. But first there was the hooting owl."

"I heard the owl, nothing else. You did seem a little jumpy, Ian."

"I might have been, a wee bit." He looked at me with those dark eyes Helen had called *dreamy*. I could see a sudden glitter of anxiety. "That bloody owl. I've been going to the pub most nights, you know. Most times I walk home. Three times now, I've heard the owl."

He paused, as if waiting for me to say something. I had no logical explanation, but I gave it a try. "Maybe you pass the owl's tree and disturb him. And he hoots. Maybe it's as simple as that."

Ian gave a vigorous shake of his head, his dark curls bobbing. "It wasn't the same place along the road, not tonight." He reached back for the desk chair and eased himself into it.

"Are you all right?" I said. "Why don't you drink some more tea."

He did. "I was feeling a bit weak in the knees. Maybe I'm not mended, after all."

"I'm sure you're not mended. Not yet. It's only been a few hours. You need to rest."

He looked into his teacup. I sensed he was embarrassed to look at me directly as he said, "Y'know, one of the legends in my book has an owl as a harbinger of death. A man is acquitted of a crime, but he's guilty, and the guilt he carries inside him drives him to madness. The owl comes to him three times." He stopped but did not look up.

I said, "And the third time?"

"After the third time, he plunges a dagger into his own heart."

I caught my breath. "Well, you didn't do that."

A smile curled on Ian's lips, and he raised his eyes to mine at last. "No, I did not."

"Are you carrying a big load of guilt about something?"

"No, I am not." His smile widened.

"Ian, I know you're a very imaginative writer, but—you don't *really* think the owl we heard has anything to do with your story, do you? Or with the shooting?"

He gave a sheepish look. "All of it does seem a bit mad, doesn't it? Forgive me. Sometimes we Irish get too much into fanciful things."

"All the same, I'd like to read your story."

"It's on my blog," he said. "I posted two of my stories, and that's one of them."

Your blog keeps coming up, I thought, but I didn't say it. He was touching his arm, wincing.

I went to the door. "I need to let you have your breakfast. Take it easy now, and I'll see Molly about that ticket."

CHAPTER 9

We were on our way to the town of Cashel in South Tipperary, site of the castle ruins known as the Rock of Cashel, only a half hour from Thurles. I should not have been surprised that Doreen Quinn was going with us.

I had knocked on the Quinns' door to see Molly about getting Ian a ticket for her performance. How she had beamed! Doreen, from somewhere in the room, had called out, "Better hurry, Jordan! Alex will be waiting. We're going to the Rock of Cashel."

"Right," I'd said, unable to keep the irritation from my voice, refusing to admit that Alex hadn't consulted me about his plans. I was happy for him to make our itinerary—his book was our *raison d'etre*—but was he just a *wee bit* influenced by what Doreen wanted to visit?

Alex was standing at my door when I came upstairs. "Jordan," he began in that particular tone that bordered on apology—but not quite.

"Better hurry, Alex," I said. "Doreen tells me we're going to the Rock of Cashel. I can be downstairs in ten. Does that work? Doreen didn't give me your exact timetable." Alex looked as if he would speak, but he simply pursed his lips and nodded, and I muttered, "Oh, it's all right."

Doreen, who had visited the attraction previously, and Alex, with his fistful of brochures, provided me with a comprehensive lesson on the historic site as I drove the twenty-five kilometers, mostly on the M8. Even with my head full of facts, the magnificent icon made my breath catch when it came into view, some distance from the town.

Doreen, leaning between us from the back seat—though I had mentioned the seatbelt to her several times—said, "There 'tis, like the Devil dropped it from the sky, don't you see?" She'd told us the legend, that the Devil was flying overhead and saw St. Patrick founding a new church, and in his anger, he dropped the Rock, creating the spectacular sight.

"What a photo op! Alex, get your camera," I said.

"Ah, you'll have plenty of chances for pictures," Doreen said, "from anywhere in town."

"But this view! So majestic."

"Watch the road, Jordan. I'll take care of the photos," Alex said, raising the camera for a shot. I slowed the car to a crawl, until I realized I was holding up a string of cars behind me.

As she had done in Kilkenny, Doreen gave directions for parking in the vibrant little town. I had to admit that whether the Rock of Cashel was Doreen's idea or Alex's, it was an excellent one. "This is a tour I don't mind taking again," Doreen said. "It starts at the Tourist Office, there at the Town Hall." She led the way, walking at a brisk pace past quaint little shops. I took advantage of the photo ops everywhere. My first shot was of the huge Celtic cross in the Victorian town center.

Though I was expecting a tour guide, I was glad to see we would be purchasing an audio tour, using headphones. "This is nice," I said. "It allows each of us to speed up or slow down."

Doreen said, "We should all stay together, don't you think?"

Alex glanced at me and then fixed Doreen with a serious look. "I don't want to make you ladies wait for me. Maybe we should just decide on a meeting place and a certain time for all of us to come back together."

Thank you, Alex! For all the times I was annoyed with him, I had to say he'd made remarkable progress since we'd first traveled together. He could listen to a tour guide drone on all day, the more intricate the details, the better, and he'd expected me to do the same. Now he seemed to accept that whether I was touring a museum or a town, I was happier making my own discoveries. The audio tour was the perfect tool for someone with my particular attention span—short or long, depending on whether I was being active or passive.

But Doreen was not easily put off. "Oh, you're every bit as fit as we are," she said with a playful slap on Alex's arm. "No reason you can't keep up. You had no trouble on the Kilmacoliver Walk."

"You're kind to say so, Doreen, but I meant that I'll be making notes. Jordan will be taking photos—from an architect's vantage point—and you should feel free to do whatever you like as well." He smiled, and I was certain he was certain he'd made his point.

"I'll just stay with you then," Doreen said. "You take all the time you want, and don't worry your head about me."

I would have been more amused if Alex had not made the effort to liberate me from Doreen's cloying presence—and now he was stuck with her. "I won't get too far off track," I promised, "but if we *happen* to get separated, let's meet at the Heritage Centre." The Heritage Centre Museum, Tourist Information Office, and Town Hall were all in the same general locale. Alex had read a description of the museum from his brochure. Not only did it house a craft shop, featuring local textiles, but it also featured a full-scale model of the town of Cashel in the 1640s. That was on *my* list of things to see, and I wouldn't want to be hurried.

"It's settled then. We should get started," Alex said. He put on his earphones and turned on the audio. Doreen did so, too, but with some hesitation. It meant she had to stop talking.

The first point of interest—and all three of us stopped to take notice—was the main entrance of the Town Hall, where the stocks from the late 1700s and 1800s remained. At that time, it was customary for the townspeople to take matters into their own hands, throwing rotting vegetables and eggs at the lawbreaker detained in the stocks. The narrator on the audio tour suggested that this kind of public discipline might be just the thing for delinquents and petty criminals in modern times, as it was then. Everyone on the tour—maybe fifteen in all— smiled at almost the same time. We were all just getting started, all at the beginning of the recording.

But at that point, several tourists hiked ahead at a fast clip, clearly heading up the steep path toward the castle ruins that dominated everything. That was my inclination as well. Alex was scribbling in his little notebook, with Doreen at his side, blissfully content to stroll at a snail's pace if her placid expression was any indication. I doubted they would notice if I forged on ahead. Still, I found myself stopping at each shop along the long, steep path, perusing linens, woolens, and jewelry, waiting, making sure Alex and Doreen were not too far behind.

"Cashel, known as the City of Kings, has a glorious past. Kings of the Munster Province ruled from the Rock for five hundred years until, in 1101, the king handed over his fortress to the Bishop of Limerick," explained the female narrator with a most engaging Irish accent. I found myself more intrigued than I had anticipated as she described significant events associated with the Rock of Cashel, events that had helped shape Ireland's history, from the stirring speech by Daniel O'Connell, the great Irish liberator, in 1847, to Queen Elizabeth's visit in 2011. *"A concert by John McCormack in 1929 might be called the first mass*

pop concert," said the narrator. *"The famous Irish tenor sang to some 25,000 to 40,000 fans from the Rock of Cashel."* Here, St. Patrick first used the shamrock to explain the Holy Trinity, and Arthur Guinness was said to have developed his famous brew at Cashel. All of it fascinating!

I looked over my shoulder and saw Alex and Doreen making their way past the Irish woolens shop. No reason for me to wait for them to catch up.

Up ahead, the ancient ruins beckoned.

Most of the buildings on the site dated back to the twelfth and thirteenth centuries. Walking through and around the limestone remains, perusing what was called *"one of the finest collections of medieval art and architecture in the world,"* I found the audio tour a tremendous asset. Alex would be astonished when I told him how much I was enjoying the tour.

Sometime later, I heard him call my name. I was outside, taking photos of the rolling pastures and the town of Cashel below. A little break from the helpful narrator. I turned and saw Alex and Doreen remove their headphones. Alex retrieved his handkerchief and wiped his face.

"Are you all right?" I said.

"Just a little out of breath."

I thought of the angina attack Alex suffered in Provence, the night after he had walked up a steep path, but that hike was much longer than the one from the town center to the castle ruins.

"I can almost see those wheels turning in your mind, Jordan," Alex said. "Please, don't worry about me. I may have let myself get overheated, but, really, it's nothing serious."

His cheeks were flushed, but I knew not to argue. Doreen rolled her eyes as if to say, *Didn't I tell him?* I looked around for a section of rock wall that was low enough for sitting, and Alex didn't balk at my suggestion. "Perfect for viewing the Golden Vale of South Tipperary," I said, stretching out my hand to indicate the encircling plain that seemed to extend forever. Alex raised his eyebrows in surprise. Yes, I had been paying attention. I returned a smile.

I busied myself capturing the panoramic scene on film: the little town with its charming houses, the sheep in the green pastures, low rock walls and narrow roads making patterns throughout the valley, all of it set under a clear blue sky. After a cool morning, the day had warmed up and the breeze was mild. I didn't mind sitting here as long as Alex needed to rest.

But that wasn't long. He stood up and consulted a map of the structure. "I understand the oldest building here is the eleventh-century Round Tower," he said. "The rocks were laid without mortar. You have to see that, Jordan."

I frowned. "I did! I was going to show off and tell you all about the dry stone method."

"We must see the original St. Patrick's cross," Doreen said, leading the way.

We all put on our headphones.

An hour passed before we knew it, much of the time spent in Cormac's Chapel, with its magnificent vaulted ceiling and Romanesque frescoes, the oldest wall paintings in Ireland, and an exquisitely carved sarcophagus that might be the tomb of King Cormac himself, or possibly his brother. Alex—and Doreen, sticking close by him—lingered in the museum of the Hall of the Vicars Choral, where artifacts excavated from the site were on display, while I gravitated to the five-story Tower House and the Cathedral with its lancet windows and ornate wall tombs. Eventually, all of us viewed everything. It was early afternoon before we made our way down the hill. We had a hearty lunch—shepherd's pie, in my case—at one of the restaurants on Main Street, shared a pot of tea, and recalled for each other the highlights of the day so far.

Alex seemed fine, after the earlier episode of "overheating," but I said, "We need to give ourselves some time to unwind before we go to Molly's performance this evening."

"I'm quite unwound," Alex said, lifting his cup of steaming tea, "and there's so much else to see. The Folk Village is supposed to have an excellent reconstruction of shops and houses from the past. Some of the finest examples of thatched roofs in Ireland, I understand." We compromised. Alex went to Folk Village, and I went to the Heritage Centre, specifically to see the model of Cashel as it was in the 1640s. Doreen elected to accompany me, saying that she'd seen the Folk Village on her previous visit and didn't care to pay admission again.

As we headed toward the museum, she said, "Your uncle is a dear man, sure as the day is long, but he is a wee bit stubborn, don't you think?"

"Oh yes," I said. She didn't know the half of it.

We arrived at Shepherds in the middle of a "row," as Helen would have called it. The door to the office behind Reception was ajar, and voices were easy to hear.

"We just got back! Don't I get to take a breath before you put me to work?" The petulant Enya, no doubt.

"I have to go to the market." Grace's calmer voice. "Little Jimmie will wake up any time now, and I'm just asking you to take care of him till I get back. He'll need his snack. You know the routine, Enya. It's not so hard."

"We'll see to Little Jimmie. It's not a problem, Mam." Patrick's voice.

"It *is* a problem! You never take *my* side," Enya complained.

"We had a night in town, Enya."

"So I'm being punished for having some fun? And where's Colin, by the way? He's always sneaking out somewhere."

"My God, Enya!" Patrick raised his voice.

"I'll be as quick as I can." Grace came out of the room and closed the door behind her. By this time Alex and I were nearing the top of the stairs. We might have already been out of earshot, but I was following Alex, who was taking each stair with a heavy step, slowing our progress. Doreen had entered the other wing by a door that stayed unlocked during the day.

Grace saw us and called up to us. "I apologize. Just trying to get away to buy the week's groceries. I usually shop on Friday, so I'm running out of everything."

I stopped on the stairs and turned to look down at her. Friday morning had started with the police at the door, asking for Bridget. Grace had spent much of the day waiting, wondering whether her daughter would be arrested for murder. No wonder she hadn't bought groceries.

"Would you like for me to go to the market with you?" I said.

"Jordan, you simply *won't* behave like our guest."

"I thought we'd covered that. As a matter of fact, I need some fruit and water and granola bars to take on our day trips, to keep our energy up." My mind flashed back to Alex's damp brow and flushed cheeks. I saw he had gone on to his room. "Let me tell Alex where I'm going."

Grace didn't object. She simply said, "I have to get my list."

I knocked on Alex's door, and he called for me to come in. He was already sitting on the bed, taking off his shoes. I fussed over him for a minute, worried that the visit to the Rock of Cashel had been *too much*, but I gave up when he lay back on top of the covers and said, "I'm taking care of myself, Jordan. Now *please*—stop acting like my nursemaid. I just need you to go, so I can take a nap!" He sounded quite vigorous.

I left him to his rest and turned in the hall to see Ian Haverty in his doorway.

"I've been listening for you to come in," he said in a quiet voice.

"Molly has a ticket for you, so we're on for tonight." I walked over to him, keeping my voice just above a whisper. Alex's door was closed but sound carried easily through the thin walls, a product of the renovation Colin had described. "Alex is trying to nap."

"I heard," he said.

I studied his face, his tousled hair. He looked as if he'd spent the day in bed.

"How's your arm?"

He touched his sleeve. "Sore is all. Grace cleaned the wound again today."

Ian's expression was worrisome. He must have needed to tell me something, but I knew Grace was waiting for me. I said, "Grace and I are going to the grocery, but I'll check with you when I get back—when I find out what time the performance starts."

"Ah—sorry." He stepped back into his room. "Don't let me keep you."

And then I couldn't resist asking, "Is something wrong, Ian?"

I was surprised by his answer: "Yes, I think so." He added, "But it can wait till tonight. I'm looking forward to getting out of my room."

On the way to buy groceries, Grace said, "How could Enya say that Colin is always 'sneaking off'? What a little bitch she is! Forgive me for that, Jordan, but Colin has been nothing but kind to our spoiled daughter-in-law. As for sneaking off today, he went out into the country to see someone about a used mower. Ours keeps breaking down. It doesn't make sense to keep buying parts—but used mowers aren't cheap." This was another time that Grace had stopped before delving too deeply into their financial situation. She'd lifted her shoulders and laughed—a laugh without much merriment in it. "Oh, the joys of running a country inn!"

It felt a little like a girls' afternoon out. Grace was more relaxed by the time we returned. Patrick and Enya were in the backyard, swinging Little Jimmie. Grace said in a near-whisper, "You might be right, Jordan. Maybe Enya would like a baby of her own."

"One thing's for sure," I said. "You can't do anything about that."

"No, I can't!" This time her laugh was bright.

In my room, as I was choosing what to wear to the concert, my phone jingled. I checked the caller ID. Though "Caller Unknown" appeared, I recognized the string of digits, the country code—France—and the city code—Paris.

The number belonged to Paul Broussard.

I let the phone ring and ring and ring, and then I let the message go to voice mail.

Monsieur Broussard, wealthy and charming patron of the arts— how complicated it was with this man! We'd had an adventure and almost a romance in Provence. Almost. We'd danced under the stars. He'd saved my life. Our time together ran out, but there would be another chance for us—there was *supposed* to be another chance. In Savannah, his calls made me a little woozy, like a teenager, the sound of his voice: *It won't be long now, Jordan, and this time we will not be foolish. We will not let anything get in our way.*

In January he came to the States to promote an extraordinary young artist named Emil. The first gallery showing was in New York. With Alex's influence, a gallery in Atlanta also showed Emil's work. There was a fabulous, highly successful reception. Emil was there, smiling his shy smile, expressing great appreciation for everyone's helpfulness. Alex was there. I was there. I had waited three months for that night. But Paul Broussard was not there.

An urgent personal matter, he had said.

Another call two weeks later, and he had said, *It is not possible yet to explain everything, but please trust me.*

Now I went to voice mail and felt that familiar stitch in my chest when he spoke. *Jordan, I hope you will not be too angry with me. I called your home in an attempt to reach you. Your daughter said you were in Ireland. Do not blame her. If you must, blame me for my insistence. It is not a long flight from Paris to Dublin, and I want very much to see you. Please, call me.*

A pause, and then *Au revoir, Jordan.* My lips formed a silent, "Au revoir, Paul."

CHAPTER 10

The concert was magnificent. Alex expressed what I'd been thinking when our little group of four stretched our legs during intermission. "I think I was expecting to hear what the Atlanta Chamber Music Society plays—or what they played when I used to buy season tickets. I would have enjoyed that, but this is a delightful surprise!"

"And Molly—I can't say enough about her talent," I told Doreen. "She's made me fall in love with the violin." It wasn't empty flattery. Molly's performance was flawless, not only the classical pieces we had expected, but the pop, light rock, and jazz pieces she had played with just as much skill. Billed as "an eclectic program for a large ensemble," the concert expanded on the string quartet Alex and I both had associated with the violin. In addition to violins, viola, cello, and bass, the ensemble featured trumpet and saxophone, clarinet and flute, harp, piano, and one female voice, a soprano who would sing the operatic arias we had not yet heard.

"Molly's very good," Ian said. He'd been quiet—distracted—but now he smiled at Doreen. "Ah, to play an instrument the way she does, any instrument, it would be such an accomplishment."

"Or to write a book, Ian. Writing stories is a gift, too," Doreen said. She patted his arm. "Oh, that's not your sore one, is it? Thank God."

It was refreshing to see Doreen like this, not so self-absorbed.

The lights flickered. We made our way back to our seats, four together in the center, not more than a dozen rows back.

Molly, as first violinist, had a solo part on the Mozart concerto that introduced the second half, and then the soprano came out for an aria from one of Bellini's operas. The extensive program allowed for smaller groupings of instruments so that each section got to shine on one piece or another, but Molly's violin was rarely excluded. When the strings performed Beethoven's String Quartet in D, Alex gave me a nod, as if to say, *This is the kind of chamber music I know something about, and I approve.* The soprano sang another lengthy operatic aria. A suite of Beatles classics might have ended the evening on a high note, judging from the enthusiastic applause, but the Celtic music, saved for the finale, took it all up a notch. The audience, faces all aglow, clapped in time with a merry Irish tune. A colorful jig followed, with more wild applause. The final piece, performed by the entire ensemble, was "Londonderry Air."

As I listened to the familiar melody, played with the deep emotion that perhaps only Irish musicians could give to the song, I studied the faces around me. Doreen's eyes glistened. Ian looked as if his heart might break, and he was not alone. Around us, the rapt expressions of men and women alike made me think of the days when sports events all over America began with everyone singing the national anthem. Not a professional, a celebrity, a superstar, a diva, but ordinary people, with hands over our hearts, joining voices in patriotic pride. "Londonderry Air" brought out the essence of the Irish people—the passions, the memories, the shared spirit. I was beginning to understand something that Ian had tried to explain. I felt my own throat tighten. Alex had closed his eyes. The sweet music, like a singing voice, ended, and we all rose to our feet in spontaneous applause that thundered on and on, until the conductor signaled an encore. We sat down again, and the ensemble entertained for another few minutes with another lively tune, "a drinking song," according to Doreen. More clapping—and laughter this time.

Hard to believe nearly three hours had elapsed since we'd gathered in the performance hall. We stood around, as did many others, waiting for the musicians to pack up their instruments, recalling the high points of the concert. Doreen was complimentary of the conductor who also served as the music director of the ensemble, and who had arranged most of the music as well. "I hope the college can hold on to him after the great success of this concert season," she was saying as Molly came into sight. Molly was radiant, still experiencing the performer's adrenalin rush, no doubt, but I suspected part of her excitement came from knowing Ian had been there to hear her play.

"You played very well, Molly," Ian said, and the color intensified in her cheeks as she thanked him. Alex and I lavished praise, too, but she didn't blush over our compliments.

"Last night there was a lovely reception," Doreen said.

"That was opening night. Nothing tonight. Nowhere I have to go," Molly said, looking from her mother to Ian to me, and finally to Alex when no one spoke up immediately.

"Shall we go somewhere to celebrate?" I said, not certain how to read Alex and Ian, neither being quite as transparent as Doreen and Molly.

"I think I'll have to ask you to drop me back at Shepherds, Jordan," Alex said, and then he turned to the others. "How I hate to admit it, but I may have overexerted myself today. You know this niece of mine keeps insisting that I take care of myself. Tonight I think I should."

Ian was quick to add, "I'm feeling I should do the same. I'm sorry, Molly. You deserve to celebrate, but I wouldn't be much fun tonight."

The hope fell from Molly's face, as surely as if the blow had been a physical one. As I was trying to decide whether Molly would have any desire to celebrate with her mother and me, the young woman who had played the cello came by, asking, "Are you going to join us, Molly? Not sure where yet. And you, Mrs. Quinn?" Molly's friends apparently knew her mother well.

"Oh, sure! You don't mind, do you, Jordan?" Doreen said.

"Not at all." I hoped I didn't sound too relieved. "Will you be all right, getting home?"

"Don't worry about us." She took hold of her daughter's arm. "Come, love!"

Doreen and Molly left to catch up with the cellist—Molly, looking downcast, and Doreen, oblivious to her daughter's disappointment.

Driving to Shepherds, I couldn't help thinking that last night, at about this time, we were walking along the same dark road, when we heard shots. Or was it just one? I couldn't recall. Maybe Ian was thinking about it, too. I asked, "Are you asleep back there, Ian?"

"No, but I could be if the drive were a bit longer," he said.

A few minutes later, back at the B&B, Alex remarked, "The O'Tooles must have turned in early tonight." Reception was dimly lit, two lamps, both turned low. No crack of light showing from under the door to the office.

"Everyone deserves a night off," I said. True especially of Grace and Colin.

Upstairs, Alex was first to unlock his door and say goodnight. "Sleep well," I said. My room was across the hall from his and Ian's rooms, but I took my time with my key, and when Alex's door closed behind him, I turned to Ian. "I'm sorry I had to rush off to meet Grace this afternoon. I had a feeling you were going to tell me something."

When Grace and I had returned from the grocery, Ian and Charles were bent over the chess board—surely they had finished the game from two nights ago. I'd told Ian to meet Alex, Doreen, and me at seven o'clock and he'd said he would. That was the extent of our conversation.

"I wanted to show you something, but I think I took it too seriously. It's probably not important." Ian fidgeted with the keys in his hand, his room key on a chain with other keys.

"Are you sure it's not important?" I said.

He sighed. "Come in. I'll pull it up on my laptop."

I followed him into his room, to the desk where I had set his tray at breakfast. His belongings were more cluttered than they'd been this morning, but this time he didn't apologize. He turned on his computer and struck a few keys.

"This comment showed up on my website at 10:35 a.m. today." He stepped back, and I moved closer to the desk, leaning in toward the screen.

The message read: *If you were meant to be dead, you would be.*

I caught my breath. "This is serious, Ian," I said.

"It could be a joke," he said, but without confidence.

"What does that mean—*pending*?"

"I have it set up so I can read the comments and make sure I want to post them. And a good thing it is. No one else has seen this."

"I don't think it's a joke. This message has to be from the person who shot you."

Ian breathed a long, deep sigh. "I did not want to believe *I* was the target. I still don't understand why. Who would do this? I don't have any enemies."

Obviously, he did have an enemy. I said, "You need to take this to the police."

"Oh, Jordan," he said with a little laugh, "you've been watching too many crime shows on American television. I know about *CSI*. I spent a month with my sister's family in Chicago last summer. Her husband is addicted to those shows. What's the other one that has the girl with the pigtails—Abby? And Mc-Gee. Oh, sure, Abby and McGee might uncover a terrorist cell from a hotmail account like this one, but you can't be expecting the same from *an garda síochána.*"

"Maybe Patrick could help," I said. "I hear he's a computer whiz. He teaches computer networking, doesn't he?"

"Something about computers at LIT Tipperary." Ian closed down his laptop.

"I still think you should go to the police. They know about the shooting. If they have a suspect in mind, they could check that person's computer to see if the message came from it."

"And do you believe they have a suspect, Jordan? You really do watch too many crime shows," Ian said, the corner of his mouth turned up in a half-grin.

I raised my hands in a helpless gesture. "I'll let you get some rest," I said, "but please think about contacting the police—the Guard."

"I'll give it a think," he said. "At least I know the shooter wasn't trying to kill me."

Not *that* time, I thought.

Back in my room, I listened to Paul Broussard's message again. *I want very much to see you,* he had said. Meet in Dublin? So tempting. I almost made the call. But I didn't.

Sunday morning I was up early again, eager for the scrumptious Irish breakfast that Grace always prepared. Before the performance last night, we'd had cheese, fruit, and tea, not a hearty meal. This morning Colin and Enya were scurrying from the kitchen to the breakfast room and back. I saw Patrick at the kitchen table, tending to Little Jimmie's breakfast. Not seeing Grace, I wondered at first if she might be sick, but no, she'd gone to early mass. "Father Tierney must be heaping on the guilt this morning," Colin said. "Grace is usually back by this time—it's why she goes to the early mass—but the Father's homilies have been getting a bit long-winded."

The coffee was ready. I filled a cup from the coffee urn. Maybe I was *too* early, but before Enya had delivered all the platters, Alex arrived, and the Prescotts were not far behind. I couldn't help thinking that Molly would be delighted to see our four-top table filled. She and her mother would have to go to another table, and likely Ian would join them.

"Was the concert simply wonderful?" Helen asked.

"It was," I said. "Simply wonderful."

"We should go to one of the performances," she said to Charles. "I wonder how many more there are?"

"I know there's a matinee this afternoon," I said.

"I'm afraid it's out of the question today." Charles peered out the window. The sun was bright and the sky was blue. Perfect day to be on the golf course.

Mr. Sweeney was the next to arrive. I made a point of saying, "Good morning!" and the others at my table did the same. He might have wondered if we had a pact, all of us determined to extend a jolly greeting that he'd be so obviously rude to ignore. We had no such pact, but he was obliged to say, "Good morning," and he did. He filled his plate and sat at an empty table. A minute later Ian joined him and actually engaged him in a few words of conversation—about Dublin, it seemed—though it was evident to anyone paying attention that Mr. Sweeney couldn't wait to eat and run. By the time Doreen and Molly came to breakfast, Mr. Sweeney was wiping his plate with his bread.

"Thank you for going to the concert last night, Ian," Molly said.

"Thank *you*. I enjoyed it very much," Ian said.

Mr. Sweeney stood up with a careless toss of his napkin onto his plate. "You play the violin?" he asked with a quick glance at Molly, and when she answered yes, he said, "My son did."

I was astonished that he'd offered that personal information. As I tried to eavesdrop without being conspicious, Helen said, "Do you, Jordan? Because we should go on and make arrangements," and I realized she'd already asked me something that I had ignored.

Alex said, "The Cliffs of Moher are certainly a sight I don't want to miss. If Finn is taking a group, that might be the way to do it."

"Nothing has been arranged. That's why I was asking," Helen said. "Finn mentioned it again last night, and I said I'd ask some of the other guests at Shepherds. What do you think, Jordan?"

"I think it would be fun," I said. I couldn't keep from glancing at the other table, where Doreen and Molly were settling in on either side of Ian. Mr. Sweeney had hurried from the breakfast room. I had the impression he had shocked himself by mentioning his son.

"I'm sure Ian will want to go, too," Helen said, "and Molly and Doreen."

"Molly's ensemble is performing a couple of afternoons," I said.

Helen stood, picking up her teacup. On her way to the buffet, she stopped at the other table and a minute later she was sitting at the fourth seat and had taken charge of the conversation.

Charles shook his head. "You know she means well," he said.

I had a glimpse of Grace in the kitchen when I was leaving the breakfast room. Alex and Charles were still at the table, discussing the future of the British monarchy. Grace waved. She and her family seemed quite busy, rattling pots and pans. I went up to my room.

A few minutes later Grace knocked on my door.

"Busy morning," she said, adjusting the apron she wore over her church clothes. I invited her in. She stepped just inside the door. "Can't stay. I'm needed downstairs. I just came to ask if you'd like to go for a walk with me this afternoon."

"A walk—where?"

"I thought we might go out to Red Stag Crossing."

The light in her eyes said it all. She was going to see about her daughter.

"I'd love to go with you." I didn't finish my thought—*but I'm surprised you've invited me on this errand that seems so personal.*

She must have read my mind. "I want Bridget to come home. We can get her some professional help if she'll just come home. You know her story, and you have daughters, Jordan. I'm hoping you can give me some—advice, maybe."

My four daughters and I had certainly experienced our ups and downs, but nothing that would qualify me to give advice on this serious matter. "Not advice," I said. "But support, yes, of course. Whatever you need, Grace." I put my hand on her arm and squeezed.

"Support, then," she said.

CHAPTER 11

Grace drove. We took the main road a short distance toward town and then turned onto a narrow lane, the lane so obscure that I hadn't ever paid attention to it when we were driving into town. But now, as we turned, I said, "Back there, I think that's where Ian was shot."

I remembered the trees and the hooting owl. The shooting had happened not long after we'd passed that point. "It didn't register before, but there aren't many trees along the road. This was definitely the place."

"Ireland doesn't have many forests," Grace said. "There are just a few wooded areas around Thurles." She gave a bitter little laugh. "Someone like Lucas Riordan will probably buy up these woodlands before long and cut the trees and pour concrete over it all." She'd come incredibly close to describing what Helen had divulged about Lucas's planned development.

The lane may have just *seemed* to wind on and on because we were proceeding so slowly on the uneven dirt surface. Grace said it was less than a mile from the main road to the place we'd have to park and walk the rest of the way.

"What was Alex doing today?" she asked.

"Organizing his notes from our trip to Cashel," I said. "He likes to write as he goes, while everything's fresh in his mind. I told him what we were doing. You don't mind, do you?"

"Not at all. I trust you and Alex. I just think it's best to keep our family secrets from the other guests as long as possible. If

Bridget comes home with us—we'll deal with that if it happens. *When* it happens, I should say," she added, on a cheery note that seemed forced; then her level-headedness took over. "I'm trying to be optimistic. I have to hope." A minute later she pulled the car to the side of the road. There wasn't much shoulder. I thought she was parking dangerously close to a ditch in which a thin stream of water flowed, but she knew this location far better than I. "Now we walk," she said.

She took a wicker basket from the back seat, and we headed into the woods on foot.

Red Stag Crossing, they called this place, and I could see it as a habitat for deer. All kinds of woodland creatures might scamper from the underbrush or dance on the branches that hung over our footpath, a somewhat-defined trail but rough, with roots and rocks that might trip up an unsuspecting hiker. The sunlight filtered through the delicate leaves of medium-size trees with gray, spotted bark. What I had imagined as a dense, dark forest when Grace and Colin had talked about Red Stag Crossing was not like that at all. It was airy and luminous.

I remarked to Grace about the purplish air.

She laughed. "It's the alder trees. Their small, scaly clusters have a purple tinge in the spring. That's what makes the purple sheen."

"Alder," I repeated. I remembered something about the alder tree from Ian's story.

"From the birch family," Grace said. "The Irish have all kinds of stories about the alder tree. It's associated with death, the guardian of travelers to the Otherworld. Legend has it that its branches were used to measure graves. And it's said that when the alder is cut, the light-colored wood changes to orange and then red, as if it's bleeding."

"You'll have to tell Ian about the alder," I said. "You may know he's collecting legends for his book. He's been talking to old men in the pubs, but he needn't have left Shepherds."

"Anyone who lives in Ireland as long as I have is bound to know the legends, whether Irish-born or not," she said. "There's another one about a man who cut down a giant alder tree that was inhabited by a tree spirit, and he was cursed by the hag, Famine, with a hunger he couldn't satisfy. In the end, when food would not relieve his hunger, he devoured himself."

Grace rearranged her red wool wrap that she wore over a light sweater and shifted the basket to her other arm. I couldn't help thinking about Red Riding Hood. The woods had the aura of fantasy—magical, but eerie, too. I could almost imagine a leprechaun popping out from one of the thickets.

"Wonder where Dr. Malone's body was found." Grace jolted me from my thoughts.

I said, "I don't suppose anyone knows why he was out this way."

"Seems the coroner is now saying the doctor's body was moved—brought out here from somewhere else. That's what Colin heard. A good thing for Bridget. *She* couldn't manage to do that. Oh, I just pray to God it will all be cleared up soon." Grace directed an anxious gaze at me. I understood. No matter that the old woman, Magdala, gave Bridget an alibi or that Bridget couldn't have managed to move a man's body. Grace's worries would not go away completely until the truth was known, until someone else was charged with the murder.

We walked in silence for a minute longer until Grace said, "There it is."

The gray stone cottage blended into the trees so that I had to blink twice to make it out. A little "Oh!" escaped me. I wasn't sure what I'd expected, but this was something from a fairy tale—*Once upon a time.* It was the teeny-tiny cottage in the woods depicted on the pages of children's stories, except that in those illustrations, the cottage was usually colorful. This ancient structure must have been limestone, whitish-gray, similar to the bark of the alder trees. The thatched roof was a shade darker. I wondered if the roof was water-tight. It seemed impossible that anyone lived in this small dwelling.

Grace had drawn her lips together in a tight line. She pulled at her wrap again, readjusting, and I felt a shiver, too. I hugged myself, rubbing my arms through my thick sweater. Had the temperature dropped? The sun was no longer shining through the trees. The cottage sat back twenty yards or so from path we'd followed, a path that continued on into the woods through overgrown scrub—to other neighbors? Colin or Grace had mentioned a neighbor, someone who had contacted Dr. Malone once when Magdala was seriously ill, when Bridget was volunteering at his office. That was how she had met the old woman.

The ground around the cottage was nearly as bare as the chicken-pecked yards of rural Georgia that I remembered growing up, but random clumps of something wild and green were not surprising here in the Emerald Isle. Grace's steps grew heavier as we approached the cottage. "I hope Magdala doesn't shoot us," she said under her breath, just before the door opened.

It was Magdala, no doubt, much as she had been described, a woman with a stoop, dressed in layers of clothes that had not seen soap and water lately. Steel-gray hair that hadn't seen a comb lately. She'd pulled it back, but loose strands frizzed around her face. She might have had a head of curls as a young woman, many decades ago, judging from her wrinkles.

She didn't speak as she stood in the doorway, which barely framed her, though she looked to be no more than five feet tall. People were smaller centuries ago when this cottage must have been built. I could not quite make out the old woman's expression. She looked at us straight on, her right eye veering off slightly, but there was nothing particularly sinister about her. It seemed more likely that her eyesight was poor and she was trying to figure out who we were.

"Hello, Magdala, it's me, Grace O'Toole." Grace raised her voice as if she believed the old woman was hard of hearing. "Grace O'Toole. I've brought a friend. We've come to see Bridget."

Magdala said nothing. She turned and walked back inside. She'd left the door open so it was likely Bridget was coming out or we were supposed to go in. Bridget did not come out. We waited a moment, and then Grace proceeded to the doorstep. She first peered inside and then went in without further invitation.

I stopped in the doorway, studying the room. No electricity, I remembered, and not much natural light coming in from small, high windows. The cottage had a pungent smell about it, like wild onions.

Magdala was bending over a heap of covers. "Yer mam," she said.

Grace threw caution aside and hurried to the bed—I would have called it a *futon* in a more modern setting—even as Bridget's hoarse moan came from the covers: "No. Go away."

I could only imagine how Grace's heart broke, seeing her daughter like this. At first, Bridget turned her face to the wall and drew the covers up to her ears, but in the end she responded to Grace's soft murmurings—"Bridget, please, please, love"—and the gentle hands that pulled her into her mother's arms. I could see the girl's fragile face clearly as Grace embraced her, rocking back and forth, as if she were a child. She looked small enough to pass for a child, but her hollow eyes were older than her twenty years. Her long tangled hair was light, like Grace's, as far as I could tell in the dim room. She wore a blouse that appeared stylish, maybe expensive, oddly out of character with everything else in this place, but naturally she had brought her own clothing with her.

After a moment, she pulled back from her mother and said in a weak voice, a whine, "Why are you here?"

"I had to see you." Grace tried to touch her daughter's face, but Bridget turned away.

Magdala, who had taken only a couple of steps away from Bridget as Grace had moved in, spoke to Grace for the first time, pointing to the wicker basket that sat on the floor. "What'd you bring?"

"Cheese and bread, apples, peanut butter and jam. It's for both of you." To Bridget, Grace said, "Are you hungry?" Bridget shook her head.

Magdala picked up the basket. Her attention had finally shifted. She set the basket on what was apparently the kitchen table, square, rough-hewn. The sparse furnishings consisted of the table and two chairs, a rocking chair, a tall cabinet, and a smaller cabinet with a pan of water sitting on it. And a fireplace. Though not large by American standards, the stone fireplace seemed out of proportion with everything else in the cottage. Magdala could at least make a roaring fire that would warm this small space. I could see into another room to what must have been Magdala's bed, neatly made up with a patchwork quilt on it. It was then that I noticed the other accessories in the main room, a hooked rug on which Grace was kneeling and an afghan draped over the back of the rocking chair. A faded picture of Mary and Baby hung over Bridget's bed. In the other room, over the other bed, a crucifix adorned the wall. Large brown water stains on the walls confirmed my initial impression that the thatched roof was deteriorating.

Magdala emptied the basket, setting the jam and peanut butter on one of the shelves above the table, alongside other jars— canned fruits, vegetables, soups? Had Dr. Malone or neighbors brought these to her? A kerosene lamp sat on the other shelf, with cans of soft drinks that someone had to have supplied. Grace had brought a large plastic bottle of water. Magdala set it on the shelf, too. She had already bitten into one of the apples. The others she placed in a bowl that she took from the tall cabinet, which contained other dishes as well. I was beginning to see something about Magdala that had not been immediately apparent: vestiges of domesticity that made it seem the old woman might be simply hanging onto ways of the long-ago past. Maybe there was not as much wrong with her mind as people surmised. Something here had drawn a twenty-year-old woman who was accustomed to a comfortable home and nice things.

"You remember how we talked about Jordan and her uncle," Grace was saying, "how they were coming to Shepherds. And they did. They arrived this past week. See, I brought Jordan with me. She has four daughters, and a son, too." As she spoke, she moved from her kneeling position beside the bed to sitting on it. "Come, Jordan, meet my daughter."

Bridget straightened up until she was sitting. I said, "Hello, Bridget."

I had visited the sick under many different conditions, but what did one say in a situation like this? Bridget managed a trace of a smile that hinted of how happy, healthy, and lovely she might have once been. Maybe Grace had made a smart move, bringing me with her. Maybe she'd thought that in front of her mother's friend, Bridget would be on her best behavior and be more likely to go home with us. But there was something to all of this besides stubbornness. I wasn't sure Bridget was strong enough to make the trek to the car.

"I've been so anxious to meet you. Grace and Colin are friends from a long time ago—so I hope it's all right." The words tumbled out. I stopped short of saying *all right that I'm visiting you when you're like this.* How incredibly awkward the situation was.

Bridget's voice was still soft, but polite, no longer complaining. "It's all right."

"Are you sure you won't eat something?" Grace said. "Peanut butter and jam sandwich?"

Another weak smile, this time directed at Grace. Apparently Grace had hit upon one of her daughter's favorites.

I jumped on the opportunity. "Let me make a sandwich for you."

"Lots of jam," Grace said.

I looked for a place to wash my hands, forgetting for a moment that there was no indoor plumbing, no kitchen sink. The pan of water did not entice me. Magdala took down the jars of peanut butter and jam that she had just put on the shelf and produced a plate and a knife. I made the sandwich while Grace and Bridget talked—mostly Grace, but Bridget did ask about Jimmie. Grace reported that he was healthy, active, and "growing like a weed." She sounded like her younger Southern self as she used the phrase. She told of ordering summer clothes online, but she planned to take him into town in a few days to buy new shoes. Grace spoke as if Bridget hadn't seen the child in weeks, when, in fact, it had been just a few days ago that Bridget snatched Jimmie from the backyard of Shepherds. Maybe when Bridget had those erratic episodes, she didn't remember later, or maybe Grace was just trying to block out that memory for both of them.

"Here's your sandwich. I hope it's how you like it," I said. Three steps from the table to the low, narrow bed, where Bridget was changing her position, curling her legs under her. She might have been more comfortable sitting at the table, I thought, but it wasn't my place to suggest it. I noticed for the first time a paper bag with paper handles sitting on the floor at the head of her bed. Full of pill bottles, from what I could tell.

Bridget took a small bite of her sandwich. Unlike Magdala, who chewed noisily on her apple, Bridget showed no pleasure in eating. She put the sandwich down after a couple of bites and handed her mother the plate. "I'll finish later," she said, and she lay back down, burrowing into the covers.

"I was hoping you'd come home with me," Grace said.

Bridget didn't say no. Maybe that was a good sign. "I'm tired," she said.

I took the plate from Grace and set it on the table. I peered into the picnic basket, on the chance that Grace had thought to bring plastic wrap, but the basket was empty.

"We need to get you to a doctor," Grace said. Bridget began the snuffling sound that children make when they're starting to cry. "It's an awful thing," Grace went on, "what happened to Dr. Malone, but you know he'd want you to find another doctor." Bridget buried her face in the covers and continued to whimper and sniffle. Grace said, "Little Jimmie needs you. He needs his mother to be healthy. That's what we all want. We want you to get your health back."

Bridget dabbed at her eyes with the quilt. Still sniffling, she said, "I'm no good to Jimmie."

"Oh, Bridget, love, you mustn't think that," Grace said, near tears herself.

It seemed a good time for me to go outside, to give them some privacy. I was surprised that Magdala followed, but when we were outdoors, she walked away from me, to a tree. From a pocket somewhere in her layers of clothing, she retrieved a pack of cigarettes, tapped out one for herself, and struck a match from a matchbook. She began to smoke, taking heavy draws on the cigarette that she held between her thumb and forefinger.

On the chance that she'd talk to me, I took a few steps toward her. She cast a suspicious look at me—or in my direction, the best I could tell, given her wandering eye—but I spoke anyway. "Does anyone live close by?"

She took another drag on her cigarette. After a moment, she grunted something that sounded like "Owen" and swung her thumb toward the path that continued on past her cottage.

Perhaps the same person who brought her cigarettes. It didn't seem likely that Dr. Malone would provide cigarettes for her.

I noticed wood stacked against the house, not much, but it was May now. "Does Owen keep you in firewood through the winter?" Her nod was almost imperceptible.

So much for small talk. I stepped closer and said in a confidential voice, "Bridget needs a doctor."

"He's dead," Magdala said.

"Dr. Malone is dead, but Grace and Colin can find another doctor," I said.

A bird twittered in the tree above Magdala. We both looked up. Magdala said, "She has the medicine."

"It won't last," I said. "She'll have to find a doctor to give her more, and to give her the right kind of medicine. She needs to go home with Grace so she can get medical care. You've been kind to her. She trusts you. You might be able to persuade her."

Magdala frowned at me again, and I wondered if she'd followed all of that. "The spirits watch her," she said. She tossed her cigarette on the ground and stamped it out with her heavy shoe. "We have what we need."

"Maybe *you* do, but Bridget is very sick. She needs medical attention, and she needs her family—her child."

I had said too much. But it didn't matter because Grace appeared in the doorway, wiping her eyes. The empty wicker basket swung on her arm as she stepped into the yard. "Let's go," she said to me. She looked at Magdala as if she wanted to say something, but Magdala turned toward the cottage. Grace and I went to the footpath.

CHAPTER 12

Back at Shepherds, we entered through the rear, the family's entrance, and found Colin in the kitchen with Little Jimmie. The child was in his high chair eating chocolate ice cream, looking as if most of the ice cream had gone on his face and bib. Grace set down the wicker basket, kissed the top of her grandchild's head, and said in a playful voice, "I can't leave you and your granddad for a minute."

"Nothing wrong with giving the boy ice cream," Colin said.

I didn't intend to stay. Grace would want to tell Colin about the afternoon. I asked if Colin had seen Alex, and he said he hadn't. As I left the kitchen, Grace was saying in a sorrowful voice, "She wouldn't come with me, Colin. I couldn't persuade her to come home."

"It's me," I said, knocking on Alex's door. He told me to come in. He was on his bed with pillows propped behind him, reading a brochure.

"Are you all right?" I said. "I thought you might get out, this beautiful day."

"I sat outside earlier," he said.

"Are you all right?" I repeated.

"Just a little tired. I'm resting up for tomorrow." This didn't sound like Alex. He may have caught the worry in my face because he sounded more chipper as he said, "Ian and I talked about going to the Hedge School tomorrow. How does that

118

sound to you?" He didn't give me a chance to answer. He flashed the brochure and began to tell about the site not far from Thurles that commemorated the secret hedge schools of the eighteenth and nineteenth centuries.

I hadn't been in Alex's room. It was as orderly and uncluttered as I would have expected. One thing caught my eye, a clear plastic zip bag on his bedside table with what looked like half a dozen pill bottles. I didn't know Alex took any medicine except the occasional nitroglycerine tablets when his angina flared up.

I interrupted his description of the Hedge School. "Alex, what are all of those pills for?" Immediately I regretted being so nosy. Maybe if I were his daughter I'd feel more obligated to know his business, but I was his niece, and he was—he was *Alex*.

I thought he'd be cross, but he chuckled. "Doctors have a pill for everything," he said.

"So it seems," I said, and I thought of Bridget's paper bag full of pill bottles.

Letting the topic of pills drop, Alex suggested that we go into town for an early dinner. He sat up, swung his legs off the bed, and wriggled his feet into his slippers. "I think I'll go downstairs and check some of the menus, unless you already have a restaurant in mind."

"Whatever you choose is fine," I said. "I think I'll go to my room and try to call home."

Meeting Bridget had made me want to talk to my own children. Catherine, especially, was on my mind. Just a year younger than Bridget, she was planning to spend the summer in Savannah, work part time for a doctor who was a long-time friend of our family, and volunteer at a free clinic some evenings. She was on the pre-med path, eager to make her way to med school. Bridget had wanted to be a nurse. Grace had said she had the temperament for it. It was hard to imagine that the frail, lethargic girl in Magdala's cottage who said, "I'm no good to Jimmie," had once volunteered in Dr. Malone's office and dreamed of going into nursing.

"What a pleasant surprise!" I said when Julie answered the phone. "I'm glad I didn't have to leave a message."

"We're both here," Julie said. "Catherine is making breakfast. Pancakes from scratch, if you can believe it."

"I'm impressed," I said. "She hid that talent from me when she lived at home."

"She's not a bad cook," Julie said. "Last night she made lasagna. She didn't even use your recipe. Just threw some things together, and it was good. Oh—you had a call, and I can see why you'd go for that French accent."

"Paul Broussard," I said, trying not to give anything away with the words.

"I told him you were in Ireland. That's all right, isn't it? He said he hadn't been able to reach you. Aren't you getting his messages?"

"Thanks for the information, Julie."

"What's going on? He sounds very charming."

"I don't ask questions about the men in your life," I said.

"The men in my life? Sure. As if I've had a date since I came back to Savannah."

I jumped at the opportunity to change the subject. "I'll bet some of your friends will be back in town this summer, don't you think?"

She bemoaned the fact that her friends from high school who were now college graduates, as she was, all had real jobs in other cities. Poor Julie. She'd had a job in Santa Fe, where Claire lived, but due to a buyout, the newest employees were let go, and she was back home. It was a relief when Catherine took the phone. Julie's job situation was a sore spot.

"Guess who we saw on River Street last night," Catherine chirped.

"The President," I ventured.

"Mom!" My children had a way of dragging the word out, making it two syllables. "That's not a real guess."

"Why don't you just tell me."

"Uncle Drew. He came out of one the bars, with another guy that was older, probably even older than you, and they had a couple of *very young women* hanging all over them." In the background I could hear Julie saying something. Catherine said, "Julie wonders if they were dancers from one of those show-bars. They were pretty but a little too *made-up*. Not the classy kind of women that Uncle Drew usually goes for."

I let the *even older than you* part slide by, and I didn't debate the *classy women* statement, either, though I knew my brother better than my daughters did.

"He didn't introduce us, or the people with him. Couldn't *wait* to move on. He hugged us and told *us* to be careful. It was kind of funny."

Not that funny to me, but I said, "Let's just hope, for my brother's sake, that the very young women were at least eighteen." On the bright side, Drew hadn't called me even once with a business crisis, so I assumed he hadn't run our company into the ground while I was gone.

Catherine was excited about reporting to the doctor's office on Monday for her summer job, to meet with the office manager. "I don't know yet what they'll want me to do—maybe whatever anyone else doesn't want to do—but I don't care. Just as long as I get to be part of what's going on in a doctor's office."

I thought of Bridget again. The image of her on that low, rumpled bed was replaying in my mind when Catherine asked how my trip was going.

So much to tell—and so little I could tell my daughters. Not about Bridget or the gunshot that had injured Ian or my concern over Alex's health. Not about Paul Broussard.

"We've been to a castle and to the ruins of another castle, and last night we went to an amazing concert," I said.

"Sounds like fun! Bring lots of photos," Catherine said.

"Of course I will." But then I had no photos from the concert, only memories of the extraordinary performance. How did you share that sort of thing when you went back home?

I asked about Winston, and Catherine assured me that my big, lovable, clumsy mutt was getting plenty of attention. We said goodbye and disconnected. These long-distance calls had an odd effect. As good as it was to hear voices from home, the conversations never seemed quite *enough*. You never said exactly what you'd like to say. It would be the same with Paul.

Breakfast was becoming a favorite time of the day. Besides the meal itself, the hearty Irish breakfast that Shepherds provided, morning was an occasion when all the guests showed up in the cozy breakfast room and discussed their plans for the day. Except for Mr. Sweeney. He was there, bending over his plate, shoveling in his food as if it were an obligation rather than a pleasure, but unless someone asked him a specific question, he was silent. He had his own car. Wherever he went or planned to go, he kept to himself. But all the others were eager to talk about their plans. Somewhat like a family.

"You must know about the hedge schools that came about as the result of the Penal Laws in the 1700s. The Curreeny Hedge School was one of many, all over Ireland," Ian was saying. He shared a table with Molly and Doreen. Alex and I were at a table with Helen and Charles. Mr. Sweeney had chosen to sit by himself in the corner. Typical seating arrangement for our group. Sometimes the seven of us switched around, but not Mr. Sweeney. "Alex was kind enough to say I could go with him and Jordan to visit the memorial site. It's not far from here," Ian said.

"It's too bad we can't go along," Doreen said. "Molly has another performance this afternoon, and rehearsal this morning."

"For schoolchildren," Molly added, her eyes bright as she gazed at Ian across the table.

"That's a very good thing," Ian said.

At our table, Helen announced, "I have at last persuaded Charles to go to Cashel today."

"You won't be sorry, Charles," Alex said.

"I'm sure." Charles shook his head to get his obnoxious shock of hair out of his eyes. "It isn't that I haven't wanted to go. I hear it's a rather splendid site."

"You haven't wanted to miss a day of golf," Helen said, rolling her eyes.

"That's true. I won't deny it."

I wondered what was different about today, but I didn't have to ask.

"You see, Lucas Riordan will be at the doctor's funeral mass," Helen said, addressing Alex and me, "so Charles would have to pay his own fees on the course if he played today."

"Helen! What a thing to say! As if I didn't pay my own fees yesterday." Charles turned his gaze to Alex and me. "Is it so hard for my wife to believe I might want to show respect for Lucas's family?"

"It's quite *impossible* for me to believe that is why you're not playing golf," Helen said.

These two seemed to enjoy their bickering, especially when they could draw someone else into the middle. But for the someone-in-the-middle, it was awkward. Alex excused himself and went to the coffee urn for a refill. I smiled what must have been a vacuous smile, as if I had momentarily forgotten where we were in the conversation, and said, "I suppose the whole town will turn out for Dr. Malone's mass."

Grace had come in from the kitchen with the rolling cart. "Colin plans to go to the mass," she said, loading a couple of empty platters onto the cart.

"I understand the wake was private," Charles said.

"Apparently Dr. Malone's wife wanted it that way, just a banquet room at one of the hotels for a little while last night," Helen said.

"Not the typical Irish wake," Grace said with a smile.

Helen leaned forward and spoke to me confidentially, "The doctor and his wife were separated. And with the murder investigation going on, you can imagine! Lucas told Charles that his sister was having a very hard time of it. I don't blame her, really, for wanting her privacy."

Grace said, "Does anyone need anything else?"

No one did. It was a good time to excuse myself.

Ian followed close on my heels. On the stairs, he said, "I've been thinking about the message on my website, and you're right. I doubt the Guards can help, but I'll go anyway when we get back from the Hedge School. They might surprise me with their computer skills."

Repeating a line from Alex, I said, "It's the twenty-first century everywhere."

The drive to the Curreeny Heritage Hedge School took us through more narrow lanes edged in rock walls, past more emerald meadows dotted with sheep. Gradually, the landscape became more hilly. Ian, from the back seat, directed me as we twisted and turned and finally came to our destination atop a short, steep road. Alex gave a loud sigh and said, "Who needs a

GPS?" For the first time since we rented the car in Dublin, I had tried to set the GPS and realized it wasn't working properly. Most of the time Alex preferred a map anyway, but we didn't have a map to the Hedge School, just sketchy directions from Alex's brochure that Ian had managed to follow.

A small bus was parked in front of a simple church-like building. Children who looked to be middle-graders were coming out of the building. A woman with pretty red shoulder-length hair was apparently the teacher. Attractive as she was, she had that demanding school-mistress manner about her. A roundish man with gray hair and beard locked the door and came forward to meet us. His smile was welcoming, his blue eyes friendly. He was a Programme Specialist from LIT Tipperary, and these were children from a local school, here on a folklore field trip. Ian introduced himself as a teacher from a boys' school in Dublin, and the two men chatted like old friends reunited, until all the children were loaded on the bus and the teacher was glaring from the bus door, her arms folded.

In the meantime, Alex went back to the car for his jacket, and I took out my camera. Each photo op in Ireland seemed to surpass the one before. From this high vantage point, in the midst of green rolling hills, I could see the distant slopes of mountains. The valley below was a patchwork that must have been small farms, separated by hedgerows and rock walls. Alex returned, his windbreaker zipped up against the whispering breezes, cool and gusty. I had learned that layering was a necessity in Ireland. You could always pull off the heavier jacket. I'd worn one today, over a sweater, and I was glad.

Alex took a couple of photos, too, but not twenty—or more—as I had done. His camera was also digital, but he was as selective about his picture-taking as if he had a Kodak Brownie with film that was good for only thirty-six shots.

"Imagine children walking from their homes in those hills,"

he said, "walking miles in rain or freezing temperatures—and the great risk to their families as well as the schoolmaster."

I didn't interrupt his reflective mood. His smile was wistful as he went on. "Though on a day like today, in a setting like this, I can see why the open-air classroom would have been more attractive than a computer room without windows."

The bus had pulled away. I looked around for Ian. He was standing on a patch of ground with a monument at its center, a low rock wall around its perimeter.

Alex said, "That's the memorial," and we headed that way.

The monument was the bust of a schoolmaster, complete with jaunty cap, atop a slab of stone with an inscription in English and in Gaelic: *Dedicated to all hedge schoolmasters who provided education in the eighteenth and nineteenth centuries. If caught teaching they faced imprisonment or death.*

After a moment, Ian spoke. "The laws were not just about prohibiting Catholic education, you know. The intent was clearly to demoralize Ireland. The English government schools were all about proselytizing, teaching Irish children to be good English citizens and know the *true* religion. They considered us a *deluded* people, you know," he said. He looked at me as if he wanted to make sure I understood. I had read Alex's brochure about the hedge schools, but I gave an encouraging nod, and Ian went on. "The Irish wanted their children to learn the language and the history of our country, to hear our music and stories, but it had to be accomplished in secret, in the shadow of hedges or in caves or ditches." Ian turned his gaze back to the monument, and I thought his eyes were as hard as the stone face of the schoolmaster.

"The hedge schools demonstrated that Ireland would *not* be demoralized," Alex said in his professorial voice. "They showed how far the Irish would go to protect their culture."

The wind kicked up for a minute and then died down again.

Without a word, we all turned away from the memorial.

"Feels like a sacred place up here, doesn't it?" Ian said a few steps later.

"Is that a church or a school?" I asked, indicating the small, simple building on the property. It was about a hundred yards from us.

"A schoolhouse, built in the early 1800s," Ian said, and he and Alex continued to talk about how, after the penal laws were repealed, the government had finally established a system of small country schools that many Irish families accepted. The Programme Specialist from LIT Tipperary had told Ian that this particular school remained in operation until the 1960s.

"I know it's locked, but I wonder if I can see anything through the windows," I said.

Alex and Ian followed, lagging behind, still talking. I heard a car and turned to look past where our car was parked, but I didn't see anything. Then the engine cut off, maybe someone parking, another visitor to the memorial, I thought. I went to one of the windows of the schoolhouse and peered in. "Rows of old-fashioned desks," I said.

A gunshot and the sound of breaking glass pierced the air all at once. I ducked next to the building, yelping. A window was shattered next to me, but not the one above me. I saw Alex and Ian crouched on the ground, there in the open. Had they been in the line of fire? I couldn't tell. We called to each other. No one appeared to be hurt. Alex told me to stay put. A minute later, a car motor started up. The men waited another moment and then stood, and I rushed to them.

Alex was brushing himself off, trying to appear unflustered, but he was breathing hard. Ian rubbed his arm. Maybe he'd landed on it, diving to the ground, or maybe he was just remembering the gunshot that had grazed that arm just two nights ago.

I asked again if they were all right.

"Just mad as bloody hell," Ian said. He jerked his phone from its clip on his belt and punched in 999.

CHAPTER 13

Not more than fifteen minutes later, two officers arrived, dispatched from somewhere locally. It didn't take long to tell them what happened. "A shame it is that someone would shoot out the window of the old schoolhouse," the younger of the two men mused.

The other exchanged a look with Alex that said the shooter likely had something in mind besides the window, and Alex followed up with an explanation about the incident Friday night. "You can check with the Thurles police. We made a report."

"Do you know who might want to shoot you?" the older man asked Ian.

"I would have told you, first thing, if I did," Ian said. "I have no idea, same as I told the Guards in Thurles."

I gave Ian one of those *meaningful* looks that mothers learn to do so well. He met my gaze, blinked, and looked away. It wasn't my place to tell about the message that had come to his website—*If you were meant to be dead, you would be.* Had he changed his mind about telling the Guards?

The local officials didn't keep us long. They didn't seem to know what else to ask us, so they said we could leave and they would contact us if they needed us. Yes, of course they knew Shepherds. They had heard good things about the O'Tooles.

"Are the crime scene investigators coming?" Alex asked. His question was met with frowns. Certainly you couldn't blame the men for not knowing that we all kept up with *CSI*. "You should be able to recover the shells and determine what kind of gun was used." Alex must have heard how he'd sounded. "My apologies," he said. "We'll go so you can do your work."

The older man winked. "Don't you worry now. We'll be in touch with Headquarters."

On the way to the car, I said to Ian, "Headquarters? Is that Thurles?"

"It is. The locals are nice enough, and they do fine when it comes to breaking up a brawl in the pub, but this is something the Guard in Thurles will take up."

"Is that why you didn't say anything about the message?"

"What message?" Alex asked.

"Ah, Jordan, you can be trusted to keep secrets, I see," Ian said.

He explained to Alex, who was not annoyed with *me*, as I'd predicted, but rather at Ian. "And this happened two days ago? My boy, you *must* go to the Guard."

"After what happened here—I will indeed. As soon as we get to Thurles," Ian said.

Grace was alone in Reception when we arrived at Shepherds. She seemed to be sorting through mail. Alex greeted her briefly before he headed upstairs—for a nap, I suspected. We had dropped Ian off in town. He was going first to the police station—called the Garda station—and then, he said, "I'll be stopping in at Finn's. I could use a pint after all that drama."

"Maybe he'll get a ride back if he stays until after dark," I'd said to Alex, thinking about the road where Ian was shot Friday night. Alex had told me Ian would take care of himself and he didn't need me to be a mother hen.

"How did you like the Hedge School?" Grace asked.

I didn't know how to break the news except to just say it. "There was another shooting."

"Oh, you can't mean it!" Grace looked horrified. "Was anyone hurt? Where's Ian?"

"He's at Finn's, and no one was hurt," I said, "but I'm still shaking inside."

"For good reason! Oh, I am so sorry, Jordan. I'll make us some tea," she said.

We had our tea in the keeping room, that warm, inviting family room off the kitchen. I filled Grace in on the events of the afternoon. "What do the Guards plan to do?" she asked. I had no answer. Then we heard Colin come through the rear entrance, whistling. Grace looked surprised. Maybe Colin had not whistled much lately. She called to him, and he appeared in the doorway, shedding his tie. Sunday clothes and Colin O'Toole did not exactly go together.

"Aren't you a little too cheery to be coming from a funeral?" she said.

"Ah, I suppose you're right," he said. "It was sad, of course."

"Get yourself a cup and join us. We have a pot here," Grace said. "Jordan will tell you what happened at the Hedge School."

I told the story again, and Colin's reaction was the same as Grace's. Nothing like this *ever* happened in Thurles. No shootings. No murders. This was supposed to be a peaceful little town! And all of these incidents while Alex and I were visiting. Not what they'd hoped their American friends would experience in Ireland! They were both profuse with apologies. They didn't mention Bridget, but their daughter's troubles had to weigh heavily on their minds.

"None of it is your fault," I insisted, "and the two of you could not have been more gracious to us! We love being at Shepherds."

"It's a wonder Alex can think about writing a book," Colin said.

"I think he's getting what he needs. We've packed a lot into a few days, and we have nearly a week left." I stopped short of saying anything about the tiredness that seemed so out of character for Alex. Colin and Grace didn't need one more thing, one more source of worry.

"Maybe I can spend more time with you and Alex this next week." Colin shook his head. "Mother of God, I hope nothing else comes up!"

"What about the funeral?" Grace asked. "You came in whistling."

"And to think, I almost talked myself out of going because I knew the whole town would turn out—and I'm not much for a starched collar and tie." He glanced at me. "But out of respect for the doctor, who was good to our family, I went anyway. And sure, the whole town was there." He turned his gaze back to Grace. "And so was Liam Riordan."

"Mr. Riordan!" Grace exclaimed. "I thought he was seriously ill."

"That's what his son would have us believe, isn't it now?"

"He wasn't sick?"

"Hard to say. Sure, he looked a bit pale. I went up to him after the mass and expressed my condolences. Told him our family appreciated Dr. Malone, and Mr. Riordan said, yes, his son-in-law was a good man. I said, 'I'm glad to see you out and about. I hope you're over what was ailing you,' and he just chuckled and said, 'I fear my ailments were much exaggerated. I'm not an easy man to put down.' And then he said, 'I'll be back in the bank soon.'"

Grace's face lit up. "Lucas can't keep you from talking to him if he's in the bank. And Mr. Riordan will be reasonable. Oh, Colin, that is very good news!"

Colin's eyes twinkled, like a mischievous lad's. "Ah, but I haven't got to the best part. I said I'd be glad to see him back at work and started to walk away. Lucas was giving us the evil eye from across the room. But Mr. Riordan stopped me. Put his hand on my shoulder and said, 'Don't you worry, Colin. We'll figure something out for you and Grace.' "

Grace gave a noisy, relieved sigh, clasping her hands as if to contain her joy. "I never doubted he would work with us, but I was afraid he was so sick that he'd never come back to the bank, and we'd have to deal with Lucas."

"I'm sure that's what Lucas was hoping," Colin said. He glanced at me as if he'd forgotten I was there. "Forgive us, Jordan, for boring you with all of this business talk."

"I'm sure Jordan has caught on that we have a problem at the bank," Grace said. She explained to me, "Lucas Riordan wants this place. That's the bottom line. And we've got a big payment coming up. But if Mr. Riordan can give us just a little more time—as I've said before, we have a big summer already booked. We'll be grand."

"Lucas Riordan wants Shepherds?" I said.

"I don't know exactly why he wants us to go under, but he's been sniffing around," Colin said. What Helen had said struck a chord in my memory. Something Lucas Riordan was planning that the public didn't know about, but it involved a golf course. A resort development? Was that why Lucas Riordan wanted Shepherds? It had to be.

"I've heard talk that he's optioned a couple of properties around here," Colin went on, "and another thing—I saw Kevin Conner after the mass. Lucas got his claws into the Conner farm, not far down the road. Kevin said he's taking his wife and new baby to Dublin, hoping some relative there will help him find work. Small farms are having a hard time of it."

"Kevin Conner." I repeated the words. "I think we heard him playing at Finn's."

"I expect you did. He's a fine musician," Colin said.

"What about his father? They all live there together," Grace said.

"The old man's going to stay with Kevin's sister, in Galway, for a time, anyway." Colin shook his head. "Kevin said his dad was taking it hard. He was born on that farm."

Grace said, "I wonder if Mr. Riordan knows what Lucas has been up to. I just can't believe he'd approve of Lucas's heavy-handed way of doing business."

"How long has Mr. Riordan been sick?" I asked.

"I've been trying to see him for at least a month." Colin drained the last of his tea, and then—typical Colin—his voice had a lilt as he said, "But the winds have shifted. Everything is going to be fine for us now. Whatever Lucas has done to others, Mr. Riordan is not going to let it happen to us."

I took a short nap myself. Alex and I decided we'd have dinner at Ryan's Daughter, a small restaurant in the town center, popular with the locals, Colin said. The doors opened at six, and if we went early, we should not have trouble getting seated. I was fine with going early. Somehow, in all the excitement at the Hedge School, we had completely forgotten lunch.

Colin was at Reception when I went downstairs to wait for Alex. "I called a friend at Ryan's, just to be sure," he said with a wink. "It will be their pleasure to serve you."

"You're too good to us, Colin," I said.

"And why shouldn't I be?"

Helen came in the front door. She and Charles had been to Kilkenny, and she couldn't wait to give a report on their visit.

"Yes, Alex and I were there Thursday," I said when she took a breath.

She held up her camera and began clicking through her photos. "You'll like this one, Jordan. I took it from Castle Park, and you can see all the rooftops, how they represent so many different architectural periods and styles—but you know about that, don't you?"

I nodded. "Good composition. You're quite the photographer."

She looked pleased. "You're kind to say so, Jordan. I do enjoy my little hobby." She held another frame up to my face. "I loved this watercolor in the Butler Gallery. You know the castle was the Butlers' Irish residence. They owned it for six hundred years, until 1967, when they presented it to the people of Kilkenny for fifty pounds. Actually *gave* it away. Remarkable!"

"Remarkable," I echoed.

"It was a lovely tour. Charles even liked it. He's really quite interested in history and culture, but one wouldn't know it, the face he puts on."

"Where *is* Charles?" I asked.

"Out in the car park. Talking to Lucas Riordan."

"Lucas Riordan?" Colin put in. "Sweet Mother, what could he be doing here at Shepherds? He must have come straight from the cemetery."

"We drove up at the same time," Helen said. "They're golfing friends, you know, Charles and Lucas. They go back *years,* to their wild youth." I nodded, as I'd heard this several times.

"I would think he'd be consoling his sister. She just buried her husband," Colin said.

The irony in Colin's tone seemed to have escaped Helen. "Actually, I don't think Lucas was close to his brother-in-law. Not that he wasn't sorry about his death—I'm sure he was, *naturally*—but his sister and the doctor were getting a divorce. I have to say the Riordans have been quite civilized about all of this, don't you think?"

"All of this?" I asked, though her question may have been directed at Colin.

"The wake, the mass, behaving as if the doctor and Lucas's

sister were still married—they *were* still married, of course, but they were not living together. The Riordans could have behaved quite differently, but they have conducted themselves with dignity."

The expression on Colin's face said he would have had plenty to say about that if Helen had not been a guest at his establishment.

The door opened and Ian came in, followed by Charles and then Lucas Riordan. Ian had brought fish and chips for dinner in his room. He thanked Lucas for the ride from town and went upstairs. I met his gaze; he gave me a thumbs-up. I would be anxious to hear what the Guard had said about the message on his website. Charles and Helen continued to stand around, with Helen expressing condolences to Lucas over his family's loss. Lucas's response was cool: "One of those things, isn't it now?"

I moved to a chair, out of the way. Lucas glanced at me, as if wondering who I was and concluding that I wasn't anyone important. He left the Prescotts' side, edging toward the Reception desk, where Colin stood, exceptionally straight-backed, I thought. Colin said with strained courtesy, "I didn't get to speak to you at the mass, Lucas. It was a fine funeral."

"Ah, but you did speak with my father, didn't you, now?" Lucas said.

"I did."

"And I've come here to tell you, Colin, you need to stay away from him."

Colin tilted his head and narrowed his eyes, as if sizing up the shorter, thicker man across from him. Surely Colin wasn't thinking of throwing a punch, but I could sense his blood beginning to boil. "I don't understand the problem," he said, each word sharp-edged.

"Understand this," Lucas said. "My dad is in poor health and he's just had a shock, with James's death, and I don't appreciate it that you took the occasion of the funeral to ask for help with your loan. Is that clear enough now?"

"I did no such thing," Colin said. "I told him I was glad to see him out and about. I told him I was sorry about Dr. Malone. I see nothing wrong with that."

Lucas leaned in closer to Colin's face, but Colin didn't back away.

"I expect I know what you talked about, and I'm giving you fair warning. You stay away from my father. You have no business with him. What business you have is with me, and we'll conduct it at the bank. Don't you be going behind my back." Lucas straightened his lapels in a pompous manner and said, "You have a nice evening now, Colin."

Colin said, "Mr. Riordan told me he'd be back at the bank soon. I can wait for him."

I winced, thinking, *Oh, Colin, that was the wrong thing to say.*

"We'll be seeing about that," Lucas said. He bid the stunned Prescotts good evening, reminding Charles of their tee time the next morning.

Silence took over for a minute, until Charles spoke. "I must say, I've never quite seen that side of the old boy."

CHAPTER 14

For the first morning since I'd been at Shepherds, I was not ravenous when I woke.

Ryan's Daughter, a small restaurant just off the square, had turned out to be another charming Irish eatery, warm and welcoming. Our entrees—roast beef for me, curried chicken for Alex—had come with huge portions of mashed potatoes, mashed carrots, and mashed turnips, all delicious. Best of all was dessert, which I could not resist because of the way the friendly young waitress described it: "Rich chocolate cake with fudge sauce, topped with raspberries and whipped cream. Homemade, of course." Alex and I decided to split the item, but it was not fifty-fifty. I was the one who polished off most of the decadent dessert.

"Another rave review," Alex had said, scribbling in his little notebook as we finished with coffee.

This morning I thought I might just stick with coffee, bread, and strawberry jam. And one scoop of scrambled eggs. But the hash browns did look so appealing. I passed up the blood pudding and baked beans but still found myself with a full plate. I had no trouble eating it all.

Helen was rounding up a group to go to the Cliffs of Moher with Finn on Saturday. Alex had not come down yet, but I told Helen to count both of us in. Ian said yes, he thought it would be enjoyable. Molly said, "I'll go, sure! And my mother will, too." I was shocked to hear her speak for Doreen.

"I can get tickets for our concert this afternoon, if you'd like to attend," Molly said, while it was just the four of us—Helen, Ian, Molly, and me. "This is one we'll be doing for the schoolchildren. We performed yesterday for one of the schools, but today it should be much more entertaining. The children are performing, too. They go to a heritage school where they learn Gaelic and Irish music. We've shortened our program, so the children can show off their talents. Would you like to come?"

It was the longest speech I'd heard from Molly. Her mother had not yet arrived, to intimidate her—or whatever Doreen's effect was—but this was also something she was passionate about. I said I'd love to attend. Once again, I spoke for Alex. I was confident he'd enjoy the concert, too. Helen and Ian said yes, and Molly's face shined with delight. We'd all go together that afternoon.

One by one, the others arrived for breakfast and everyone lingered for a while—except for Mr. Sweeney. All of us somewhat like a little family, I thought—except for Mr. Sweeney. I waited for Alex to finish, since he'd started late, and when he excused himself, I left as well. I'd noticed he hadn't eaten anything but bread and jam. That was all I had intended to have, of course. Nothing wrong with that. But I asked, "How are you feeling this morning?"

Before he answered, Grace called to us. "After I finish a few housekeeping chores, I'm going to take Jimmie out in the stroller," she said. "We haven't gone out like that in a while. Do you want to walk into town with us?"

"Thank you for the invitation, Grace, but I must beg off. I need to work on my notes this morning," Alex said. With a cheery smile, he reported that we were going to see children from the heritage school perform in the afternoon. He seemed well enough, I decided.

"Sounds delightful," Grace said. "What about you, Jordan?

Are you up for a nice walk? Leave in about forty-five minutes?"

"Sure," I said. "It's a gorgeous day."

"The fresh air will do us good," she said.

Now my day's schedule, which had been blank before breakfast, was full.

It was, indeed, a splendid, sun-splashed day, with low humidity and no wind. Little Jimmie settled back in the stroller and put his fingers in his mouth for the ride. When we passed the narrow lane that led to Red Stag Crossing, Grace darted a brief glance in that direction, and a shadow came over her face. Obviously she was thinking of Bridget, but after a moment she continued our conversation about the two shootings that apparently targeted Ian. "I can't imagine who would want to do Ian harm," she said. "Surely it can't be anyone from Thurles."

"I wouldn't think he's been here long enough to make enemies," I said.

"He's from Dublin. It's more likely connected to Dublin, don't you think?"

"Mr. Sweeney's from Dublin," I said, "and so are the Quinn ladies."

"I didn't mean anyone from Shepherds! I certainly hope not!" she said.

Before we knew it, we were approaching the town proper. The trip didn't seem long at all in daytime, with the bright sun beaming down on our shoulders. Now and then Grace waved to someone in a passing car. So different from that other journey on a chilly night, walking on the dark, lonely road.

We stopped in front of the beautiful Cathedral that dominated Cathedral Street so I could admire it. Grace said, "I should have invited you to mass with me Sunday. You would enjoy the architecture, not to mention that Father Tierney always delivers a thought-provoking homily."

"Maybe I can just go inside and look around sometime before

I leave Thurles," I said. "Alex would probably want to come with me. He'd *definitely* be interested in the history."

"The history is fascinating," Grace said. "Originally the Cathedral for the diocese was located on the Rock of Cashel. After the Reformation, the seat of power changed. I'm fuzzy on all the details, but I know our Cathedral of the Assumption was built in the mid-1800s." She gave a little laugh. "I'll tell you who knows all the facts and will talk your head off if you ask him about the history—Father Tierney. If you and Alex decide to visit the Cathedral, I'll give him a call and see if he can meet with you."

We moved on toward the town center. Grace suggested that we take a break and have a cup of tea. There was a nice little tea house, she said, on one of the side streets. On the corner as we made the turn, she pointed out, "That's Dr. Malone's office and his apartment above. It *was.*"

The words had scarcely passed her lips when the door of the office opened and a woman appeared. She was carrying a box of files, about half the size of a banker's box but still an armful. Smartly dressed in designer jeans, a tailored jacket, and short-topped boots, she was a little on the heavy side but might have had a very pretty face, had she not been scowling. Her dark hair was cut in a short, severe style. She said, "What are you doing here, Grace?"

"Just passing, on our way to the tea house. This is my friend Jordan Mayfair. Norah Malone."

I said hello, and Norah Malone nodded, but her expression did not soften. Grace pushed the stroller closer to her and said, "Norah, I didn't make it to the funeral, but I want you to know how sorry I am about Dr. Malone."

Norah was looking Little Jimmie over. He continued to suck on his fingers, staring back at her with a look that seemed oddly disapproving for a twenty-two-month-old child. He was accustomed to seeing smiling faces when people approached him, and he always smiled back. I wondered how Norah Malone could be so unfriendly toward this little boy. A thought flitted through my mind: She and Dr. Malone didn't have children— not to my knowledge. Someone would have mentioned it if they did. She may have wondered why Bridget O'Toole, who had yet to prove herself as a mother, deserved a child like this.

"We'll miss the doctor," Grace went on. "Everyone in Thurles will miss him."

"No doubt you will," Norah said with a piercing gaze. Then she turned back to the door and shook the doorknob. "Everyone loved my husband, didn't they now? The whole town was over the moon for him." Grace opened her mouth but Norah raised her palm and said, "*Don't.* Don't say any more, Grace. And now you'll have to excuse me. I have things I must do." She shifted the box in her arms and crossed the street to a black SUV parked at the curb.

Grace turned to me with an expression of bewilderment. "Did I say something wrong?"

"Certainly not," I said. "I don't understand that, either."

"Unless," Grace said, "it's about the exchange her brother and Colin had yesterday when Lucas came to Shepherds. Lucas warning Colin to stay away from Mr. Riordan. You heard, didn't you?"

"I was there in Reception. Lucas was insulting. And now his sister has been just as rude. All very odd."

Grace began to push the stroller. "Do you think Norah believes Bridget had something to do with Dr. Malone's murder? Even though the Guard has cleared her?"

I wouldn't have said the Guard had cleared Bridget, not entirely, but I didn't say that to Grace. "If Norah does believe it, yes, you're probably right. That could account for her behavior toward you."

"And toward Jimmie." Grace had noticed, too.

We were at the tea house, a charming, frilly little place, filled with ladies who all smiled at Little Jimmie as we threaded through the tables.

He took his fingers out of his mouth and rewarded each pretty lady with a happy grin.

After our delightful excursion—delightful, except for the encounter with Norah Malone—we returned to Shepherds with a little time to spare before I needed to get ready for the afternoon performance at The Source. I checked on Alex, who was engrossed in writing and obviously did not have time for me. Fine, because I just wanted to know he was all right. I had become quite the worrywart about my uncle since I'd seen all those pill bottles in his room.

I knocked on Ian's door. He answered, and when I expressed my surprise that he was in, he said he was writing. "So was Alex," I said. "He didn't want to be bothered, and you may not, either."

"No, it's quite all right, Jordan. Come in," he said. "I've been looking for a chance to tell you about my visit to the Garda station yesterday."

"That's why I came by," I said. "I didn't want to bring it up in front of the others."

"I told Charles and Helen about the Hedge School incident last night when we were at the pub," he said, turning the desk chair around to face the bed. I noticed that his computer was gone. He'd been writing on a legal pad.

He indicated the chair for me, and he sat on the foot of his bed. "So yes, I went to the Garda station, and there's a Sergeant Casey who has taken an interest in these shootings."

"Good," I said, remembering that Colin had mentioned

Sergeant Casey as one of the officers who came to Magdala's cottage to speak with Bridget. Colin had been impressed with how the Sergeant dealt with her.

"As I expected, they have no leads so far," Ian said, "but the Guards who met us at the Hedge School had already reported to the Thurles station, and someone was going out there to investigate. The Sergeant said they should get much more from that location than they'd obtained from the place where I was shot. Which, as you know, was bollocks. I have to wonder how hard they looked. But at the Hedge School, the Sergeant said, they'd get shell casings and tire tracks and footprints."

I nodded, but without too much enthusiasm. That evidence would be of little use unless they had a suspect and a car and a weapon to match. Ian had to be thinking the same thing. "I know, it's not much, but Sergeant Casey said they'd also be willing to look at my computer—the message that came to my website. So I took it in to them this morning."

"How long will they have to keep it?" I asked.

"Normally they get help on things of this nature from the Dublin office. But they're going to send their best IT person over to LIT Tipperary this afternoon to get some help." He laughed. "Wouldn't it be ironic if Patrick was the expert they consulted?"

As I got up to leave, Ian said, "Did you ever read the stories on my blog, Jordan?"

I had to confess that I hadn't had a chance—or hadn't taken the time.

Ian walked to the door with me. "You know there's a computer in Reception for guests to use. It's old, but it works. I may go down later myself and check my website."

"Don't forget the performance this afternoon."

"Oh, I wouldn't," he said.

"I think I'll go down right now," I said. "I should have just enough time to read the stories on your blog."

Ian beamed as he told me how to access his website.

I settled at the computer in the corner of Reception. It was probably five years old—an ancient relic! The legends on Ian's website were well written. He was quite the storyteller, as I'd already concluded from hearing him tell about the man with the cows who hid the priest and the man driven to suicide by the hooting owls. The written versions supplied some vivid details that had not come out in what Ian had told us. In the first story, Cromwell's men had gone to the cottage on several occasions looking for the priest, but he was hidden in a "priest hole," a secret hiding place that was often built into houses during the sixteenth and seventeenth centuries, when Catholics had to practice their religion in secret. I remembered studying about hidden chambers, including priest holes, in architecture school. The significance of the owl in the other story was clearer to me when I understood what the owl was hooting—actually, what the guilty man was hearing: "Who-o-o? You-o-o!" No wonder the owl had so alarmed Ian last Friday night, the night he was shot.

Ian's website was attractive and informative. There were photos of his students in the classroom and engaged in various casual activities. He had photos from soccer games and dramatic presentations. It was apparent that Ian was far from the stuffy schoolmaster stereotype. He appeared in some of the photos himself, in a tug of war, giving a student a high-five, and sitting under a tree with several boys as one of them seemed to be reading aloud from a notebook.

His website encouraged comments, and many were posted. Considering that he had to approve all the comments, it wasn't surprising that all were positive. As I read Ian's posts to his readers, I saw that he wasn't too concerned about privacy. Privacy was an issue I'd discussed with my young adult children who didn't mind sharing with the world, via social media, far too much personal information. I hadn't convinced them that too much sharing was not only unnecessary but it could be dangerous, and Ian apparently didn't believe it, either.

"I'll be on holiday tomorrow," he'd written. *"Don't expect much blogging for two weeks. I'll be gathering material for my book."* And what if someone takes advantage of these two weeks to burglarize your apartment? I scrolled back farther, to where he'd first announced his plans to spend his holiday in Thurles, spend time talking with the townspeople who might know of legends that he could use for his book, and stay in a quaint little bed and breakfast called Shepherds Guesthouse.

Anyone who'd been on Ian's website knew how to find him. Anyone who wished him harm.

Was that what Mr. Sweeney had read?

"What is it?" Colin was standing nearby, smiling.

I realized I'd been shaking my head, trying to comprehend.

I logged out and moved back from the computer. "What do you *really* know about Mr. Sweeney?" I said, keeping my voice low. No one was around, but better to take precaution.

"Very little," Colin said, also in a quiet voice. It occurred to me that he may have felt my question was inappropriate, and maybe it was. "Why do you ask?" he said.

"You said he'd read something on a blog about Shepherds and he'd insisted on booking a room here. Ian had something on his blog about spending his holiday at Shepherds." I hunched my shoulders. "I doubt there's any connection."

"Sure, Mr. Sweeney did insist on a room here," Colin mused, "but you're not saying *he's* the one shooting at Ian, are you, Jordan?"

"I'm not accusing. Just wondering," I said. Though the message Ian had received on his blog clearly had some connection to the shootings, it was a stretch to suspect Mr. Sweeney was in any way involved. Poor man who had just lost his wife. I was wondering if I should tell Colin about the message Ian had received—Ian had told the police, so it wasn't a secret—when the phone rang at the Reception desk. Colin reached for it but paused before answering.

"Mr. Sweeney is a wee bit strange but he seems harmless enough," he said.

I nodded, thinking I had let my imagination run wild.

CHAPTER 15

The afternoon performance at The Source was a delight. Though the music by Molly's ensemble was wonderful, as one would expect after the Saturday night performance, the twenty or so bright-eyed, fresh-faced children from the heritage school stole the show. They played Irish music on wooden flutes and whistles. They performed Irish set dances. They sang and recited poems and acted out a folktale about an old woman beside the road—all in Gaelic. The oldest students were just ten years old. We could not stop talking about them as we waited for Molly.

She joined us, with more high praise for the children. "Wasn't it thrilling? Those lovely children, singing in our own language?"

It was the ensemble's last performance at The Source, but the young people were going straight to the Seniors Centre to play again. "You can come, too. Please do!" Molly said to us, the Shepherds group. Doreen did not hesitate. She hooked one arm around Molly's and grabbed Alex's arm. At first he looked mortified, but then in the spirit of the occasion, he gave me a look—*Why not?*—and let himself be pulled along.

Ian held back a little, until I reminded him that he'd get to meet some of the older people in town who, no doubt, had a lot of stories. He nodded and said, "Ah, I see your point."

As we turned on a side street with a narrow sidewalk, Molly broke loose from her mother and our little procession continued with Molly and Ian walking together, Helen and me bringing up the rear. Doreen seemed to have a natural sense of direction.

Molly told her the address, and she said, "I know the street. Remember, love? Grace directed us to a place for lunch, our first day in Thurles." Molly didn't reply. She was smiling up at Ian.

And so, after enjoying the talents of the children, we assembled in a large hall surrounded by some fifty elderly citizens. They could not have been more hospitable, as they directed us to the tea and biscuits and put out extra folding chairs for us. Molly's ensemble entertained for no more than fifteen minutes, after which the white-tufted gentleman in charge announced that the music had been grand but now it was time for dancing.

The floor was immediately crowded, and the Irish step dancing began. The footwork was incredible. Men and women much older than Alex performed intricate steps. Most astonishing was that no one seemed to be breathing hard. I commented to Ian that they were all amazingly fit. "Makes me think I should take up step dancing instead of tennis," I said.

"The thing is to do manual labor all your life and walk or ride a bicycle everywhere you go. And hoist a pint or two every night," Ian said.

The step dancing ended with a solo performance by a woman who had won some kind of national title. The announcer told her age, which was eighty-three. And then the others came back on the floor for set dancing, which was what we'd seen the children do at The Source, but somehow it was even more impressive, performed by these dancers in orthopedic shoes. The footwork was not so fancy in these figure-dances, but the movements required precision, grace, and—yes, a high level of energy. Memory was apparently not a problem with these seniors.

After the first dance, the announcer invited all the visitors to join in. Molly had continued to play all the tunes with the musicians, but the others from the ensemble were eager to participate

149

in the dancing. Doreen popped up and said to Alex, "Let's give it a whirl!"

"Not on your life, Doreen," Alex said with an expression that indicated he was serious.

She laughed, gave him a dismissive wave as if to say he was being very silly, and found another partner immediately. One who took a liking to her, if I judged correctly.

Ian caught the eye of the woman who had performed the solo, and they joined one of the squares. Two *very* elderly men presented themselves to Helen and me, and we could not refuse. My partner was so small, he could have passed for a leprechaun. What a pair we made, with me at five-foot-ten and him at about five feet. But he was a splendid dancer and had a great knack for leading, so that I always knew what I was supposed to do. The only trouble we had was when he had to twirl me, and I had to stoop low to make it under his short arm.

When we joined Alex again, I said, "I'm embarrassed that I'm out of breath and no one else seems to be."

"I am!" said Helen. "But isn't this just lovely? Remarkable!"

Alex had been writing in his notebook. Most tourists would never know about this kind of thing—this unexpected pleasure— unless they were to read Alexander Carlyle's account in his travel guide.

The group from Shepherds went to the Star of India for an early dinner and had another noteworthy meal. It was just beginning to get dark when we left the restaurant. Molly said she wanted to catch up with her friends who were going to The Monks pub for their last night out. "You're welcome to join us, Ian," she said with a demure smile.

"Sure, I would enjoy it," Ian said.

"Don't worry about me, Mam," Molly told her mother before Doreen could speak up. I was certain Doreen was about to insinuate herself between Molly and Ian, but she had the good sense—this time—to stand still and keep quiet.

"I'll see Molly home safe and sound," Ian said.

Helen, like Doreen, sometimes missed the obvious, but not in this case. "Oh, Doreen, let the young people have their fun," she said.

I had driven into town, with Alex, Ian, and Helen. Doreen had gone on to The Source much earlier. On the way back to Shepherds, Doreen, who had remained silent—a little sullen, actually—until she climbed into the back seat with Helen, said, "I don't know how safe Molly can be with someone who's been shot at twice."

"All the more reason for Ian to be *very* careful," Alex said. "He will be. Count on it."

"Don't you remember how it was to be young and in love?" Helen said.

Doreen gave a cry of horror. "In love? Molly's not in love with anybody!"

Helen cleared her throat. "Perhaps—infatuated. Surely you've seen it, Doreen."

"I don't know what you mean about *that*," Doreen said. "Molly is a sensible young woman who's going to have a grand career, not a husband and a houseful of whiney children to take care of. I've raised her to aim higher than that."

No one spoke. I think we were all shocked by Doreen's pronouncement. She seemed to realize what she'd said. "Not that there's anything wrong with children," she went on after a minute. "Molly has been my *whole life*. My great joy. But she has a talent she should not waste."

"What *is* Molly going to do when she graduates?" I asked.

"If I have my way about it, she'll take the offer to stay in Dublin and play in the symphony and give music lessons at UCD. She will continue to nurture her gift."

"I have four daughters and a son," I said, "and we mothers

don't always get our way, not when they become young adults and have their own plans."

"Molly has taken education courses to teach young children," Doreen said. "Sure, children look very well when they perform, like today. But I ask you, does it take a gifted violinist to teach schoolchildren? Can't those with no ear for music do that? Why should it be my Molly, taking off for Sligo!"

"Sligo?" Helen and I echoed at once, as the word had come out of nowhere.

"Up in the Northwest, in the wild country. Molly has had another offer, a teaching position in Sligo! And I think I'll just lay down and die if she goes!"

It was just as well that we were coming upon Shepherds.

Patrick was behind the Reception desk with a cheery greeting when we arrived. He asked how our day had been. Alex said, "The best yet! I'm sure Jordan will enjoy telling you all about it." He was exceptionally slow, climbing the stairs.

"I thought Ian went with you to the performance," Patrick said. Doreen scowled and departed without an answer. Helen trilled a little laugh and left as well. I remained, and Alex was right. I enjoyed telling Patrick about the performance at The Source and the unexpected experience at the Seniors Centre.

"Ian and Molly went off to join Molly's friends at The Monks pub," I said. Leaning closer to the counter, I lowered my voice. "Doreen was not too happy about that."

Patrick laughed. "I can't say I'm surprised—not about Ian and Molly, and not about Doreen. I expect they'll be in late, so I'll just see him tomorrow."

Probably Patrick had news about Ian's computer, but I resisted prying. As I was about to say goodnight, Patrick said, "Ah, Jordan—my dad said you were wondering about Mr. Sweeney. I suppose I've wondered myself why he wanted a room here at Shepherds and took the third floor when he could have booked a very nice room at another B&B in town. I don't have an answer to that, but I did find out with a few keystrokes that he does confidential investigations."

The door to the office was ajar. It opened wide, and Enya stood there, frowning. "Why do you need to know about Mr. Sweeney?" she said to me.

"Enya, don't be rude!" Patrick said.

"Maybe it's *rude* to ask too many questions about a man who has done nothing but mind his own business," she said.

"Stop it, Enya," Patrick said. "I've seen him trying to talk to you, and you don't act very friendly to him, so why are you saying this now?"

She walked up to the counter and stood beside Patrick. She had not stopped frowning, but her voice softened. "I do know him. What I mean is, I knew him in Dublin when I was younger."

"Why didn't you ever say anything?" Patrick said.

"Why should I? Nobody said anything about him to me. Maybe you and Colin talked about him, but you didn't talk to me."

The change in Patrick's expression was barely noticeable, but I sensed that he was hearing Enya's underlying complaint. I didn't want this to become a marital spat. I asked, "Did you know he was a private investigator?"

She took a deep breath. "Yes. My family and the Sweeneys lived on the same street when I was growing up. It was not a posh neighborhood, but it was all right. My dad did very well in business and we moved to a better part of Dublin. Tim—that was his son—he was maybe ten or eleven years old when we left. I didn't really know him. I didn't know about his death—or Mrs. Sweeney's—till Mr. Sweeney came to Shepherds."

I blinked, taking it all in. "He lost his son *and* his wife?"

She nodded. "Both within the last year. I was sorry, of course.

But when Mr. Sweeney recognized me, he seemed to want—I don't know what he wanted from me."

Just a listening ear, I thought, a little sympathy from someone who had known his family.

"My parents have not gone back to the old neighborhood, and I haven't," she said.

She looked at Patrick, her eyes asking for understanding. But his words were edged with sarcasm. "So I guess you didn't want to talk about the old times on the old street."

"I didn't know what to say. He kept asking me things about Tim, but Tim was younger than me. 'Did you ever hear him play his violin?' Mr. Sweeney said. I never did." Her voice was full of frustration now. "He said his wife had been very ill, and after Tim was gone, she just gave up. About a month ago, I think. He said my mother sent a card, but *I* didn't know about any of it. I've been out here in Thurles! And Mam never mentioned it when we were in Dublin."

"And Mr. Sweeney didn't know you were at Shepherds?" I asked.

"He did not! I don't know why he's here, but I have nothing to do with it."

After a moment, Patrick turned to me. "So now we know a bit more than we did but not why he came to Shepherds. Maybe it does have something to do with his work. It's Sweeney Confidential Investigations if you want to look at his website. Not much to it, though."

Enya's glare seemed to dare me to pry any further.

It was nice to be in early, to just reflect on all of the day's experiences. I was straightening up my room, which I had left in a mess, when my phone rang. It was Drew. I wasn't always delighted to hear from my brother, but tonight I felt a smile coming on as I answered with a greeting that he was used to hearing when we'd been apart for a while. "Hello, Drew. What's wrong?"

"You're funny. Hilarious. As a matter of fact, everything's great," he said.

"I'm glad to hear it."

"When are you coming home?"

"We have another week here. Missing me?"

"Of course, Jordie! Are you having a good time in the Emerald Isle?"

"I am, indeed." There was no point in trying to tell him any particulars. I hoped he was being truthful, that nothing was wrong, but he wouldn't be calling to hear about my trip. I knew my brother. He had something to tell me. So better to get on with it. "What's going on in Savannah?" I asked.

"Nothing much, you know, the regular. Actually—I don't suppose you've talked to my sweet nieces, have you?"

There it was. "As a matter of fact, yes. They said they'd seen you on River Street."

"Right. Saturday night. I'd had dinner with some friends at Rocks on the River."

"Some *very young* women, your nieces said."

"Okay, okay," he said when it was clear he couldn't keep up the pretense. "I figured Julie and Catherine got the wrong idea. Those girls—not girls, I didn't mean that—those *young ladies* were friends of the guy that invited me. Walter Sutton, but you wouldn't know the name. He's not from around here. He's living on Hilton Head and has his eye on some property here in Savannah, on Whitaker. I thought we were going to talk business."

"Funny business," I said. "So what did he want from you?"

"You are so suspicious! That's a real flaw in your character, Jordan."

"What's the story, Drew? I know there's a story."

155

Drew had a long story about how he'd met Walter Sutton at a golf tournament and had gone out on his boat twice before that night on River Street. It was good to know my brother had been staying busy since I'd left town. The man was from Ohio, but after a messy divorce he'd decided to go South, for the weather. "He hasn't spent a summer in Savannah yet," Drew laughed, to which I had to add an Amen. Even the natives wilted in the humidity during July and August.

"The thing is, back in Ohio, his family owns some land that has an old house on it. Really old, probably early 1800s." I smiled, thinking what *really old* meant in Ireland. "The house was literally falling down," Drew went on. "Then somebody discovered a secret room that nobody had ever known about. They're thinking it's part of the Underground Railroad. You know, the Underground Railroad," he repeated.

"I know about the Underground Railroad, Drew," I said.

"So now they've got the historical society involved, and somebody's going to make a documentary."

"Where's the hidden room?" I couldn't help myself. "Was it part of the original structure or added later?"

"I don't know all the details, but there's something about a false wall and a hidden staircase. And they found a shoe and a scrap of paper with a name on it, somebody at *another* stop on the Underground Railroad. Pretty cool, huh?"

I had to admit it was. "So I have to ask again: What does Walter Sutton want?"

"I can't believe you! Does there always have to be a catch?"

Usually there was, with my brother and his pals, but he sounded sincere when he said, "There's no catch. I just knew you went for stuff like this. I told Walter about you and how you were *the best* when it came to historical renovations, and he said he'd love to take us to see the house. Did I mention that he has a private plane? And if he lands the real estate deal on Whitaker, you might get the renovation."

"I'm properly scolded, Drew," I said.

"I hope so. You really need to work on that suspicious nature of yours." Then he said, "So about that night on River Street," and I knew we had probably arrived at the *real* reason for his call.

"I'll tell Julie and Catherine it was strictly business," I said.

I was wide awake for a long time, and when I did go to sleep, my dreams were fitful, centered around a secret chamber housing slaves on the Underground Railroad. But, like most dreams, mine were confusing, with priests, not slaves, in the room, hiding from Oliver Cromwell's men.

CHAPTER 16

Ian and I were the first to breakfast on Wednesday morning. Enya had unloaded the rolling cart. As she left the breakfast room, she said to Ian over her shoulder, "Patrick said to tell you that your computer should be back at the Garda station this morning."

"Ah, thank you, Enya. I don't suppose Patrick knew what they found," Ian said.

"I wouldn't know," she said, and she disappeared into the kitchen.

Ian gave a little shrug. "I suppose there's a protocol to follow."

"Good news that you'll know soon," I said. Though the report might be that the IT people could not trace the message, I thought.

We finished at the buffet and sat down. I couldn't keep from asking Ian, "Did you have a good time last night?" The light in his eyes told me he didn't mind the question.

"Ah, it was all very fine," he said. "Molly is a bit young for me, you know. I'm thirty-two, more than a decade older than she is, but I'd like to keep going about with her in Dublin if it wasn't for her mother. Doreen might put up a hard battle to keep Molly to herself."

I wondered how much he knew about Molly's offers following graduation, but I said, "Mothers sometimes give in when they realize the cost of winning the battle is too great," and left it at that. Ian gave me an inquisitive look and then began to nod that he understood. Helen came into the room and took over, as she was inclined to do.

Alex didn't come down for breakfast. I waited for him, but eventually Grace and Enya cleared away the food. I kept out some toast and jam for Alex and went up to his room with the plate and a cup of coffee. He was dressed when he answered the door.

"Just moving more slowly than usual this morning," he said.

"Alex, what's wrong, exactly?" I asked.

"What do you mean?"

"You know what I mean. You're not yourself. Something must be going on or you wouldn't be taking all those pills." I glanced at the plastic bag on his bedside table.

I was sure he was going to berate me for trying to "play nursemaid," but he said, "You're right, of course, that I don't quite have the *starch* I should have. I assure you, though, there's no mystery disease that I'm keeping a secret. And the medications—I'm not sure myself that I need all of them, but I'm not a physician." He settled at the desk with his breakfast and began to butter his toast.

I sat on the foot of his bed without invitation. The bed was made, everything in its place. Very Alex. "What does Reuben say?" I asked.

"Don't you remember that I told you Reuben went skiing somewhere in the West and broke his leg? I was supposed to have my physical—I *knew* about Reuben's accident but I wouldn't have thought he'd be out of the office for two months—so I was surprised when his nurse called and gave me the names of some other doctors who might see me." Alex took a bite and seemed to be remembering as he chewed and swallowed. "I don't recall the name of the young doctor. It would be on some of the pill bottles. Good fellow. I might have waited for

Reuben to get back to work, but this trip was coming up, and I wanted to mark my doctor's visit off my list of things to do. It was just my annual physical. Nothing was wrong with me."

"*Just* your physical?" I said.

Alex cut his eyes at me, and I realized I'd better be quiet if I expected him to level with me. He sipped his coffee. "The young man couldn't *believe* I didn't have any prescriptions." I started to speak but stopped myself, and Alex added, "Yes, Jordan, I did tell him about the angina, the nitroglycerine *as needed.* He spent a lot of time with me. Very thorough."

More spreading butter, spreading jam. No hurry to finish his story.

"What did he find *wrong* with you, to make him prescribe those meds?" I asked.

"I suppose the main thing was my blood pressure. He said it was a little high, and we shouldn't let that get out of hand. I mentioned heartburn—nothing serious—and he prescribed something so I wouldn't have to worry on this trip about trying anything I wanted to eat. And I had that flare-up with bursitis—you wouldn't have known about that." Alex held up his finger as if he'd just remembered. "And the insomnia."

"You suffer from insomnia?"

"*Suffer from* is a little overstated, Jordan. I think sleeping problems are common as we advance in years."

I raised my eyebrows. Alex wasn't usually willing to concede that his age might be a factor in anything.

"My friends all complain that they have trouble sleeping," he said. "It *is* annoying."

"So the doctor gave you something to help you sleep," I said. "What else?"

He took a moment to answer. "My bloodwork came back showing my cholesterol was out of whack. Though it wasn't *that* high."

"Would you mind if I looked at the meds?" I asked.

Alex was looking a little irritated, that wrinkle between his heavy brows. "I suppose if you think it's necessary. I really don't need you to play nursemaid, Jordan."

There it was, but we'd gone this far so I wasn't giving up. I reached for the plastic bag. "A lot of pills for somebody who wasn't taking *any* medicine before you went to the doctor."

I recognized a couple of brand names but not the generic ones. There were over-the-counter pills, too, for allergies, the hay fever that always kicked up in the spring, Alex explained. And over-the-counter cough syrup. I held up the bottle and remarked that I hadn't heard him cough. He said, "It's only a problem when I lie down. The antihistamine has that drying effect and I wake up coughing. For heaven's sake, Jordan, I'm not a drug abuser!" He pushed back from the empty plate and cup on his desk, the frustration obvious in his face.

I put the bottles back into the plastic bag and zipped it. "Don't be mad at me, Alex. I just wonder about possible drug interactions."

"I wondered the same thing." He began to look a little smug now. "I called the doctor's office and they had me back in for a follow-up."

I had to wrench it out of Alex that he'd experienced some light-headedness that had caused him to contact the doctor again, and the "young fellow" had changed his blood pressure medicine. He was adamant that the doctor went over all the prescriptions again, but he also admitted that he simply hadn't thought to mention the cough medicine or antihistamine.

"I think you ought to make an appointment with Reuben when you get back," I said.

Alex rubbed his face. After a moment, he said, "I'm not anxious to tell Reuben about this. He may think I should have

161

been more discerning. But that young doctor seemed so *trustworthy.*"

I said, "He was probably well meaning. If you did a survey of your friends, I'll bet you'd find most of them taking these prescriptions. Didn't you say doctors have a pill for everything?"

"Not Reuben—no, he's very conservative. Several times I've asked him to prescribe something to help me sleep, and you know what he says? *Warm milk.* What adult drinks warm milk? But I suppose—he *is* my primary physician." He grunted. "I'll make an appointment."

I set the plastic bag back on the night table and asked what he had in mind for today.

"I think I'll just stay around Shepherds," Alex said. "No excitement, no drama. I think a day of quiet will do me good. Feel free to go sightseeing without me if you like, Jordan."

Fine with me to stick around Shepherds, too, I said. No excitement, no drama.

We made an exception and drove into town for a late lunch at one of the many small, cozy eateries. It was located on a side street, between a bookstore and an Internet café. Alex was up for browsing in the bookstore for a while after lunch. He purchased a book written by a local author on the history of County Tipperary and was eager to get back to Shepherds to read. We drove by the Cathedral and I mentioned what Grace had said about the building's history. Father Tierney would be a good one to talk to, she'd said, and she'd offered to give the Father a call. Alex said he'd enjoy it, but not today.

The scene at Shepherds was not exactly as it had been the day Alex and I had first arrived, but it felt like *déjà vu* when the screen door banged and Grace rushed outside, followed by Enya, with her cell phone to her ear.

"It's Jimmie," Grace said. "Bridget has taken Jimmie again."

It was easy enough to persuade Grace to let me take my car. I remembered the other time Jimmie had disappeared, just over a week ago, and Helen's description of Grace—not *worried* as much as *bothered.* This time Grace was clearly *worried;* perhaps it was that the stakes were higher now, with all that had happened in the past week.

She said Colin had gone to buy a mower from Davin Callahan's father. Grace had reached him at the Callahan farm, some ten kilometers from town, and Davin had offered his all-terrain vehicle for the trip to Red Stag Crossing. "They'll have to load it on Davin's lorry and unload it, but in the end it should save time in the woods," she said.

"And make it easier to bring Jimmie back," I said, trying for an optimistic note.

"And Bridget," she said. "We *will* bring her home. This can't go on!"

She had put Little Jimmie down for his nap, she said, and a while later, she couldn't say what it was, but something had made her go check on him, to see that he was all right. He was not in his crib. "Not Enya's fault this time," she said with a bitter laugh. "My watch, this time."

We made the first turn onto the narrow, twisting road, and soon came to the place where we had to park the car. It was quite a hike from that point, as I remembered. On this journey, I paid little attention to the flora and fauna. I focused on the uneven path in front of us, the roots and rocks that made our trek difficult. Grace was quiet, so I remained silent, too.

A few minutes had passed when we heard the soft roar of an engine, growing louder. "It's the ATV," Grace said with her arm out, pushing me to the side of the path. It was a good thing. They came roaring toward us and lurched to a stop just short of where we stood.

Colin jumped out and said, "Get in." He gave Grace a hand as she climbed in next to Davin, the young man I recognized from that first evening at Mitchel House. Colin helped me as I squeezed in beside Grace. "Don't put your foot out if you feel it's about to topple," he said, and leaped behind us into the cart that was part of the vehicle, like a small truck bed.

It was a bumpy ride, but Davin maneuvered the four-wheeler with skill, and in less than five minutes, we were at Magdala's cottage. The sunny morning had turned into an overcast afternoon. We did not need rain to complicate our mission, but it looked like we might get it.

Davin pulled across the hardscrabble ground, up to the doorstep, before shutting off the engine.

Grace didn't knock at the door of the cottage. She went inside, with Colin just behind her, calling, "Bridget? Are you here, Bridget?" I held back a little, standing at the open door, taking in the room with one sweeping gaze. Everything was reminiscent of our visit the past Sunday, except that no one lay on the low bed. It was a jumble of covers. Magdala sat in a rocking chair, her hands folded, looking not at all surprised to see her visitors.

"Where is she, Magdala?" Grace said. No answer, just the squeaking of the rocker. Grace hurried to her and knelt down. "Magdala, please tell me where Bridget is. She has the baby, you know. Little Jimmie."

Colin didn't wait when it appeared Magdala was not forthcoming. He went into the side room where Magdala must have slept and looked around. I followed. The room was so sparsely furnished that I couldn't see how anyone could have been hiding anywhere in it.

"I'm begging you, Magdala. Tell me!" Grace continued.

"You're not helping Bridget or Little Jimmie. You may think you are, but you're not."

I saw that Colin was climbing a short, steep ladder, and I went to see where it led. Colin was peering into a small loft, in a dark corner. "Nothing here," he said.

"Is that a sleeping loft?" I asked.

"Maybe. For a child. Not long enough for a man."

I imagined that in the centuries since the cottage was built, there were times that it was full of small children, for whom the loft made a nice, warm bed.

We returned to the other room. Grace had stopped pleading with Magdala. She was opening a cabinet, peering at the dishes. No one could have hidden in the small cabinet, but Grace's desperation was taking over. She said to no one or to all of us, "I know they're here. I know they are. They *have* to be somewhere around here."

The door was still open to the outside, and I saw that Davin was looking around in the edge of the woods. Good idea. There just weren't that many places in the small cottage that Bridget and the baby could be.

Colin came to Magdala's side. Glaring down at her, he struggled to keep his voice modulated. "Bridget is very ill, Magdala, I'm telling you, and she might hurt Little Jimmie without meaning to. Mother of God, woman, don't you have any concern for the baby?"

Magdala stopped rocking. She looked up at Colin, her wandering eye more evident than it had been, and spoke for the first time in a hiss. "He's *hers*!"

Grace rushed back to Magdala, wailing, "Bridget gets it in her mind that Little Jimmie is in danger, but she's confused! He's in danger *now*, wherever she's taken him!"

"She's not able to take care of her baby," Colin broke in. "If she could, don't you think she'd be back with us right now, acting like his mam? No, she's running about like a madwoman! Doesn't that tell you something? Won't you help us, Magdala?"

Something in the old woman seemed to shut down. She took up rocking again.

Colin threw up his hands and marched to the door. "I'll look around outside," he mumbled, and then he called to Davin, "See anything out there?"

Grace went into the side room and climbed the short ladder, as Colin had done.

"Can you think of some other place she might have gone?" I said, trying to think of anything that might help. "Could she have taken Little Jimmie into town or to a friend's house?"

"She has no friends," Grace said. "She did, when she was in school. Davin is the closest to a friend she has. No, she's here somewhere. I feel it. Trust me. Magdala knows."

As Grace tried once more with Magdala, I climbed the ladder to the sleeping loft myself, for what reason I couldn't have said. Back at the door to the outside, I took another long look at the room, from the low futon-like bed around to the fireplace. The stone hearth and inlaid mantelpiece. The big fireplace seemed so out of proportion for such a small cottage, but as the only source of heat, it probably was no different from others built in that time period.

Grace said, "If harm comes to them, Magdala, you can be sure you'll answer to God."

We left the cottage. Colin and Davin returned to the ATV, and we all stood around it, looking at each other, helplessly, for a moment.

"Let's go," Colin said. "My phone won't work here. I need to get to a place where I can call the Guard."

A light mist began to fall. Davin, Grace, and I were in the enclosed part of the little vehicle, but Colin was in the back, unprotected from the rain. We couldn't have been far from where my car and Davin's truck were parked when Davin brought the ATV to a stop and Colin jumped out and stood beneath a leafy tree with a purplish hue—an alder, I remembered—to make his call, to keep his phone dry, I surmised.

Grace had not spoken since we left the cottage. She sat between Davin and me, her shoulders sagging, her expression unreadable. I could only guess. She'd been so sure they would find Bridget and Little Jimmie at Magdala's cottage. She'd said she *felt* they were there. I went over and over the room—both rooms—in my mind. There was nowhere to hide.

And then a thought began to take shape—several thoughts bumping into each other like gathering clouds. Secret chambers. The place on the Underground Railroad that Drew had mentioned. What had he said about a hidden staircase? Ian's story about the priest, how Cromwell's men had searched for him in the cottage. Where had he hidden? Memories of long-ago studies about artfully contrived spaces where priests could be concealed for days.

"Did you ever hear of priest holes?" I said.

Grace looked up, suddenly attentive, as if recovering from a daze. Davin said, "Of course. It's part of our history."

"In a cottage as small as Magdala's, would it be possible— no, let's say it *is* possible—where would a priest hole be?" I said, feeling my heart beat faster.

Hope sounded in Davin's voice. "Sometimes behind a false wall. Or a place around the chimneys."

Colin was back, squinting as the rain picked up. "The Guards are on the way," he said, climbing into the cart.

"We need to go back," I said. "We missed something."

Davin turned the ATV toward Magdala's cottage.

Chapter 17

Magdala was standing at the cottage door when Davin shut off the engine and we climbed out of the ATV. The expression on the old woman's face was a giveaway—or maybe I was just hoping. She'd remained so calm, even detached, when we'd arrived earlier; now anxiety danced in her eyes. "Why'd you come back? You're not welcome here! Go away!" she spat.

The thought skittered through my mind that we should have left the ATV in the woods and returned in silence, but we'd been so eager to get back that no one had considered how the engine noise would alert Bridget to hide again—assuming she'd come out of hiding after we left.

"We know about the hiding place, Magdala," Colin said with great confidence, incredibly convincing, "and we're going in to get them, so move out of our way."

"No!" She spread her arms. "You can't have the gold!"

"What're you talking about, woman? I'm not looking for any gold." Colin pushed her to the side. He could have exerted much more force, but he didn't need to. She looked confused and continued to babble but she didn't try to stop us as we filed into the cottage.

"The little men will get you! It's their gold!"

As we'd come back through the woods, we had discussed where the priest hole might be. I was almost certain that it was somewhere around that huge stone fireplace, but I didn't know how to get to it. How did Bridget get into it? I took a long, deep

168

breath, trying to clear my head. Was I delusional—was this some fanciful notion? Colin and Grace believed I was right, that Bridget was here. Grace had said once again that she'd *felt* it, and Colin had said, quite seriously, "Not a good thing to argue with a mother's intuition."

Colin and Davin began sounding the wall around the large mantlepiece.

I looked up into the dark chimney, even crawled inside the fireplace, into the soot and ashes, examining the flue. No sign of a way someone might gain access to a hidden chamber unless it had to do with removing bricks, a task I couldn't see Bridget accomplishing.

"If there's a hollow space, it has to be *behind* here," I said, "and the access would have to be from the other room."

Colin hurried past Magdala, who was beginning to shriek. Grace took her by the arm and led her to her rocking chair. I was surprised at how easily she managed. Magdala put up no resistance. Her shrieking turned to wailing and finally died away into unintelligible mumbling about little men and gold.

Colin was pounding on the paneled wall behind the fireplace when I looked up again to the dark sleeping loft. What if the access was up *there,* a trap door? I hadn't thought of that when I'd checked out the loft before. One would have to have a way to lower himself—or herself, in Bridget's case—into a small space between the fireplace and wall. It was possible.

I went up the ladder, climbed into the flat loft, and began sounding the boards.

"Listen!" Grace called, raising her hand to halt us. "Did you hear that?"

All of us froze, holding our breaths, the four of us that had gathered in the small room, but Magdala's mutterings from the other room were so distracting, I couldn't hear anything else.

"I'll take the old woman outside," Davin said.

We didn't have to wait for complete silence. The sound Grace had heard grew louder and more persistent. It was a baby's cry.

The next minutes were heart-rending.

We knew it was Little Jimmie. We knew he was there, somewhere, *in the wall*, but how to get to him? Colin kept up his examination of the wall just behind the fireplace. He shouted, "Bridget! Come out! For Little Jimmie's sake, girl, please give it up! I know you can hear me!"

Grace called to Bridget, too, wiping tears all the while. "How can you do this to your baby? Can't you tell how terrified he is? You must be terrified, too, Bridget. Please come out!"

"If we don't get anywhere soon, I'm going to find an ax and break the wall down," Colin said. "I don't want to risk hurting them but we've got to get in there."

"Why won't Bridget answer? What if something has already happened to her?" Grace said. "Oh, Colin, I think you have to risk it! Get them out."

"Are you finding anything up there?" Colin called to me.

"No," I said, and then, "maybe—yes, I think so."

The panel was so skillfully concealed in that dark corner that I might have missed it entirely if we hadn't heard Little Jimmie's cries, if we hadn't known we had to keep on looking. By the time Colin had come up the ladder, I had removed the panel, such a small rectangle that it seemed impossible an adult could squeeze through. Bridget was tiny, but a priest? Not a well-fed one. "Ask Davin if he has a torch!" Colin called down, and Grace rushed outside.

A few minutes later, Colin shined the flashlight into the secret chamber. He closed his eyes for one anxious moment, and I feared the worst. But then his face altered, like the sun breaking through dark clouds, and he said in a lilting voice, "It's your

Grandda, Jimmie, come to get you. You can quit your crying now." And Little Jimmie did.

We were soaked and chilled to the bone when we made it out of the woods. The temperature had dropped. None of us had dressed prepared for this sudden shift in the weather. We'd already found Bridget and Jimmie when the Guards appeared at the cottage in their own all-terrain vehicle. In the flurry of activity, Magdala disappeared into the woods beyond the cottage. The Guards said they would stay and look for her, as they couldn't very well leave an old woman out there, exposed to the elements, though Garda Mallory declared, "She's a tough old bird, she is." He told Colin, "We'll find her. We'll take her to the A&E. You take care of your family."

The rest of us piled into Davin's ATV, Grace holding Little Jimmie as if she would never let him go, Bridget wedged between her mother and Davin, Colin and me in the back. We'd gathered up all the covers we could find at Magdala's cottage. Bridget and Little Jimmie were both wrapped in blankets. Colin and I pulled quilts over our heads as rain pounded us.

I had thought to grab the paper bag beside Bridget's bed, the one that contained her medications.

I gave Colin my car keys so he could drive his family to the emergency room, since his car was still at the Callahan farm. "Bridget will go to hospital, no doubt about that," he said. "I hope Jimmie will be fine to come home with us, but we have to get him checked out."

I handed the paper bag to him. I'd tried to protect it, holding it under my sweater. "Bridget's pills," I said. "Maybe you'll get some answers from these."

Davin loaded his ATV on his truck, and he dropped me at Shepherds.

Everyone, it seemed, had gathered in Reception, Alex and all the other guests, even Mr. Sweeney, and Patrick and Enya. Colin had called Patrick with the good news, but it was clear from the anxious faces awaiting me that everyone wanted a firsthand report. I must have been a sight to behold, wet, smudged with soot, with stringy hair, a dirty quilt wrapped around me.

"For heaven's sake! Look at you!" Helen said, her hands on her cheeks. "It's a very good thing I've had a pot of tea waiting for you."

The hot tea was welcome. I drank it, standing in the middle of Reception, too wet and dirty to sit anywhere. Patrick sent Enya for a couple of clean towels, after which I noticed that she went back to their quarters. Patrick had explained to the guests about Bridget, as they were all so worried about Jimmie. "Nothing gained now by keeping them in the dark," he said. Though I imagined he'd painted just the broad strokes of the picture, I was relieved. He'd made it possible for me to tell what had happened at Red Stag Crossing without fear of betraying a confidence. Mostly, the guests wanted to know that Jimmie was not harmed, nor was Bridget. Probably they were curious about why Bridget was hiding at Magdala's cottage, but no one asked. I didn't mention the priest hole, which would have said too much about Bridget's mental state. I would tell Alex later—yes, I should tell Ian, too—but I headed for a hot shower when I finished my tea.

As the spray of hot water on my shoulders eased my chill, I began to wonder about Magdala's rantings. What had she meant about the little men and their gold? Why had she chosen that moment to slip into hallucinations about leprechauns? Something else I would tell Alex and Ian.

I hadn't shared with the other guests most of the details that cluttered my mind, that might not fade from memory for a long time. Little Jimmie's tear-streaked face when Colin brought him up, the confusion in his eyes, his tiny bell voice when he said, "Grandda." The way he had simply laid his head on Grace's shoulder and put his grimy fingers in his mouth.

Bridget had handed him up, but it had taken a while longer to coax her out. Colin was about to go down and bring her up, though the space was almost too tight to allow it. Eventually, her haunted face appeared in the rectangle where the panel had been, and Colin grabbed her frail shoulders, pulling her out, pulling her to him. I would not forget the unnatural glitter in her eyes.

Colin returned to Shepherds with Jimmie a couple of hours later, much sooner than I would have expected. I had to marvel at how unflappable Colin was. His clothes still damp, his hair plastered to his head like a dark red helmet, he sang out, "Fine as a fiddle, the boy is. The nurses at the A&E pampered him something awful, gave him juice and peanut butter and jam and ice cream, and a banana after that! Now he'll be needing a good scrubbing."

"Enya and I will take care of this scamp," Patrick said, and Little Jimmie bounded into his uncle's arms.

I couldn't help wondering about the repercussions of this afternoon, the damaging effects on this gentle-spirited little boy. Would he remember being snatched from his crib? The flight through the woods? The pitch-black, claustrophobic hole? Would he remember the terror that must have prompted his cries? Or would the love that surrounded him here at Shepherds be enough to wipe out those nightmarish memories?

"Is there anything I can do to help, Colin?" I asked.

"If you don't mind, you can drive me to get my car. It's at the Callahan place," he said. "Alex might like to go along, to see a real Irish farm. He might use it in his book." I was astonished that Colin would think of that—now, with all that had happened.

I was happy to be useful, and Alex was glad to ride with us. "You know about farm holidays, don't you?" Colin said. "Very popular. Worth a mention in your book." Alex made a note. The rain had stopped, and everything had a freshly washed sparkle. Though we didn't get out of the car, Alex and I both delighted in the pastoral scene, pristine little farmhouse with rock wall around it, emerald pastures and darker green hedgerows, and someone—and a dog—driving spotted cows to the barn. I thought of Ian's story, the man with a spotted cow and a white one.

"That would be Davin's younger brother," Colin said.

I remarked that Davin's ATV had been a big help. "A great help it was. I hope Davin wasn't too late for his shift at Mitchel House," Colin said. Only for an instant did a shadow cross his face. Then—he was planning on making a stop at the pizza place on the way back, he said, and what kind of pizzas did we like? We could not dissuade him. He was treating all the guests at Shepherds tonight, so touched he had been by how everyone had put aside their plans today and had waited for news of Jimmie. "Such caring they showed, people who don't really know us. Even Charles Prescott came from the golf course when Helen called him," he laughed.

"Even Mr. Sweeney was there," I said.

By the time Colin arrived at Shepherds with boxes of pizza, it was dark. Patrick said it was no trouble at all getting Little Jimmie to sleep. Enya did not come down.

After everyone had finished their pizza, Alex and I lingered in the breakfast room with Colin. I had started clearing things away when Grace called Colin to come and get her.

"Bridget's in hospital, in good care. It's Grace that needs a rest now, I'm thinking," he told us. "She says she's desperate for a hot bath."

"You might consider the same, Colin," Alex said.

We had a much-needed laugh.

Grace was cooking breakfast as usual the next morning, Enya loading platters onto the rolling cart, Little Jimmie in his high chair with bowl and spoon. He had a smile for me when I peeked into the kitchen and said good morning. Grace returned the greeting, but something in her somber expression was troubling. I asked, "Any news about Bridget this morning?"

"Colin went early to the hospital, hoping to talk to the doctor on Bridget's case. He called a few minutes ago. He was told Bridget had a comfortable night. She was still sleeping. I'm sure sleep is good for her right now. She's so weak." Grace scooped some eggs into a chafing dish. "Colin also said the Guards haven't found Magdala."

I hadn't expected that. The officers at the cottage had seemed so sure they'd just go out in the woods and bring her in. Now it had been—I calculated silently—more than eighteen hours.

"Colin heard it from one of the nurses whose husband is a Guard. It's a small town." Grace managed a smile. "He said they sent out others to search through the night but haven't had any luck so far."

Enya broke in, impatience peppering her voice. "Are the eggs ready?"

Grace finished with the eggs. Enya took the chafing dish and rolled the cart from the kitchen.

"That old fool, Magdala, she thought she was helping Bridget, I'm sure," Grace said.

"Maybe they'll find her, now that it's daylight, and she can get the medical care she's needed all along," I said.

Grace nodded, and I was sure her thoughts were the same as mine: *If she's still alive.*

Ian was at the table with the Quinn ladies, but he left the

breakfast room as I did. "Beautiful morning," he said. "How about a walk?"

"Any place in particular?" I said.

"Red Stag Crossing, I was thinking." He winked. "I hear things. Grace told me that the old woman out there was missing. The old woman someone suggested I should see. And Colin and Grace's daughter, Little Jimmie's mam, was staying at her cottage, I understand. And I suppose you've known about that all along." He gave a mock scowl.

"I did know about Bridget, but I couldn't say anything, Ian. Now I can tell you some things about the old woman, Magdala, and about her cottage. Have you ever seen a priest hole?"

On our way to the place where we had to leave my car, I told how we'd found the secret chamber only because of Jimmie's cries.

"My God," Ian said. "What a terrible thing for the little boy."

He didn't make a judgment about Bridget, but I felt I needed to say that she was quite ill, not at all herself. I was not surprised that Ian's questions turned to the priest hole.

"Some of them were scarcely more than a wall's thickness," he said. "Did you get a look inside?"

"Not really. I held the flashlight and directed it into the space for Colin to see, but I wasn't in a position to look. It was all— confusing," I said, trying to remember the moments following their rescue. I probably could have examined the hole, but it wasn't my priority.

I parked beside a couple of official-looking cars. "It's still a trek, from this point."

The woods were less menacing today, more like the afternoon Grace and I had made the first visit to Magdala's cottage. Sunlight filtered through the delicate leaves of the alder trees.

"Alders figure into many Irish legends," Ian remarked. Probably he knew the legends Grace had mentioned.

I had expected we would come upon some of the officials looking for Magdala, but they'd been searching for a long time now; they had likely made a thorough search of these woods and had expanded their territory.

When we reached the cottage, Ian was not as fascinated as I had been. He'd seen other old—very old—dwellings. But when he tried the door and it opened, his face lit up.

"Do you think it's all right to go in?" I said.

"Why not? We're not breaking in, are we? It's not a crime scene, is it?" He winked. "You're much too influenced by those crime shows on American television, Jordan."

I supposed he was right. Still, I called out, "Magdala?" Not surprisingly—silence.

Ian examined the fireplace for a moment before following me into the other room.

"That's it," I said, pointing up. No one had taken the time to replace the panel.

Like a child drawn to a favorite climbing tree, Ian made his way up the ladder. "I wish we had a torch. Why didn't I think of that?" he said, crouching at the small rectangle in the wall. "I'd like to go down, myself, to see what it's like."

"Imagine a priest squeezing through that space," I said, climbing the ladder, and I thought of Bridget, small enough, but with Jimmie in tow. The thought made ice in my blood again.

"I heard one tale of a priest hiding for more than a week, with only an apple to eat." Ian peered into the opening. And then his face contorted into astonishment. "Sweet Mother Mary!" he said in a hoarse whisper. "I see eyes! Someone's down there!"

Sometime in the cover of darkness, Magdala had returned to her cottage and had hidden in the secret chamber. Was she thinking the Guards would finally just go away—or just not thinking?

Ian tried to place a call to the Garda station, but he had no cell phone service. I told him Colin had the same trouble but was able to get service out on the path, not far. I was surprised that Ian had to go no further than the yard to make the call. "Different carrier, I suppose," he explained. "The Guards are on their way."

The minutes dragged by as we waited. From time to time I called down to Magdala. I *thought* it was Magdala all along but was not absolutely sure until she cursed at me and grunted something about gold. Tough old bird. Ian was determined to get a peek at the hiding place. We did, when it was all over. Just a black hole with rungs on the side, between three and four feet wide, a thickness of barely eighteen inches. One might sit, but could not lie down.

It was an ordeal, but a small female Guard finally managed to get Magdala out.

The old woman was dirty, wet, and reeked to high heaven, but otherwise seemed much as she'd been when we last saw her. Though physically unharmed, she continued to babble about the little men.

And she was holding on tight to a gold chalice.

CHAPTER 18

"A gold chalice. I suppose it all makes perfect sense now," Alex said.

Ian and I sat across from Alex at Tara's, over plates of baked salmon, mashed potatoes, peas, and carrots, their lunch special.

"You're a hard one to impress," I said.

"Oh, I am definitely impressed!" Alex said. "It's *most* impressive that you had a hand in recovering a gold chalice that has to be centuries old—both of you."

"I would love to know how long the old woman has known about the sacred vessel," Ian said. "Her whole life, do you think? I would love to know the story that was passed down. It seems clear enough that a priest left the chalice that he'd used in a secret mass. The communion—the wine. You said you're Catholic, so you'd know."

Alex and I exchanged a look. I was not a very *good* Catholic, though I'd tried to raise my children in the faith. I doubted Alex had attended mass or gone to confession in decades.

"Why did the priest never come back for the chalice? Was he captured by priest hunters?" Ian paused with his fork in midair and said, in a lower voice, "Could it be *my* story?"

I had wondered the same thing.

"A lot hinges on the age of the chalice," Alex said. "The Guard will surely contact the church, and they'll find an expert to date it."

"It *has* to go back to Cromwell's siege," Ian said. "Otherwise, why the secret?"

"What about Magdala?" I said. "Do you think she'll receive any compensation? Surely, if the chalice has been hidden in her cottage for centuries, she can claim some ownership."

"Ah, poor old thing," Ian said. "From what I saw of her, I'd say she'll be spending the rest of her days in care. Going on about the little men like that."

"If she'd been shrewd—in her younger days—she could have found a collector and sold the chalice for a pretty penny," Alex said. He responded to my frown. "I'm not saying she *should* have, just that some people would have done something with it besides keep it hidden."

"She thought the gold vessel belonged to the leprechauns, if you pay any mind to her mad ravings," Ian said.

"I wonder when it was that her mind began to go in that direction," I said.

Our conversation went on like that for a bit, and then as we were leaving the restaurant, Ian said, "I didn't tell you what the Guards said about my computer, did I?"

Everything that had happened the previous afternoon had taken precedence. The shootings, the message that had come to Ian's website—all of it seemed long ago, but Ian's report of the Guards' findings renewed my interest.

"As expected, it was impossible to identify *who* sent the e-mail, but we know where it came from," Ian said. "Right here in Thurles. The Internet café."

Grace had gone to the hospital up in the morning, and Colin had returned to Shepherds. He'd been working in the office, he said, when Alex and I came back from lunch. We'd left Ian in town. He was going to make a personal call on the proprietors of the Internet café to see what else he could learn.

"I was just about to make myself a cup of tea," Colin said. "Join me?"

We followed him to the kitchen. Alex told him about our lunch. "I should be getting tired of potatoes, but I'm not. Tara's mashed potatoes may have been the best yet."

Colin smiled, a little distracted, I thought. He busied himself with the teapot.

"Have you had lunch?" I asked.

"I'm not hungry," he said. "Grace and I had some scones, waiting for the doctor."

Colin was taking his time. I'd seen his method before, telling about the visit of the Guards to Magdala's cottage, what Bridget knew and didn't know, what the Guards said about Dr. Malone's murder. Colin had to have his tea first. He'd say what he had to say, eventually. He told us the doctor on Bridget's case, Dr. Hogan, was a woman, very professional, it seemed, but young. Probably early thirties, though she didn't look much older than Bridget. Ponytail and glasses shaped like cat eyes with sequins on the frames.

Bridget was much more "clear-headed" this morning, he said, but very tired. Not saying much. Grace was going to help her with a shower. Bridget didn't object; she just didn't seem to care much whether she cleaned up or not.

Colin made the tea and sat with us at the table, stirring the cream into his cup, and finally he came to the point.

"Bridget had a lot of drugs in her system. I can't remember what they all were. A whole pharmacy, it sounded like, when Dr. Hogan began to rattle off the names." Colin put down his spoon and picked up his cup, but he didn't bring it to his lips. "The doctor said it was no wonder Bridget was in such a state. She'd been taking barbiturates that bring her down and amphetamines that make her high. Antidepressants and I don't know what else. Some of the pill bottles from the cottage were empty but clearly she'd been mixing up all kinds of medications."

He sipped his tea at last, and I took the opportunity to say, "Prescriptions."

Colin waited a moment before answering. "I looked at the bottles before I handed them over yesterday. Some had the kind of label you get at a pharmacy, though they didn't have a name of any pharmacy. Must have meant they came from Dr. Malone's office. A few of the bottles just had a piece of tape with writing on it: *Oxy* was one I recognized. The painkiller. One of Patrick's friends when we were back in Dublin was in a motorcycle accident and tore his back up bad. He got addicted to Oxycodone. First time I'd heard of that." Another sip of tea. "So the question is, where did those come from?"

We all pondered the question. Alex said, "Did the doctor—Hogan, you said—was she able to shed any light on the matter?"

"She was baffled," Colin said. "She knew Dr. Malone but not well. She hasn't been in Thurles long. You know doctors aren't apt to speak ill of each other, but when I told her Bridget had been in the care of Dr. Malone for more than two years and I was sure he was supervising her medications, she got a very strange look and said, 'I can't explain it.'"

Colin's phone sounded, and he answered. Mouthing "Grace" to us, he stood up and walked over to the kitchen sink to talk. I gathered up our teacups, gave Alex a look, and he got the message that we should give Colin some privacy for his call.

Colin caught up with us as we started up the stairs. "I thought you'd want to know the latest. Dr. Hogan thinks Bridget should be moved to Dublin. She mentioned a couple of hospitals. I'm going to call my brother for advice. He's a surgeon in Dublin, I think I told you."

Things moved quickly. Before time for dinner, Colin had set

off for Dublin with Bridget. Grace was back at Shepherds. She had packed Bridget's bags and was now on the phone at Reception, arranging for Alex to meet with Father Tierney the next day, to talk about the history of the Cathedral of the Assumption. "Eleven o'clock, and stay for a light lunch?" she said to Alex, and Alex nodded. "He'll be there, Father, and he's looking forward to it. Thank you."

"What a juggler you are," I said to Grace. "Taking care of everybody."

She laughed. "That's just the way it has to be. Alex, you're sure to enjoy Father Tierney."

We spoke about Bridget, and though Grace tried for a cheerful tone, it was clear that she was frustrated. "I would have gone to Dublin myself, but it made more sense for Colin to go. It's his brother, arranging things, and he can sleep over in Donal's flat after he gets Bridget settled in. And Lord knows I can cook a better breakfast here than Colin can!"

I had a thought, and before I could consider whether it was a good idea or not, I said, "Would you like to go to Dublin tomorrow? I'll drive. I might try to meet a friend there."

Alex raised his eyebrows. I gave a wave of dismissal. "Whether that works out or not, it doesn't matter. We can drive to Dublin for the day."

"That's a possibility," Grace said, her face brightening as she worked it out in her mind. "Colin would like to come back home in the morning. He's so behind in the office. But with things up in the air with Bridget, it would help if I could be there tomorrow. Maybe we can get some good professional opinions."

"Then we'll plan on it," I said.

"Enya will just have to take responsibility for Jimmie until Colin gets back. Since the day he went missing in her care, she doesn't like to be *in charge,* but I'll talk to Patrick. And I wonder if Helen would give you a ride to the church," Grace said to Alex, covering all her bases.

"Please don't concern yourself about *that*. I can walk," he said.

I glared at Alex. "I vote for asking Helen."

Mr. Sweeney had just come down the stairs. Alex turned to him, "Oh, Mr. Sweeney, you're just the man I wanted to see. I might need a ride into town in the morning. Would you be able to help me out, at eleven o'clock?"

Mr. Sweeney's persistent frown eased a bit. "I s'pose I could," he said.

"Fine! It's all taken care of," Alex said.

Mr. Sweeney went on his way. Grace excused herself, as it was time to begin dinner for her family.

"Any ideas about what *we* should do for dinner?" I said to Alex.

"I'm thinking I'll do some reading and turn in early. Maybe try a glass of warm milk."

I smiled. "I think I'll just pick up a snack at the market, then, and I should probably make it an early night, too."

"In preparation for your day trip tomorrow."

"Right."

"And meeting that friend of yours."

"If that works out," I said.

Alex couldn't possibly know, but somehow I had a feeling he did.

When Paul Broussard answered, I couldn't help wondering why I had waited so long.

I had thought I knew, but in that moment, my reasons made no sense.

"Jordan," he said. "It is so very good to hear your voice."

"Yours, too," I said.

And then there was an awkward pause, but Paul was always able to handle that sort of thing. "Are you still in Ireland?" he asked. I said yes, and he asked, "How long will you be staying?" We would be leaving Thurles Monday, flying out on Tuesday, I said.

So little time left.

I told him about our friends in Thurles whose daughter was hospitalized in Dublin. I planned to drive my friend to the hospital, I explained. "Tomorrow," I said, "just for the day," knowing as I said it that it wasn't reasonable to hope a man like Monsieur Broussard would simply drop everything and fly to Dublin in what amounted to a few hours from now.

He said, "And are you saying that we might meet in Dublin—tomorrow?"

Hesitating, I said, "I was just hoping. I took a chance." And then I began to stammer about how I realized this was short notice and he probably wasn't free, and certainly I could understand if he couldn't—but he interrupted me.

"Jordan, please. The answer is yes. I will meet you in Dublin." I could hear the smile in his voice. "As it happens, I have nothing on my schedule that cannot wait, and I do have a plane, as you know." Yes, I knew.

"The flight is not very long. I can be in Dublin in time for a late lunch in the Temple Bar area."

We made plans for lunch at The Bank on College Green. I would have no trouble finding the elegant restaurant. I had commented about the splendid red sandstone building as Alex and I had strolled through the touristy Temple Bar area to a traditional Irish pub named Gogarty's for the music on our first evening in Ireland.

Paul seemed to know The Bank well. "Exquisitely restored Victorian architecture, and the food and service are excellent," he said. "It's my favorite restaurant in Dublin." I imagined he knew the finest restaurants in every European capital, and beyond.

"Sounds lovely," I said.

Sometimes I believed Paul Broussard could read my mind, even as we spoke on the phone. He said, "Yes, it is a fascinating restoration that I hope you as an architect will enjoy seeing. But you are not too concerned about where we go and what we will order for lunch. I understand. We have much to talk about—the thing that lies so uneasily between us."

"Like a heavy concrete barrier," I said, and I was thinking I didn't know how we'd get over it or around it. Paul laughed, that warm, rich laugh of his, and it made me hope.

"You are delightful, Jordan," he said.

"I'm glad we can do this," I said.

"So am I. I won't—what is your American expression?—stand you up. I won't do that again," he said.

CHAPTER 19

I drove to Dublin in the rain.

Grace's silence when we left Shepherds Friday morning spoke of her uneasiness, and who could blame her? She had so much on her shoulders—all that went with running the B&B, not to mention the trouble with the Riordans at the bank, trouble that had slipped behind other pressing issues but had not gone away. Trying to make sure that Little Jimmie's life was as normal as possible. Dealing with Enya. Wondering what the future held for Bridget.

I began telling Grace about Paul Broussard as a diversion. By the time we reached the M8, the worry lines on Grace's face had eased, and she was caught up in the "soap opera" of Jordan and Paul. Her words, "soap opera." She had plenty of questions. I was glad I'd succeeded in making her smile—laugh, at times—but some of her pointed questions were hard to answer: "What do you hope for, out of this relationship?" she asked. "Do you want a long-distance romance? *Very* long distance. Is it enough to be together a few times a year? Are you just wanting a fabulous fling? Sounds like you almost had it in Provence, so maybe you just need to finish unfinished business. Or do you hope this could lead to marriage?"

"Marriage? Oh, no. I'm not thinking along those lines at all!" I said.

"You need to figure out what you want," she said, "and be honest about it. I remember when you said those very words to me, back in Atlanta about thirty years ago. Something Colin had done, and I was pouting, and you said, 'Tell him what's on your mind! How will he know, if you don't tell him?' It was great advice. Sure, men are *supposed* to know, but they don't."

"Paul is very perceptive," I said.

She gave a wave of dismissal, shaking her head, as if she did not believe any man could be *very* perceptive.

But Paul had to know what it meant when he'd missed the gallery opening in Atlanta and hadn't explained. He'd said, just last night, *I won't stand you up again.* He understood, all right.

"I had arranged everything, with Alex's help," I told Grace. "Alex had the Atlanta connections. I'll never forget how it felt that night, wearing my little black dress *and* my stilettoes *and* my brave face. The gallery owner, his assistant, a reporter doing a story for the arts section of the newspaper who was so excited about interviewing Monsieur Broussard—all of them had the same expression when they looked at me. As if they *got it* that Paul was just a player, and I had been foolish to think otherwise. Even the artist, Emil, knew something, I think."

"Something like—another woman?" Grace said.

"I don't know. A man like Paul Broussard—I think he would have handled that kind of thing very differently. He's had a lifetime of experience with women coming and going."

"He has said that?"

"Oh no, Paul would never say a thing like that, but I just know. You would know, too, if you spent five minutes with him."

Grace laughed. "I think I will need to meet this man some-day."

It was easy to talk to Grace about things I hadn't confided to anyone. Yes, Paul had called the afternoon before the reception at the gallery, profuse with his apologies. *An urgent personal matter.* Vague, I thought, but I'd expected he would elaborate the next time we spoke.

"It was *two weeks* before he called again. Two weeks!" I told Grace. "Again, he was apologetic, but he was even more cryptic. Said he couldn't explain yet. Asked me to trust him."

"And did you trust him?"

"To a point," I said.

A car flew around me, traveling at about ninety miles per hour. The road was wet, rain coming down in sheets. I slowed down even more. Maybe the weather would change by this afternoon. What did the Irish say, that the only thing predictable about weather in Ireland was that it was unpredictable? I knew it to be true.

I wondered about Paul's flight into Dublin, in his private plane, in the rain.

"I didn't hear anything from him until a few weeks ago. More than two months. How long was I supposed to wait, to trust? I missed his call—and I didn't call back."

"Jordan! You cut off communication. That's the very worst thing."

"I thought it wouldn't hurt to let *him* wait a while," I said.

An indulgent smile played on Grace's lips. She might have been thinking I'd been too long without a man in my life, that I was no more savvy than a teenager. "He must care a lot for you," she said, "to fly from Paris just to spend a few hours with you. You do look fetching, by the way. Your raincoat—perfect color for you hair. And such style! I haven't seen anything like it in Ireland. We're very utilitarian when it comes to dressing for the elements."

So now Grace was feeling better, and I was feeling worse.

"You're lucky to have this chance to sort it out," she said.

But the question rattled in my brain: What if Paul and I couldn't sort it out?

★ ★ ★ ★ ★

St. Vincent's Hospital was not very different from any hospital in the States. The wide halls and muted colors, the sterile environment, the faint smell of disinfectant. Grace had spoken to Colin that morning before he'd left for Thurles. Likely, we had met him on the M8. Colin had said Bridget would need to go for treatment at a rehabilitation center, but she'd be at St. Vincent's for a couple of days, as they continued to do tests. Treatment, for how long? Grace had asked Colin. He didn't know.

We found Bridget's room. Nearby was a waiting area. "Take all the time you need," I said. It was about eleven o'clock. I thought about Alex and had to smile. What would Alex and Mr. Sweeney talk about, as Mr. Sweeney gave him a lift to the Cathedral?

I checked out the magazines, marveling at the great interest in American celebrities. Why did the public care so much? I found a day-old newspaper and one even older and began to catch up on what was happening in the big wide world I hadn't thought much about, these past days.

Grace returned after a half hour. "Bridget's more herself this morning," she said. "Maybe she's got all the drugs out of her system. She'll have to go into treatment, but it's very strange, Jordan. She says she only took the drugs because Dr. Malone prescribed them. He insisted, *You must take your medications.* That's what he told Colin and me—all he'd ever tell us."

I didn't know what to say. But I had my suspicions that Dr. Malone was not what everyone thought he was. Certainly, in Bridget's case, his management of her prescriptions raised serious questions.

"She's remembering some things she couldn't remember before," Grace said. "She hadn't been able to explain much about her visit to Dr. Malone that night, but it's coming back to her now, how furious she was with him. She just can't remember *why*." Grace frowned. "I know what the Guards might make of that—but no matter how *furious* she was, she couldn't have overpowered him, stabbed him, and moved him to the place in the woods where he was found."

"Good that she's regaining her memory," I said.

Grace sat in the chair across from me. "Bridget wants you to go in," she said.

I was stunned. She barely knew me.

"Is she feeling like having visitors?" I asked.

"She's much better," Grace said. "Go on in."

Bridget was sitting up in bed, with pillows behind her. Her eyes were clear, the blue made brighter by the deep blue t-shirt that bore some Tipperary sports team's insignia. Her legs were covered by a sheet, but I had a glimpse of print pj's. With clean skin and hair, she looked nothing like the young woman I'd last seen when we left Magdala's cottage two days ago.

"Grace said you were much better, but I didn't expect such a great improvement," I said.

She gave a shy little laugh. If she felt shy with me, why had she asked to see me?

"Thanks for all you've done . . . Jordan." She seemed unsure about how to address me. I preferred *Jordan*, of course. My mother-in-law was *Mrs. Mayfair*, in my mind.

"I'm just happy things are turning out well for you," I said.

She looked down at her nails, also clean. "Yes, I s'pose things are turning out very well."

There was still something in her voice—something older than her years, resignation and a wistfulness that bordered on sadness. Finally, she raised her gaze to meet mine, and said in a more confident voice, "You're a good friend to Mam. Dad, too."

191

"I've known Grace and Colin for a long time," I said. "With certain people, you can go for years without contact, but when you see them again, it seems like just yesterday that you were together. That's how it is with your parents. It's meant a lot to be able to spend this time with them."

"I haven't made it easy for them." Bridget seemed to be trying to say something that she couldn't quite get out. "You know I'll be in treatment for a while, but then I hope I can go home and be a good daughter and a good mother."

This was the young woman Grace had wanted me to know. She *was* a lovely girl. "You will," I said.

"Mam will wonder why I wanted to speak to you," Bridget said. "You can tell her I asked you to keep in touch with her, keep being a friend to her, even though you're miles apart. Everyone in Thurles likes Mam, but she doesn't have any girlfriends, you know? She just works and takes care of all of us. I can tell how much she trusts you. She would never have brought anyone else to the cottage."

"You've given this a lot of thought," I said.

I was still standing by her bedside. She patted a place beside her and said, "Please, sit here, Jordan. There's something else. I want to tell you something."

When I was settled, she said, "I want to tell you who Little Jimmie's father is."

My breath caught. My voice was not much more than a whisper. "Bridget, that's something you should talk about with your parents."

She nodded. "I will, when it seems right. I hope I can do it. I hope I can trust myself."

I didn't know what she meant. I remained silent, and after a moment, she continued. "It just doesn't feel like I should put that on them right now, with everything else that's happened and me going into treatment. I'm a bit frightened about treatment. What if I *don't* get well?" She stopped, and I wanted to reassure her, but something kept me from speaking.

"So I've been thinking," she said. "I'm *not* going to the priest. Maybe I'll come around to making my confession someday, but I'm not there yet. I couldn't tell anyone in Thurles. You're not from around here and you're going home, far from Ireland, so my secret will be safe with you." I nodded that I was on board, so far. "My parents deserve to know, and I want to tell them when I'm strong enough. I don't know how they'll take it."

At this point, I did speak up. "You're their daughter, and no matter what, they will love you. *That,* I am sure of."

"I know it's true." Bridget pulled at one of the pillows, adjusting it. "Right now, we're trying to get back, you know, like we used to be. I want to tell them—I promise I do—but I can't do it now."

I gave a slow, deliberate nod and said, "All right."

I was no priest, but if she simply needed to *say* who the child's father was—if that was what this was about—I would listen, and I would keep her secret.

"It's hard to say it, I've kept it to myself so long," Bridget said.

I laid my hand on hers. "Maybe I can say it for you."

Her eyes widened.

"James Malone?" I ventured.

She jerked her hand away. Both hands went to her chest, as if she were trying to contain herself. "How did you know? Are you saying my parents have known all along?"

"No. I just made a guess. I haven't discussed it with anyone."

"They don't know, then?"

"I don't think so."

"But—how?"

"Little things." I remembered Norah Malone's remarks to Grace and how she had glared at Little Jimmie. She must have known her husband had fathered the baby and believed Grace knew as well. Only now did I identify that it had been *contempt* in her eyes, contempt for the child she probably blamed for the breakup of her marriage.

"You were working for him when you got pregnant. His name was James."

"It was foolish of me to name Jimmie after him. But at the time, I thought I was in love with him, and I knew I couldn't have him and my baby couldn't have his last name. Dr. Malone—James—he was called Jimmie as he was growing up, he said, but that wasn't something people around Thurles knew. So I named my baby Jimmie. The town is full of men and boys named Jimmie."

"I doubt anyone made the connection because of the names, but at some point, somehow, Norah Malone found out," I said.

Bridget let her hands fall back into her lap. She seemed, at once, incredibly tired. "What a fool I was, in so many ways."

I didn't know how much longer we could talk before a nurse would make me leave, so I hurried to say, "The thing that tipped me off in the end was all the drugs in your system. The fact that Dr. Malone had been deliberate and systematic in the meds he gave you."

Her knowing look told me that she had figured out what I had figured out. She hadn't mixed up the medications herself, as the doctor in Thurles had suggested. Dr. Malone had used various drug cocktails to induce her mood swings and make her dependent on him.

Tears began to fill her eyes. Yes, Dr. Malone had provided all the pills. It had started not long after Jimmie's birth, when she began to imagine the three of them might have a life together, after all, but the doctor refused to leave his wife. "He told me he didn't love her but he felt sorry for her because she'd had a hysterectomy when she was much younger," Bridget said. "Not being able to have a baby made her a very unhappy woman and hard to live with, but he honored his vows. I know it wasn't right for me to ask him to leave her. But it wasn't right for him to refuse his baby, either."

I had my suspicions that the Riordan money might have been the primary attraction for Dr. Malone, and I said so.

Bridget wiped her eyes, and now the story came in a rush. "He told me I was suffering from post-partum depression and he could give me something for it, and he tried one thing and another. Maybe at first he was trying to help me. I think he was."

Who could say if that was true, and if so, when did he change? When did his actions become malpractice?

"And then, as I only got worse, he said I might be bipolar but he would help me with the medications so I wouldn't have to go into psychiatric care. After that, I must have just been lost."

I cringed at the severity of his manipulation. She was young and trusting. "As long as you were unstable and he could manage the drugs, he had you in his control," I said. "You wouldn't do anything to risk the arrangement you had. You wouldn't give up his name as Jimmie's father."

"I know why I went to him that night," Bridget said. "I didn't go for more drugs, but he made me take something even stronger than I'd had before. I don't remember much about getting back to Magdala's cottage. I think he took me through the woods. We had a torch."

"You said you knew why you went to his office that night."

"Above his office, where he lived. That's where I went. He took me downstairs and gave me—it was something to calm me down." She rubbed her eyes and blinked. "He took a call from someone and they were arguing."

Norah Riordan had told the Guard she was on the phone with him when Bridget pounded on the door. "You remember

195

that he *took the call*? The phone rang? He wasn't already on the phone?"

"His cell started ringing when we were upstairs, and he silenced it. Downstairs, in his office, the phone rang and rang, and he didn't answer for a time, but it kept ringing. When he finally did answer, he was very angry."

I waited, thinking the memory might come back, all clear, but she said, "It's confusing, but I know I was having a fit about Jimmie. I got it in my mind that I needed money and a lot of it so I could go away with my baby. That's what I was screaming about. I wanted money."

Bridget put her face in her hands. Some time passed, maybe just a minute, but it seemed longer. When she looked up again, she took a long breath. "If you'll do me this favor, Jordan, I'll be forever grateful. Do not breathe a word of what we've said. Sometime in the next two or three months—I'll surely be finished with the treatment in three months—you'll hear from my mother, telling you she knows everything about James Malone. I said it now, didn't I?" She gave a weak smile. "And you won't be bound by the secret anymore."

"I have to ask," I said.

"I know. What if you hear nothing?" She waited a moment, and then seemed to gather courage. "I think that would mean the treatment didn't work and who knows what would have happened to me, where I might be, or what I might be doing? I pray that won't be the outcome, but if it is, you'd know I never found the strength I needed to tell my parents about Jimmie's father. So I'd want you to tell them at that time."

"That's not going to happen, Bridget," I said. "You'll get well. You'll be the daughter you want to be—and the mother you want to be to Little Jimmie."

"I hope," she said in a small voice. Her face crumpled like a child's. I reached for her and drew her into my arms, hugging her as I would a daughter of mine. Her shoulders began to shake as she sobbed.

I could hear her father's words, and I repeated, "We must hang on to hope."

CHAPTER 20

Standing in the spacious bar of The Bank on College Grove, mesmerized by the stained glass ceiling, I was not worried that I had arrived before Paul. I was early. I had left my car in the parking lot at St. Vincent's. Taking a taxi made more sense than driving in a city I didn't know, in the rain. I hadn't imagined how quickly the taxi would get me to my destination. I had time to take in the striking interior of The Bank. Mosaic-tiled floors, intricately decorated plasterwork, sparkling chandeliers—a masterful restoration.

"The bar was once the main banking hall," came his voice, "when this was a branch of the Belfast Bank."

I turned around. "Paul," I said.

He took my hands and pulled me toward him, kissing my cheek. He held my hands a moment longer, his so strong, so alive. "You are a vision, Jordan," he said.

I was glad I'd splurged on the cerulean blue raincoat—*stylish*, Grace had pronounced—rather than one of the gray or beige boxy types that I usually bought on sale. My skirt and sweater were unremarkable, but the raincoat apparently had made a good impression.

"It's great to see you," I said. I could have said *he* was a vision. Exactly as I remembered. Salt-and-pepper hair, just long enough to be a little wavy. Strong facial features, warm smile, eyes that looked deep into mine.

Someone appeared to assist us—never a problem with

Monsieur Broussard—and took our raincoats. No one asked if we had a reservation. We were ushered to the dining room where the *maître d'* greeted us and summoned a starched waiter to seat us.

"Good to see you again, sir," said the young server in his lilting Irish accent.

Promptly a young woman from the wait staff asked if we cared for a drink.

"Shall we have a glass of wine?" Paul asked. Wine was not my customary lunchtime beverage, but this seemed like an occasion for an exception.

"I intended to be early, to be waiting for you," he told me when the servers had gone.

"You weren't late," I said.

"I made the mistake of checking into my hotel first. The rain, the traffic, and a taxi driver who may not have believed I know the shortest route to the Temple Bar area—exasperating."

I smiled. Paul was spoiled by having his own driver in Paris— even a driver in the little town in Provence where we'd met. He seemed to read my smile. He made a little dismissive gesture and said, "It is not important. I am here, and you are here."

He leaned toward me. The table, with its white tablecloth, was a small two-top. I suspected that if he'd wanted a larger one, we'd have it.

"Tell me, now, about your visit to Ireland, and Alex, and your friends," he said.

I tried to hit the highlights, telling how Alex and I had known Colin and Grace for so many years and how delightful Shepherds was. I mentioned our visits to Kilkenny and the Rock of Cashel. Paul gave a knowing nod. No doubt he'd been to both sites. As for Bridget, I kept it brief, saying she would be getting treatment in Dublin for problems with prescription drugs. And then our wine arrived. I knew it was a French wine;

I'd heard Paul order. Otherwise, I knew only that it was red and exquisite.

"So unfortunate about the young woman. I suppose that happens often," Paul said. "I can only imagine her parents' worry."

"I think she's resilient—and so are Colin and Grace," I said.

I brought the elegant glass to my lips and waited a moment, thinking how we might move forward in the conversation, acknowledge that "elephant in the room." Paul wasn't helping. He was just gazing at me, with the hint of a smile that was— sort of irresistible.

"Was the weather awful, in a small plane? Not that yours is all that small," I said.

"The sun was shining in Paris," he said. "We hit turbulence over the sea, but it was not a difficult flight. I have an excellent pilot. You met him."

I made the wine swirl a little. Paul looked at me over the rim of his glass. We could have reminisced about that *other* whirlwind flight, but I was relieved that Paul stayed in the moment. "I'll be returning to Paris tomorrow after I meet with a gallery owner I have needed to visit for some time. It is an opportunity to mix business with pleasure, as one says."

"I couldn't believe you'd fly to Dublin just for lunch," I said in a breezy tone.

But Paul was all seriousness. "Believe it, Jordan. The meeting I arranged was an afterthought. I am here because of you."

And there was the server, a pleasant young man with menus and his recitation of the lunch specials. Without consulting his menu, Paul said, "I must tell you my favorite lunch, especially on a rainy day, is the venison stew, but I have enjoyed many excellent dishes here."

"I'll take your recommendation," I said, and Paul gave a nod at my wise choice. The ordering was accomplished without much ado.

Paul and I exchanged another one of those meaningful looks, and he said, "It has been much too long, Jordan."

"About that," I said.

"Yes, about that," he said with a soft curve of his lips. "I have much to tell you, and I'm glad you have given me the opportunity to explain—at last." Was that just a hint of scolding?

"I should have returned your call," I said. I was tempted to add, *the call you finally made after two long months of silence,* but I didn't.

He seemed to be studying me. Maybe he was reading my mind.

"I apologize," I said with no great warmth.

"I accept your apology," he said. "And now it is my turn to say how sorry I am for any disappointment—or perhaps even distress—that I may have caused you. Ah, Jordan, you deserved much better than I have given you these past months. My failures have been unforgiveable, and yet I hope you will find it in your heart to forgive me."

Unforgiveable. That was about right. But the man did have a flair for the magnanimous apology. Whatever indignation I had brought with me seemed to be seeping away.

But not too fast, I reminded myself.

"I'm listening," I said.

Our server brought warm brown crusty bread and creamy butter, managing to do so with minimal interruption, but Paul waited until he was gone. "I spoke with Emil at length after the reception in Atlanta. He said the show was excellent, much credit to you and Alex. It was truly my loss, to miss that evening."

"You had that *urgent personal matter,*" I said.

Paul moved his wine glass a fraction of an inch on the table.

I took a deep breath. "Paul, we were just getting to know each other in Provence. It would have been wonderful if you had come to Atlanta, but you couldn't, and you called, and I shouldn't have made so much of it. You weren't *obligated* to me, except to be truthful." I chose my words with care. "Even if the urgent matter involved someone—what I'm saying is, if you were involved with someone—what I'm *trying* to say—is that all I expect from you is the truth."

"Jordan, I have never been untruthful to you," he said. "You are right. There was someone. But it is not at all what you think."

My throat tightened. What was I supposed to think? "All right," I said, the words sharp, betraying the fact that maybe it wasn't really all right.

"I was truthful when I told you I had business in New York that prevented me from being in Atlanta before the day of the show."

"I believed you."

"As well you should have done. But something else happened in New York, the last night of Emil's show there. A young woman introduced herself."

I turned the cool crystal stem of my glass around and around. "You can thank Emil for keeping your secret," I said.

"Emil may have noticed her speaking with me, but he did not know who she was. *I* did not know her." Paul leaned in even closer. "I was astounded—*shocked*. Jordan, I did not know that I had a daughter."

I was only marginally interested in the lunch salad with goat cheese. Paul scarcely touched his.

He had told me something of his time in New York when he was in his twenties. I knew he was divorced after a short marriage. I never knew his wife's name.

"Amanda," he said now. "I am sure the attraction for me was

that she was so *American,* or what I imagined an American to be. So exuberant! Such *joie de vivre!* Also beautiful, but—headstrong, I think, is the word. We had great passion in the beginning. We did not know each other long or well when we married, and we were young." His gaze was reflective. "Passion is a wonderful thing and much to be desired in the calm seas, but it is not enough for the storms."

He let that sink in, and I saw where he was going with it. I knew about the storms of a marriage, even when the marriage felt solid.

"After a little more than a year, we parted ways. The divorce was accomplished quickly by today's standards. I gave her a considerable sum, ensuring she would be most comfortable. All of it—the romance, the marriage—was like a dream. I woke up in Paris and could scarcely believe Amanda had ever been in my life. And that was a long time ago. I did not even know that she had died last year. Ovarian cancer. Terrible." Paul took a drink of wine that was more than a sip. "I have told you about Amanda because her daughter is much like her. Isabella. She is the young woman who came to Emil's show in New York."

Nibbling on bread with a bite of salad now and then, I listened in a kind of daze as he described that encounter and their subsequent meetings, his amazement that Isabella—*Bella,* he called her with fondness—so resembled his former wife, and his skepticism when she first revealed that before Amanda's death, she had imparted a great secret. In her last dying days, she had told Bella that the man she had known as her father, who had been killed in a boating accident on Cape Cod when she was fifteen, was not her true parent.

"She had a plausible story—but was it just *that,* a story?" Lines in Paul's face that I'd never noticed had deepened. "She knew a great deal about me. Yes, she said Amanda had told her everything she knew, but a man in my position would not be prudent to simply accept her statement. I would need verification."

I spoke at last. "It would be expected."

"Yes! You understand." He said this in a kind of rush that was not like Paul Broussard at all. Nothing I'd seen before now had shown Paul's vulnerability quite so clearly.

"How old is Bella?" I asked.

"She is thirty-four. She was born two months after I returned to Paris. Amanda and I worked through our attorneys. We did not see each other. I knew nothing about a child."

I put down my fork. "And did you get the verification you needed?"

"Yes. It is true. Bella is my daughter," he said.

Over our venison stew, Paul told about Bella as any father might, with pride and some amusement, but there was something guarded, too, in his manner. He said with a frown, "I mentioned to you once that I thought I might have been a good father. I had no idea. It is an experience like no other."

I nodded.

"Bella and I had a furious disagreement, the night before I was to leave New York." He added, "Before you and I would have been together in Atlanta."

We were getting to the heart of things, at last.

The argument, it seemed, had to do with whether Bella's claim was truthful. Paul had told her of the need to consult his attorneys. Now he insisted that he'd handled that conversation badly, but from an outsider's point of view, I could see it seemed only reasonable that he would have doubts about someone coming out of the woodwork, laying claim to his fortune. Wouldn't any intelligent thirty-four-year-old woman have realized that?

"I was at the airport, just moments from boarding, when the call came that morning. Bella's jogging partner had come by her apartment. Bella had taken an overdose of sleeping pills.

She was barely alive when they took her in the ambulance. Her friend knew I was leaving the city and she found my number in Bella's phone. Bella had confided in her about everything."

Paul finished off his wine. Our waiter who was so in tune to every nuance at our table appeared to offer more wine. Typical of Paul, he looked at my glass, still half full, and smiled. "I expect we will order coffee instead—and dessert?" I shook my head, and Paul said, "Coffee, then. *Deux.*"

He continued, describing the day at the hospital, waiting for the doctors to say that Bella would recover, waiting to see her. "The guilt and anguish I felt—I can't explain," he said. "And why could I not tell you the reason I had to stay in New York?" He turned his palms up. "My mind was—I can only say I was not myself."

"I suppose you weren't thinking about anything but Bella," I said.

"Something like that. But I have reproached myself a thousand times. As time went by, it became even more difficult to tell you about Bella—such a long story. As you might imagine, these months have been complicated."

Our coffee came. Paul took his time stirring in the cream and sugar. "I stayed in New York for another week—no, two weeks, I think it was." He gave me a significant look. It was around that time that we had talked. He still had not explained, and then he didn't call again for two months.

"I found an excellent psychiatrist for her," Paul said. "It seems Bella suffers from a depressive disorder but had never been diagnosed. Her mother's death, trying to accept that the man she believed was her father was, in fact, *not,* confronting me with the fact that *I* am her father, which took great courage, and finally my reluctance—my *caution,* as I saw it—all of these things pushed her over the edge, as they say."

Paul talked with more ease, as we lingered over our coffee.

He said, "I am not sure if it is possible to catch up when you lose thirty-four years, but we are trying."

"You've stayed in contact, then," I said.

"Indeed. She came to Paris and stayed several weeks. Every day I showed her a new sight, a museum, or a wonderful gallery. She is quite artistic herself. We met with my attorneys and took care of a number of items, as you might expect." He gave a gesture signaling the business matters were not important. Things like changing his will, making her a beneficiary on insurance policies—those things came to my mind. "I found a nice apartment for her in Paris. I want her to visit often. I would never have imagined all the things a father might do to ensure a daughter's happiness."

I didn't say a word about overindulgence. Who was I to make judgments? I had known my children all their lives, loved them from *before* they were born. Paul hadn't had that opportunity. He was certain she was his daughter. He had every right to catch up. Whatever business he was conducting that related to Bella, he could no doubt afford it. I could not say what it was that nagged at me about this new, overpowering focus of his.

Lunch ended after nearly two hours, and Paul said, "*Voila!* The rain has stopped. So it is with the weather in Ireland." He suggested a walk along the River Liffey. It wasn't far to Wellington Quay and the beautiful river. Neither of us was surprised when the sun came out, bright as a jewel. We spent another hour, strolling, holding hands. As we grew more relaxed with each other, I couldn't resist telling him about the priest hole and the gold chalice.

"The girl hid in the priest hole with her child? *Mon Dieu!*" he said. I wondered if the thought of his own daughter's erratic behavior crossed his mind. But he was as fascinated with the discovery of the secret chamber and its contents as I had imagined he would be. "If I can be of assistance with the authentication process, I can recommend an expert archeologist. I am acquainted with two men who are world-class in their field."

Of course he was.

The sunlight took on that late-afternoon glow. I looked at my watch, and I didn't have to say anything. Paul said, "I know. If you must go, we can get a taxi at that corner."

At the corner, he touched my face and turned it up to his. It was a long, lovely kiss. He gave me one of his deep, lingering gazes and said, "Let us say all is forgiven between us and leave it at that. Yes?"

"All is forgiven," I said.

A taxi pulled up, and Paul opened the door for me. He raised my fingers to his lips and kissed them. "Always, it seems, we are saying goodby, rushing to somewhere else, you and I."

And that was how we left it.

CHAPTER 21

"I think I'm home in time to put Little Jimmie to bed," Grace said when we parked at Shepherds. Conversation had been light on the return trip. Grace was pleased that Bridget was "more herself," but it would be "a long way back to the girl she was." I didn't expand on my afternoon with Paul or reveal that he had a daughter. Grace had asked that morning what I hoped for, with Paul, and I still had no answer. With Bella adding a new wrinkle to things, it might not matter what *I* hoped for.

"You look like you could use a cup of tea," Grace said as we went in. "Long day."

I agreed on both counts. Grace instructed me to make myself at home in the kitchen. I put on the teapot, but she was back before the kettle whistled, and she promptly took over. "Colin had Jimmie all bathed and dressed for bed and was reading him a story. Jimmie didn't want me to interrupt. 'Night, night!' he said, waving me away. I gave him a kiss and left them to it."

She prepared a tray, adding some biscuits, and said we should have our tea in the keeping room. She said Colin wanted me to know that Alex had gone to Finnegan's.

"I wonder how he got there," I said.

"Colin didn't say. He did say that Alex went on and on about his visit with Father Tierney. They must have hit it off. I was sure they would."

I decided I'd go to Finnegan's, too, later. It was Friday night, and our last chance for music night at Finnegan's Pub.

As Grace and I settled in the comfy keeping room, Patrick came in. "We'll be leaving for Dublin now," he said.

"You're later than usual," Grace said. "I hope you weren't detained because of minding Jimmie."

"We weren't. I guess it took Enya a bit longer to pack," he said. "Do you need anything else before we go?"

"Nothing else, Patrick. Thank you for all your help while Colin and I have been seeing to Bridget. And please thank Enya for me."

He took a step back toward the door, and then turned again toward us, his face grim. "Enya will be staying in Dublin for a time," he said.

Grace did not reply immediately. She gave a long sigh before she said, "Maybe she just needs some time to sort things out in her mind. We've been through so much—all of us."

"That's the thing—all of us have," Patrick said. "It's not just about Enya."

"She had a different life before she came to Shepherds," Grace said. "And all at once she's minding someone else's baby and getting up early to put out breakfast and spending evenings alone when you're helping out in the office. Oh, I've fussed about Enya. I won't deny it. But I can see why it's been hard on her."

"Not your fault, Mam, that Enya's a bit spoiled."

"I was a bit spoiled, too," Grace said with a reflective smile. "Wasn't I, Jordan?"

"Not the word I would use," I said. "You did have a different kind of life in Atlanta. That's true."

"I can't imagine you were selfish," Patrick said.

"You should ask your dad how hard I was to live with when he first brought me to Ireland, and his dad was dying, and his mother was so needy, and I was a new mother myself who knew little about babies. Ask Colin. See what he says."

Patrick's lips curved into a gentle smile for the first time, and he looked even more like Colin. "If you were hard to live with, I can tell you my dad does not remember a bit of it."

Patrick gave his mother a squeeze and had a quick wave for me. "You'll be here for a few more days, won't you, Jordan?"

"We'll be leaving Monday," I said.

"Ah, then I'll see you again. I'll be back tomorrow, after I've checked in on Bridget."

"If you need to stay longer, Patrick—do what you need to do," Grace said.

He shook his head. "I won't be staying."

Alex and Ian were leaning on the bar, laughing with Finn as he set new pints before them. I squeezed in beside them. Another busy night at the pub—tables full and not much bar space. It was Friday night, music in the back room. Strains of a merry Irish tune filled the air.

"Jordan!" Alex said, giving me a little hug. Not like Alex. He was not a hugger. He must have been at the bar for a while. Ian winked, as if to say, *I've been taking good care of him.*

"You're in the party going to the Cliffs of Moher tomorrow?" Finn asked.

I said I was looking forward to it.

"Irish coffee, right? You're not big on our Guinness."

"Don't you know, it's because you make such a grand coffee, Finn," Ian put in.

"That's it," I said.

"Yes, I do, if I say so meself," said Finn.

I studied Alex. "I see you've been managing fine without me. Did you have dinner?"

"I had a wonderful lunch at Father Tierney's," he said, "and I came home with a parcel of leftovers, courtesy of his lovely cook—can't remember her name but I remember her food!"

"Sounds like you and Father Tierney became fast friends," I said.

That was all Alex needed to start in on a report of his visit with the Father. He may not have remembered the name of the cook, but his memory was keen when it came to the history of the Cathedral of the Assumption and also of the town of Thurles. Incredible that he rattled off dates with such ease. I have trouble remembering my children's birthdays. After a long recitation, he said, "Father Tierney is a most intelligent and engaging fellow. I must say he did wonders for my opinion of priests, which, generally speaking, has not been high."

Ian and I glanced at each other with flickers of amusement.

I changed the subject, fearful of where Alex might be going with that. "Did you walk or ride from Shepherds tonight?"

"Helen gave us a lift. She was headed to the golf course, for Charles," Alex said.

"I expect they've had dinner at some fancy place and they'll be coming here to polish off the evening," Ian said. "In any case, you can be sure we weren't going to walk back home late at night, Jordan, not after what happened out there on that road. We'd get a ride somehow."

"It was exactly a week ago," I noted.

"Sweet Mother, has it been a week? And we'll all be leaving Thurles soon. Without knowing the answers to many of the questions that have come up, I'm afraid," Ian said.

He had not learned anything new at the Internet café, he said, nor had the Guard given him an update on their investigation of the shootings. "And the poor doctor's murder—doesn't seem they've made any progress there." Ian turned up his glass for a long drink.

"Maybe they just haven't made their findings public," I said.

He laughed. "In a town like this, word gets around. I expect we would hear."

211

A few minutes later, Mr. Sweeney came in, bellied up to the bar, and ordered from Finn's son, Brendan. Alex gave him a salute. Mr. Sweeney returned just the barest nod. I asked Alex if they'd had lively conversation on the way to Father Tierney's. Alex said, "About what you would expect. But he did offer to give me a ride back to Shepherds. We met Father Tierney inside the church to set the time, and when the Father began to show me around, we left Mr. Sweeney lighting a candle. You just never know about people, do you?"

What an assortment of guests we'd met at Shepherds. I hadn't seen much of Molly and Doreen since that evening I had come in from Red Stag Crossing, wet and dirty. I wondered about them and asked Ian, the best one to know, I thought.

Ian said, "Doreen has been dragging Molly to sites all around. Keeping her away from me, I wager."

I gave him a wry smile. "They'll be on the day trip tomorrow. Maybe we can keep Doreen occupied so Molly can have a little space."

Finn returned with my Irish coffee, and we spoke again about the trip to the Cliffs of Moher. "I thought the English woman who arranged it all would be here tonight, going over every little thing with me," Finn said.

At the far end of the bar, someone called out a harsh, "Finn! You've got thirsty customers waiting to be served, man!" It was Lucas Riordan.

"Thirsty's right," Finn said in a low voice as he bent toward us. "He's throwin' 'em back pretty good tonight."

A moment later, Mr. Sweeney edged in beside Alex and said something out of the side of his mouth. Alex glanced at Lucas Riordan and spoke in a low voice to Mr. Sweeney, who nodded and left the pub.

"What was that all about?" I said.

Alex said, "He just asked, 'Who's that eejit calling out for

Finn?' and I told him."

We heard clapping from the room where the musicians played, the fiddle predominant on a jig. I said, "We should try to get in one last set before our time in Thurles is up," and Alex and I followed the music to the back room. Ian remained at the bar, striking up a conversation with a pretty girl who had just arrived, next to him.

"I failed to ask about your day in Dublin," Alex said.

"It was good," I said.

He gave an inquisitive look, a frown, actually. We edged into the doorway of the back room, and at the end of the tune, a group at one table relinquished their seats. Most of the music was instrumental, melodies that managed to be merry and haunting at the same time. We stayed through a ballad that everyone except us seemed to know. About lost love—what else? Ian was standing in the doorway, having struck out with the girl at the bar, apparently.

"There's something about the Irish music," I said.

"It's the very air we breathe," he said.

Finn pulled up to Shepherds at 8:00 a.m. sharp, and we climbed into his van like children eager for a school trip—Molly, Doreen, Ian, Helen, Alex, and me. Grace and Colin waved us off from the front door, as if we were departing on a long journey instead of a day trip—two or three hours to the Cliffs of Moher. I had to believe they were looking forward to having the whole place to themselves for the day, with just the baby there. Charles said he had a nine-thirty tee time, and Patrick and Enya were in Dublin. Finn had said we'd be back before dark, that we'd want to spend as much time as possible at this "magnificent site."

I was sitting next to Helen, who occupied the window seat on the second row. Doreen, Molly, and Ian had the long back seat, and Alex was in the passenger seat next to Finn. At first Doreen and Finn carried on a noisy exchange over the rest of us, but as we all settled into the trip, Alex and Finn began to talk about the history of the Cliffs, and though Doreen monopolized the conversation in the back seat, Ian and Molly spoke from time to time. Dublin, the city and all its attractions, seemed to be their topic. What an attractive pair they made, Ian with his dark curls and Molly, her reddish-gold hair pulled back in a tortoise-shell barrette. The hum of the engine provided a kind of "white noise" that permeated the van, so when I spoke to Helen in a low voice, I doubted anyone was hearing.

"Are you all right, Helen?" I asked. "You've been awfully quiet this morning."

Her smile was forced. She took off her stylish, expensive-looking sunglasses and pushed her hair behind her ear. "I suppose you're right. I've been distracted." She kept her voice low, too. Somewhat surprising that she could. "I'm afraid Charles's plans to work with Lucas may have gone awry. I suppose he'll know for sure today, but from all indications, Lucas doesn't want my husband's expertise after all. He simply wants our money." She gave a brittle little laugh. "The problem is that we have no money to invest with him, even if we wanted to."

Helen did not hold back as she explained, all in just above a whisper, how they had fared poorly during the downturn in the economy. Charles had invested much of what he'd earned on the pro tour, and—"That's gone," she said with a flippant little wave. "I had family money, quite a lot in the beginning, but not so much now that it's been our only source of income. The time has come that Charles really *must* get a job. And when he talked with Lucas at Turnberry, this opportunity sounded so promising. The kind of employment that would suit Charles."

"I can imagine," I said, knowing that being just any golf pro at just any country club would not necessarily *suit* Charles.

Helen crossed her arms, rubbing them through her silky

warm-up jacket.

"Yesterday, Lucas put the screws on. Isn't that the expression? He said, 'Are you in or out?' And my husband, poor dear, he *knows* there's no money to invest, but he just couldn't say it. He said he'd talk it over with me."

"You had to put the brakes on."

"Exactly. And I don't like doing that." She gave a sorrowful look and spoke in an even softer voice. "Charles is quite a bit younger than I am. You may have guessed." She paused as I tried to find the right words, but she let me off the hook. "Never mind. We get along. He is very sweet to me, in spite of the face he puts on to others. I love to indulge him, but sometimes I have to—as you say, put on the brakes. The sort of money Lucas needs for a development of this scale—what he'd want from us is simply out of the question."

"Just how large *is* the development?" I asked, remembering what Colin and Grace had said, that Lucas wanted Shepherds and he'd acquired other properties around them.

"It has the potential to be *very* large—if he gets enough investors. A *resort*. Upscale holiday homes built around a golf course. With tennis and an upscale restaurant, boutiques—it all sounds quite lavish, actually. Eventually, he would like to get a resort hotel interested."

I could see that such a development, practically adjacent to Shepherds, had the potential to squeeze out the B&B. "Colin and Grace should know about this," I said, as if they didn't have some clue already. But Helen knew more than they did. "It's not good news for Shepherds."

"I know it's not, and you'll have to believe I've felt some guilt over all of it," Helen said. "But now that I know how deceptive Lucas was, I'll have no qualms about revealing his plans. We'll be going back to London tomorrow. What does it matter to me if Colin and Grace know?"

From the back seat came a note of laughter from Molly, apparently at something Ian had said. Doreen's dark expression did not bode well for the young couple.

We passed through the lively town of Limerick and the beautiful Shannon region, with its pastoral views. Finn pulled over a couple of times for us for photo ops. It was not long before the spectacular Cliffs of Moher came into view.

CHAPTER 22

Breathtaking was the word that came to mind, but it didn't do justice to the wild, rugged cliffs that rose high above the Atlantic, silhouetted against the gray sky. Finn pointed out the warning sign at the entrance to the car park. The white hazard sign meant to take extra caution, as the winds were strong. "Not so bad down here, but much stronger up there!" he said, pointing to the cliffs. "I hope everyone brought windbreakers or rain jackets. There's a saying that you can experience four seasons of weather in the same day, here at the Cliffs. No telling what you might get, up on the paths."

The car park was a sea of vehicles. Alex mentioned that the Cliffs of Moher were Ireland's most visited tourist attraction. "Though I hope to steer my readers to some of the less-touristy sites, like the Hedge School, I would be remiss if I didn't give this one its due," he said. I wondered how Alex would manage on the rocky cliff trails. I would stay close by him, if he'd let me, and I hoped he'd have the necessary stamina.

Finn parked the van, advising us that if we cared to use the facilities in the Visitors Centre, we might also want to view the films and exhibits that would inform us about what we could expect from the Cliffs of Moher experience. Finn was taking seriously his job as our tour guide. Alex, Doreen, Helen, and I followed his suggestion. Ian and Molly headed straight for the cliffs.

The Visitors Centre was unlike any I'd ever seen, in any

country. Built into the hillside, it was hidden under the grass roof except for the entrance and, Finn informed me, two other windows for the views. "Seventeen years in the planning and building," he said, "but you'll hear all about that when you watch the films." He turned as we were about to reach the entrance. "Ah, there you are, Mrs. Quinn. I thought we'd lost you."

Doreen, lagging behind our little group, had no clever retort. She said nothing. If she had looked over her shoulder, she would have seen Molly and Ian, holding hands, as they set off toward the cliffs. Helen had glanced back, as I had. "Come along, Doreen," she said, pausing to let Doreen catch up. "Let's find the loo and then have a cup of tea before we tax our mental and physical abilities too much."

Just inside the entrance, a woman was trying to corral two little boys, who looked to be about nine and seven. The smaller one crashed into Alex, but Alex saw the collision coming, braced himself, and kept the child from falling. "Oh ho, young fellow!" he said in a jolly voice. "Better check your brakes if you're going up on the cliffs!"

The boy called, "Mam!" and ran to his mother, wrapping his arms around her legs.

"So sorry!" the woman said. She grabbed both children's arms and shook them.

"No harm done," Alex said. What restraint he displayed! Alex was not in favor of the more permissive approaches to child-rearing. He was actually quite fond of children who sat quietly, read books, displayed good manners, and spoke politely to their elders. I was glad he didn't advise this mother to put the boys on a leash.

Helen caught up with me as the frazzled-looking mom herded the children into the coffee shop. "You don't think she'll take those boys up *there*, do you?" Helen said.

"It's a scary thought," I said, "but I don't know why they would have come here, otherwise."

"There's plenty to see besides the cliffs," Doreen said, her vinegary tone leaving no doubt that she was thinking about Molly and Ian, still miffed that they'd gone off without her.

Finn said he'd be taking a cup of tea out at the picnic tables, and he left us to our own devices.

I was eager to go up on the cliff paths, but the others—even Alex—seemed content to wait, to see if the weather might improve.

Interested in knowing more about this eco building, I went straight into the domed cave-like space that housed the interactive media displays—the Atlantic Edge exhibition. A pretty young customer service agent named Moira must have been trained to spot visitors like me, for she introduced herself and said, "Is there anything you'd like to know about?" When I said I was fascinated with the underground building, it was like turning her switch on. Moira informed me that at a cost equivalent to $32 million, the environmentally sensitive structure implemented conservation measures throughout. She explained about the use of geothermal lighting and cooling, solar panels, and gray water recycling. "Do you know about gray water?" she asked. I said I did, but she told me, anyway, how the gray water was like dishwater; it might *look* dirty but was actually safe for reuse in many instances, like irrigation. She told about the dual flush systems and aerated motion-sensor taps in the toilets. "You might not know about the waterless urinals in the men's toilets," she said. No, I did not. "Everything on the inside, as well as the outside, is in favor of protecting the environment," she said with pride.

Though I was interested enough in the renewable energy systems, I was most captivated by the structural system. The large beams that supported the structure from the roof level and spanned between the outer walls were buried within the hillside. Moira was so knowledgeable that I had to ask if she might be an architectural or engineering student, but she was not. "My specialty is ornithology," she said. "Would you like some information about the thirty thousand seabirds that nest around the cliffs?"

I might have taken her up on the offer, but I wanted to look for Alex. I located him at one of the interactive displays. "O'Brien's Tower," he said. "That, I must see."

I happened along just as the narrator was telling about Sir Cornellius O'Brien. Credited with being a man ahead of his time, O'Brien saw the potential for tourism and decided to build an observation tower for all the visitors coming to the Cliffs of Moher. The narrator added that in another version of history, it was said that O'Brien built the tower to impress the ladies.

"Maybe we should have lunch before going out on the cliffs," I told Alex, keeping my voice just above a whisper, so as not to bother the others around us who were watching the film. "It's already past noon."

"If you like," he said, still focusing on the images of the tower.

"I'll be somewhere around here when you're ready," I said. He nodded.

I made the tour of the rest of the exhibition. It had everything anyone would want to know about the cliffs—geology, plants, birds, wildlife, underwater caves—and I could see that Doreen was correct in saying there was plenty here besides walking on the cliffs. This kind of self-guided tour, I could manage, as opposed to long lectures. I got a glimpse of each area as I made my slow walk through the dome but did not stop until I came to a screen and rows of wooden seating. I saw Helen on the end of one of the rows and took a seat beside her.

"Having a good time?" I asked.

"Oh, indeed! It's all quite informative and entertaining. This is supposed to be *very* exciting. It's a virtual reality cliff face adventure," she said, half-reading from her brochure.

Virtual reality cliff face adventure was an appropriate description for the short video called "The Ledge Experience." We were *virtually* on the edge of the cliffs, looking out over the ocean, looking down on the sheer drops. When the film ended, Helen took a deep breath and exhaled. "Remarkable!" she said. "So it's actually like that, I suppose."

"I suppose, if you get that close to the edge," I said. I probably would not.

Alex found us and said he was ready for lunch. He'd seen "The Ledge Experience" earlier and was up for the *real* adventure.

"What is the name of the café with the panoramic views? If we can get in, let's have a nice lunch there," Helen said. She and Alex went on to get a table. I looked for Doreen and found her in the coffee shop, with a cup of tea.

"You're welcome to sit down," she said.

I told her Alex and Helen were waiting at the Cliffs View Café, and we wanted her to join us for lunch. She shook her head, and I took a seat across from her.

"I can't stay, but I just have to say this, Doreen. You're making yourself miserable."

She met my words with a frown, and then the frown transformed into a reflective expression. "I think Ian reminds me too much of Molly's dad. Very charming, he was. Talented and good-looking. Ian seems nice enough, but a man like that, you'll always have to worry about the young women. Like flies to honey." She sipped her tea. "My husband left us for one of his music students when Molly was just five. Since that time, it's just been Molly and me. Just us."

That, it seemed to me, was the heart of the problem. Doreen

could not imagine her life without Molly as the center of it, but I didn't think I could say that.

"It may just be a passing thing with Molly and Ian. She's enjoying the attention, and why not? Just try to enjoy yourself, too." I stood up. "I have four daughters and there have been many boyfriends along the way. Many tears, too. Not mine—theirs."

With a bit more persuasion, Doreen agreed to come along with us. Perhaps because it was already one-thirty, the crowd had thinned in the Cliffs View Café. Helen and Alex were at a window table. What a view we had! The sky was still overcast, making the cliffs seem even more ominous. I calculated that a couple of hours on the cliff paths would be enough—especially for Alex. The only thing that might make us wish we'd hurried on up there would be if the weather changed for worse, instead of better. We had light lunches all around. My bowl of chowder and slice of crusty brown bread were just right.

We visited the restrooms before taking off. Outside the gift shop, as I waited for the others, I met the little boys that we'd seen earlier. They each had a sword that I hoped was a toy. The mother followed with a bag of candy, just what the little boys needed to keep their energy up! She gave me a quick apologetic smile when the boys started fencing with each other. Toys that they were, the swords seemed too real for comfort as the hard plastic blades slapped: some twenty-seven inches from hilt to point. They could put an eye out in the hands of these little boys.

From behind me came a voice: "Where are the others?"

"Mr. Sweeney!" I said.

"Didn't you come with the bunch from Shepherds?"

It sounded a little like a reprimand. He hadn't been invited. Surely he couldn't have been surprised that we didn't ask him to join us, given his aloof manner toward all of us at the B&B.

Besides, Finn's van seated only seven, including the driver. I had no reason to apologize, but I stammered my reply: "Yes, Finn is our tour guide." That made it seem more formal. And Mr. Sweeney had said he didn't care about sightseeing.

"I'm surprised to see you," I said.

"It's my last day in Thurles," he said. I took it to mean that he'd finally decided to visit one of the sights before his holiday ended. As he spoke, he was watching the little boys and their mother, who had their attention, for a change. She must have been saying something like *We're going up on the cliffs now, but you must settle down.* I was hoping she might be saying, *We're skipping the cliffs because you're too wild!* But probably not, given that there were no tantrums.

Something else distracted Mr. Sweeney, and I followed his gaze. Molly had come in the entrance. By the time she had greeted us, Alex was there, and then Helen and Doreen joined us. From the relief that washed over Doreen's face upon seeing Molly, one might have thought her daughter was a runaway who had returned home, a prodigal daughter.

"Excuse me, and I'll see you back on the cliffs. Ian couldn't pull himself away," Molly said to no one in particular. She headed, apparently, for the restroom.

Doreen said, "I should wait and go back up with Molly," and she followed her daughter, who was not slowing down at all for her. I couldn't help wondering what those two would be saying to each other on their way to the cliffs.

Mr. Sweeney kept watching the two little boys, and I thought about the statement he'd made once, that his son had played the violin. I knew from Enya's account that his son was dead. Did those little boys trigger memories of his own child? Mr. Sweeney was such an enigma.

"We should get going," Alex said.

"We need to find out what time Finn wants to leave. He told

us he'd be around the picnic tables," Helen said.

"Going up on the cliffs, Mr. Sweeney?" I said to be polite.

But he must not have heard me. He approached the little boys, and I heard him ask, "Did you buy those swords in the gift shop?"

Clouds had begun to scuttle across the sky, and the air was cooler now.

We put on our rain jackets and hiked toward the Main Viewing Platform. Alex took his time and did not get out of breath. Helen stayed with us, telling about all she'd learned from the Atlantic Edge exhibition. The fact that Alex and I had seen the same displays—and said so—did not deter her. I thought about her glum mood when we'd first started on our day trip, and I had to admit that I preferred glib to glum. This trip was a much-needed diversion for her.

The view from the platform was nothing short of magnificent. The jagged cliffs stretched out forever, it seemed—eight kilometers, we had learned. Far below, the sea crashed against the black rocks as seabirds circled above. It was the view we'd seen so many times in our brochures and in the exhibition at the Visitors Centre, but so much more dramatic in reality. I noticed that Alex took only a couple of photos. "What's wrong?" I said. "Doesn't it just make you feel like you're standing on the edge of the world?" It was a phrase I'd heard in one of the videos.

"It's spectacular," he said.

It occurred to me that there were only so many descriptive words for the sight, and all of them overused.

"You don't seem that awe-stricken," I said.

"I am." He held up his camera. "I'm saving my photos for the cliff paths."

I was about to remind him that his camera was digital, that

he could take pictures and delete at will, when Helen spoke up. "It seems quite *safe* from here. I was expecting a more *risky* experience."

"Let's head to O'Brien's Tower," Alex said. "It's more than two hundred meters tall, the highest point around. From there they say you can see the Aran Islands—though maybe not today." He looked up. The clouds did seem to be rolling in. Maybe we had waited too long.

The walk to O'Brien's Tower was not especially dangerous or strenuous. There were steps along the way. But the wind had kicked up. At the Tower, Alex was able to listen in on a tour guide's spiel. Helen and I went on up the spiral iron staircase, for another view of what seemed like the entire five miles of cliffs. Maybe not, but a stunning spectacle. I could imagine watching for sailors to come home or looking out for Viking fleets. Not from this tower, which was less than two hundred years old, but from this site. Soon Alex joined us. We could not see the Aran Islands, as the clouds were gathering, but the wild beauty of the giant, rugged cliffs was intensified with the skies darkening above them.

Back on the path, Alex said, "Shall we go to where we can see the puffins?"

Apparently the South Platform was perfect for viewing the puffin colony on Goat Island. Alex informed us that these particular seabirds arrived from the mid-Atlantic in April and returned in July, so we were extremely fortunate to be here in May. We passed the Main Viewing Platform and continued south. This section of trail became more narrow and rocky. A sign warned: *Extreme Danger, Unstable Cliff Edge.* "Oh, my!" said Helen. "I'm not sure—well, I suppose it's all right." She admitted that this was *risky* enough for her taste. I noticed her hot pink canvas shoes were more stylish than substantial.

"I think it's fine as long as we stay on the trail," I said. There were sections of low walls where the cliff edge might have been too close to the path, but not all along the way. There were treacherous parts, to be sure. At one point a boy and a girl, probably college students, lay on their stomachs right at the edge, looking down. Flashes of my own college-age twins made my blood run cold. Alex took a photo of the couple and said he was documenting what *not* to do.

A moment later, the rain began. A mist, not a downpour, and as we pulled the hoods of our rain jackets over our heads, it seemed we might wait it out—wait for the inevitable change. But the change was for the worse, with winds that whipped the cold mist into our faces. I could almost feel the temperature dropping, degree by degree. Others began to turn around, most of them younger tourists who had dressed for warmer weather, not rain.

"Should we go back?" Helen asked, trying to hold out the edge of her hood to protect against the wind. "It's beginning to seem a little unpleasant."

"I'd like to say I did it—all of it," Alex said. His face was slick with the mist, but he stared straight into the wind like a weather-beaten sea captain, and I realized that this adventure on the cliffs was more than just sightseeing to Alex. It was his personal challenge. Maybe he had worried that he wouldn't be up to it and, if not, what impact might that have on his future travels to other demanding sites?

The South Viewing Platform couldn't be far, we agreed. I didn't think we would be able to view the puffin colony in this soupy weather, but we went on. "Watch your step," I warned. "The trail may get slick." I kept telling myself that we'd be all right because we were staying back from the edge—but the increasing winds worried me. I suspected the warning at the car park had changed now, and no one else was being allowed to come up on the cliffs. The more comforting thought was that the viewing platform with all of its protections would be a safe place to wait until the winds died down, the rain stopped, and the sun came out. Surely that would happen, given Ireland's changeable weather.

"Is that Doreen?" Helen said.

Yes, it was Doreen, coming toward us at a speed I feared was dangerous, given the slick trail. She barely slowed down when she saw us, but she called out, "I'm going to find a Ranger! It's Mr. Sweeney!"

"What happened? Is he hurt?" I wouldn't even *think* of a fall over the edge.

"No!" she cried. "He's gone stone mad!"

CHAPTER 23

Mr. Sweeney's manic voice rang out above the blustery winds. "Just say it! Admit what you did to my boy!"

I blinked, wiped the rain from my eyes, and blinked again, trying to get my mind wrapped around what I was seeing. On a point that jutted out above the boiling sea, Mr. Sweeney had Ian backed up to the edge and was jabbing at him with a sword. A toy sword! Like those the little boys had at the Visitors Centre, I realized, but he used it with the skill of an expert fencer. His stance—right foot out, left arm back—and his technique marked him as someone with experience. His quick movements with his sword arm made it impossible for Ian to grab onto the hard plastic blade or move away from the ledge.

"It's not true, Mr. Sweeney, I swear to God," Ian pleaded. "I tried to be a friend to Tim."

"You perverted him!" Mr. Sweeney made another thrust. Another inch and he would have prodded Ian's midsection with the tip of the sword. I had never realized what a big man Mr. Sweeney was. But now he was not the hunched-over figure I was accustomed to seeing at Shepherds. He was in command, and he towered several inches over Ian.

"Mother of God! You're going to kill me, man! Shove me over the damn edge!" Ian said.

"Just tell the truth is all I want—admit you're a *fag*!" Mr. Sweeney spat the word. "You perverted my boy, and he couldn't live knowing what he was! Say it. Say it!"

Molly, a safe distance from the ledge, cried out, "Say whatever he wants, Ian! It doesn't matter. Do what he says!"

"No! I am not gay, and I never touched your son. He was a troubled boy, Mr. Sweeney, trying to figure out complicated things about life. He talked to me, and I wish I could've helped him. God knows I wish I could've done something."

"I saw your website. That picture of Tim reading verses, out under a tree." Mr. Sweeney's voice was full of contempt. "Oh, I found those vulgar verses he wrote."

Ian continued to deny the accusations, insisting he never knew about any such verses. The rain grew heavier. Maybe Mr. Sweeney was only trying to scare Ian into an admission, not intending to kill him, but just one false step backward, and Ian would plunge to his death.

"I didn't even know when Tim died, Mr. Sweeney. I was in the States for a month. But I'm sorrier than I can ever say about what happened. Believe me, please." Ian's equanimity was admirable. Amazing, really. Surely his heart was thrumming even faster than mine.

"Where you were means nothing. You drove him to take his own life. Same as murder." Mr. Sweeney feigned another attack, but this one lacked the energy of the others.

After we'd met Doreen rushing to find a Ranger, I'd left Alex and Helen behind, cautioning them again about the wet trail, and I had hurried on with as much speed as I dared. Now they came up behind me. I heard Helen's excited voice, and I turned, raising a halting hand. Maybe Ian was close to convincing Mr. Sweeney to back off. The man seemed to be out of touch with reality. I didn't know what the effect might be if he realized that he had several onlookers. Not just those of us from Shepherds, but a handful of strangers. All of us watching in disbelief.

"Broke his mother's heart. Broke her spirit. I lost them both." At the mention of his wife, Mr. Sweeney's voice cracked. He seemed close to tears. I prayed he was close to letting Ian go.

Ian tried to take a step forward, but Mr. Sweeney's quick thrust prevented it. Ian raised his hands in a helpless gesture. "I cannot begin to imagine your loss, sir. I would love to tell you about Tim, the way I knew him as my student. Not any other way, I swear. Please, Mr. Sweeney." Ian's voice was so rich with genuine compassion that only a certified sociopath could have lied with such sincerely.

I was close enough to see the transformation in Mr. Sweeney's face. He believed Ian.

But his sword did not waver. A tense moment passed. His face crumpled. That, maybe, was as near to crying as he would get. A sound, something like soft keening, came from his throat, and then, after a moment, he regained his composure. He took the sword in his left hand and reached under his flapping windbreaker with his right.

And there he was, gun in one hand, sword in the other. He kept the sword pointed at Ian but made a sweeping motion with the gun.

The small, dark weapon—presumably a revolver—brought a flashback that I would not let settle into my consciousness. I had lived through that, in Provence. I heard noises around me— muffled cries, *Oh no!* I thought I recognized Molly's *Please don't!* I saw some of the strangers moving farther back, as if they expected this man to open fire on all of us. I kept clinging to the belief that Mr. Sweeney did not want to kill anyone, that the steel in his hand was simply the reaction of a private investigator asserting his authority over the tense situation, the response that felt familiar. I was aware of Alex brushing my arm as he passed beside me.

"You don't want to do that, Mr. Sweeney." Alex was calm, not at all threatening, very much the professor.

Mr. Sweeney glared at Alex, no more than four feet from

him, and then his gaze darted back to Ian. "I never meant—if I'd wanted you dead, you would be!" Words that had appeared on Ian's website. Now we knew with certainty who the shooter had been. But was it too late?

"You're not a killer. You have not gone too far *yet.*" Alex placed considerable emphasis on the last word.

"Someone must pay!" Mr. Sweeney said, still managing both the gun and sword. Anguish flooded into his face as he said it again, "Someone must pay!"

"Mr. Sweeney, no one is to blame for your son's death," Alex said, his voice infinitely patient. "Please, think about what you're doing. Put down the weapons."

It was the longest moment, a space of absolute silence. The wind had died down, and what had turned back into a fine mist made no sound at all. And then came the high-pitched voice of a child. "Look! Mam, look!" Of all times for the mother and boys we'd seen at the Visitors Centre to appear on the scene.

Mr. Sweeney lowered his arm, and the tip of the sword touched the ground.

Ian might have moved away from the cliff edge, but he seemed frozen in place, like the rest of us.

Mr. Sweeney said, "I never thought it would come to this." He mumbled something I couldn't make out except the last words: "You'll see." And then he raised the revolver to his temple.

Almost simultaneously, the sounds collided. The mother called out to the little boy, "No, Tim!" Helen shrieked, and a gunshot pierced the air.

Would it have made any difference if the Ranger had arrived a minute sooner? Probably not. He had called for assistance as soon as Doreen reported the situation. The Guards and emergency medical personnel were on their way, and would we all please stay back, just remain as we were for the moment, the Ranger said. He pushed the gun aside with his foot and hurried to Mr. Sweeney. Alex, crouching on the other side of the motionless figure, pressed his handkerchief against Mr. Sweeney's head. He said in a raspy voice, "He's alive."

The Ranger felt for a pulse and nodded. His expression seemed to indicate that it was a miracle the man was alive, and perhaps it was that, a miracle. From a kit, he retrieved a thin cover for Mr. Sweeney that looked like windbreaker material, and he provided Alex with a clean cloth in place of the bloody handkerchief, but it was apparent he had no medical expertise equal to this task. He picked up the gun and secured it in a plastic bag, also from his kit.

Alex remained kneeling at Mr. Sweeney's side as the Ranger made a call on his cell phone, keeping his voice low. Those of us from Shepherds would not have considered leaving, but the other witnesses had already slipped away before the Ranger arrived, except for one elderly couple and the woman with the two little boys, one named Tim. Given the mother's distress and the children's ages, apparently, the Ranger allowed them to go back to the Visitors Centre and wait for further questioning. My heart went out to her as they left, the younger boy wailing, begging to go home.

They might have saved Mr. Sweeney's life. As that horrific moment replayed itself in my mind, I could see that Mr. Sweeney, gun at his temple, must have flinched when he heard, "No, Tim!" The movement was ever so slight. Just enough so that his aim was off, maybe just a fraction of an inch but enough so that death was not instantaneous. He might still die. He probably would still die, I told myself. How could he possibly live after sustaining a gunshot wound to the head? I felt tears sting my eyes, thinking of the grieving man, so steeped in sorrow, so obsessed with revenge—and seeing no other way out when retribution seemed it would not ease his pain.

Helen, who appeared to have a sprained ankle, sat on a large rock that looked awfully uncomfortable, with her leg stretched out. The little boy had crashed into her and her foot had slipped, turning her ankle. She pulled a silk scarf from a zippered pocket of her rain jacket. "Would you mind terribly, wrapping my ankle, Jordan?" she asked. I was glad to do something useful. The scarf was hardly as effective as an elastic bandage, but it was better than nothing.

Doreen arrived shortly behind the Ranger and began to ask questions. She'd heard the gunshot. "I prayed it was not Ian that was shot, and I prayed for Molly," she said. "Was it cruel of me not to have prayed for Mr. Sweeney, in his state of madness?"

"You could have sent up a prayer for me," Helen said with mock severity.

"You'll be all right," Doreen said. "Next time wear some sensible shoes."

Just a few steps away, Molly leaned into Ian's arms, weeping. I expected Doreen to rush to her daughter, but she didn't.

I never thought to check my watch, but things happened as quickly as we could have expected. Within minutes two EMT-type men arrived. They gave Mr. Sweeney some immediate attention, put him on a gurney, and took him away.

Alex, who had been squatting, had trouble standing up. The Ranger helped him up and found some wipes in his kit for the blood on Alex's hands. "Must have been a friend of yours," he said, and Alex nodded.

The Ranger said, "The Guards are at the Visitors Centre, so we can go down now." He glanced at Helen and asked if she could walk. I told him we'd help her, and Doreen and I did. The elderly couple hurried on, ahead of the Ranger. The rest of us proceeded at a slow pace.

A heavy quiet settled over our somber little band as we went down the cliff path.

The sun was trying to peek from the clouds by the time we came down from the Main Viewing Platform. We might have seen the puffin colony, after all, if that had been on anyone's mind. We'd met some officials with equipment going that way. Crime scene investigators, I imagined. Someone was putting up a sign, saying the trail to the South Viewing Platform was closed.

A wide-eyed Finn met us, asking what had happened. He'd seen the ambulance leave and knew a man had shot himself, but he didn't know who it was until we told him. His exclamation may have been a string of Gaelic swearwords. *"Why?* Was he *mad?"* Finn wanted to know.

No one answered. "The authorities are waiting to talk to us," I said. *Why* was not something that could be explained in a sentence, and Finn didn't press the issue. Following our group toward the Visitors Centre, he asked about Helen's foot. "Not to worry," she said. "Just an annoying sprain."

When the Ranger led us to a restricted area inside the building, Finn left us, promising he'd call Colin and Grace.

One by one, we were questioned by two Guards, one older, one younger, in a well-appointed office. I had a fleeting thought: How many Guards had I met on this trip? The mother with the little boys and the elderly couple must have spoken with the Guards while we were still making our way down from the cliff trail. We never saw them again. Ian's interview took the longest. The rest of us waited in an area that might have been a lounge for employees until we were called. The Ranger made tea for us and applied a real bandage to Helen's ankle.

My turn came after the interviews with Alex and Molly. I had come upon the scene late, I said. I tried to remember what I'd heard Mr. Sweeney say. None of my report caused a reaction from the Guards. I had simply confirmed Ian's story. There were no questions about the shootings that had occurred in Thurles and at the Hedge School. My interview was brief.

The Ranger left the room to assist Helen when it was time for her interview, and he didn't return until he came to say we could all go. Not much conversation had taken place while he was with us. Maybe everyone else felt as I did, that rehashing what we knew about Mr. Sweeney would only complicate matters and we might be detained even longer. Maybe we were all still too shocked to make sense of anything, and silence seemed more comforting than talk.

Alex and Ian both looked bedraggled. I hadn't looked closely at myself. My hair must have been a sight, first wet and then plastered under my hood, and my makeup had disappeared, with the wind blowing the rain against my face. Molly had the benefit of her fresh, youthful face, and Doreen had come through the ordeal looking exceptionally well. Ian's tousled curls gave him a boyish appearance, but the haunted look in his eyes told that he was suffering. I was worried about Alex. He looked like a man carrying a heavy weight on his shoulders as he bent over his tea and stared into his teacup, stirring aimlessly. The cup was still nearly full. The tea had to be lukewarm by now.

"Can I heat that up for you?" I said.

"No thanks," he said, laying his spoon on the saucer.

"Tea is the best medicine," Doreen said.

Alex smiled. "I'm fine."

"I don't think you're fine at all," Doreen said.

She had missed the role Alex had played in the incident, but she was perceptive enough to ask, "You're not thinking you could have done something for Mr. Sweeney, are you?"

The straightforward question made Alex blink, as if he were coming out of a daze. He said, "I wish I could have done something, yes."

"You tried, Alex. You're the only one of us who tried," I said. I told Doreen that Alex had persuaded Mr. Sweeney to put down the sword. Ian was safe because of Alex.

Ian, who was sitting at the end of the table across from Molly, said, "It's true. It was a pivotal moment there. Even though he had a gun, I knew he would not harm me."

"I don't know. I just don't know what happened." Alex rubbed his face. "Something came over him."

"You did what you could," I said, and the others agreed.

Alex must have felt that he was becoming too much the center of attention. I'd seen it happen before. He waved away our comments. "A tragedy none of us will forget," he said with a note of finality. He stood up, picked up his cup and saucer, and went to the tea kettle.

Doreen, Ian, and Molly began to talk about their return trip to Dublin by train. I made myself another cup of tea. As Alex and I stood over the tea kettle, I said, "I wonder if he'll live."

"And, if he does, will he ever be—normal?" Alex finished my thought.

"I keep going over and over it in my mind," I said. Alex gave an earnest nod. He would have more to remember, I knew. Whatever it was that the gunshot did to Mr. Sweeney's head. The blood. The expression on Mr. Sweeney's face, whatever that might have been. Alex was right there, up close and personal.

"Do you remember his last words, Alex? I've been thinking about what he said."

"He said, 'I never thought it would come to this.' "

"And then something else I couldn't quite make out, and then, 'You'll see.' "

Alex frowned, nodding, looking as if it might be close to remembering.

I kept trying to work it out. "What could he have meant by 'You'll see.' Did he mean that we'd *see* when he'd shot himself? *What* would we see? It doesn't make sense."

"None of it does," Alex said.

I repeated. " '*I never thought it would come to this.*' then . . . something, and '*You'll see.*' "

Alex gave a little chuckle with no mirth in it. "It sounded a little like *sin.*"

Somehow I believed it was important, though I didn't know why.

A few minutes later we were finished with our interviews and released to go home. Helen would ride in the passenger seat next to Finn, as it was the easiest seat to access. Alex and I waited for Ian and the Quinn ladies to load up and climb into the back seat. As I took a step toward the door of the van, I felt Alex's hand on my arm. "I kept thinking it would come to me," he said, "and it did."

"What?"

"What Mr. Sweeney said. 'I never thought it would come to this. *It's in my notepad.* You'll see.' Sounded like *Sin my note-pad.*"

I made a little *oh* sound. "He was a private investigator. *Of course* he kept a notepad.

CHAPTER 24

Our drive through Limerick, with the sun setting behind charming old buildings, made me wish we had scheduled a day trip
here. But our time in Ireland was just about up, only one day
left, and with today's tragedy so heavy on us, sightseeing was no
longer a priority—not for me and not for Alex, I was certain.
Finn had said, on the way to the Cliffs of Moher, that we'd
make a quick tour of Limerick on our return trip. He did not
mention it this evening, nor did anyone else.

But Finn did suggest stopping in the town for pizza. I hadn't
realized how hungry I was until we entered the lively little pizzeria and smelled the aromas. When we dug into our pizzas, I
noticed that the only one who didn't seem to be starved was
Alex. Ian was quick to consume two slices and most of a glass
of Guinness, and then he flattened his palms on the wooden
table, splayed his fingers, and said, "I need to get something out
in the open. About Tim Sweeney."

Expressions ranged from skeptical—Finn and Doreen—to
sympathetic—Molly and Helen. Alex simply looked ready to
listen, and I hoped Ian saw the same openness in my face. Apparently, he had something weighty to tell us, but I refused to
believe that he'd had anything to do with the death of Mr.
Sweeney's son. I just would not believe it.

"Let me say first that I had no idea who Mr. Sweeney was. I
did not recognize the name. Many boys have come through my
classes, with all the Irish names you'd expect." Ian looked at

Finn. "I know I've had several Finnegan boys." Finn nodded, appearing more receptive to what Ian was about to tell us.

"Tim Sweeney was a good student, maybe too quiet in the classroom, but he wrote fine papers. He was a bit of a loner. Not disliked or bullied or anything like that, just not social. You know, the way boys of that age form their packs and laugh and jostle around with each other. Tim didn't seem to be part of any particular group. I did notice that. I remember something now about the violin—I can see him, carrying the case from the classroom—but I swear it didn't click at all with me that morning at breakfast when Mr. Sweeney said his son played the violin." Ian turned up his beer and finished it off. He caught the eye of the girl who was delivering a pizza to another table. He raised his empty glass, and she nodded.

"What I said to Mr. Sweeney today was the truth," Ian said. "When the school term was over, a year ago, I went to Chicago and spent a month with my sister and her family. Our headmaster sent out a schoolwide e-mail about Tim's death, must have been right after I'd left Dublin, but as I was on holiday, I didn't check my school e-mail for a couple of weeks. The headmaster did not say suicide, of course, just announced that we'd lost one of our boys, sadly, and he told when the mass would be. By the time I read about it, it was all over, and I didn't know any further details about Tim's death till I got back to Dublin."

"How did the boy kill himself?" Doreen asked.

"Shot himself in the head," Ian said.

"Oh, merciful God!" Helen said. "Just like Mr. Sweeney."

"That might shed some light on what Mr. Sweeney did," I said. "Do you know where Tim got the gun?"

"What I heard was that his father had a number of firearms in the house, all properly registered. Again, I had no idea who his father was. I'd never met him."

"Mr. Sweeney had to have felt terrible guilt that the gun belonged to him," I said.

Ian's beer was delivered, and he took a thirsty drink. "There's plenty of guilt to spread around. I hate to admit that I did nothing. Nothing, unless you count contributing a few Euros to the fund at school. Books for the library, in Tim's memory. A very nice collection it was, but—I should have made contact with the family. I should have sent a note. It's too easy to just let something like that slip by, you know."

"We've all done things like that, Ian," Helen said. "It's difficult to know what to say or do when you've never met the family members." There was a mumble of agreement.

Ian's worried expression didn't alter. I didn't think he'd told us this just so we could say comforting words, as Helen had done. I thought there had to be more, and there was.

"I was aware—I don't know any other way to say it. Tim had a *crush* on me," Ian said, enunciating the word *crush* as if it had a bad taste. "It's not just girls that sometimes get fantasies in their minds about their teachers. It's happened before with boys at the school, but never to that extent."

With his forefinger, Ian made streaks in the condensation on his glass. We waited, and finally Molly asked, "What did he do, Ian? How did you know?"

"Oh, I knew. Just a number of things that give one a feeling—but there was a particular incident that made it clear. Tim wrote a story and submitted it to our literary magazine. I'm the editor. When I read his story, I knew he was writing about himself—and me. All in his imagination, you understand, but it was so—vivid. His characters so descriptive, anyone could see it. And the setting, *my classroom,* down to the poster I have of Seamus Heaney's poem, 'Digging.' That poster was right in front of us, the day I spoke with Tim."

I could imagine the scene. The look in Ian's eyes said he was seeing it, a movie playing in his mind. He gave a deep sigh. "I tried to be very careful with my words. I told him his story was well written, but it simply could not be published in our magazine, for our students and faculty. 'It would cause the wrong idea,' I said, and then he said some things about how he'd thought I would understand. I said, 'Tim, I am not gay, and even if I were, I could never have a relationship with one of our boys. That just wouldn't do. It would be wrong.' And I went on to say that his story, if people at school read it, would make things very difficult for him. He said, 'And for you.' I had to say yes. Mother of God, I'm a schoolmaster at a boys' school! It could mean my job—my entire career—if rumors had it I was being inappropriate with one of the students."

Ian took another drink, a sip this time, took a long time swallowing, and looked in the glass as if he might find an answer there. "I suppose the truth—the painful truth—is that I was more worried about myself than I was about Tim."

"How did he take what you told him?" I asked.

"He said, 'It's just fiction.' His way, I thought, of backing down, of saying, 'You don't *really* think I have those feelings for you, Mr. Haverty!' and I can tell you I was a bit relieved, then, thinking that was a way out of it. I just said, 'I understand. You have quite an imagination, Tim, and you'll be a great writer someday.' And I sent him on his way, as if nothing had happened. That was in the winter. The rest of the term, Tim just sat in the back of my class, looking distracted—looking forlorn." Ian shook his head as if it was inconceivable that he'd left it at that. "I should've known he needed someone to talk to about his sexuality. Boys have come to me before, and I've listened, and tried to help them sort things out, but it was always theoretical, not personal."

Finn drained his beer. He'd had just one, which was a good thing since he was our driver. He stood up and said, "I imagine it's a heavy load, being a schoolmaster, trying to say and do the right thing for every lad that walks through your door."

His words of wisdom brought a weak smile to Ian's face, the first I'd seen since morning. "I just wanted you to hear the whole story, because you know Mr. Sweeney," he said to us. "And because I needed to tell it."

Helen's phone rang as we made preparations to leave the pizzeria. "Looks like my husband decided to return my call at last!" she said. A minute later, her face had a glow. "You're a darling to worry," she crooned, "but *really,* everyone is taking good care of me."

I didn't deliberately listen in, but I stood near the table where she was still sitting, so I could help her to the van when she was ready. It was hard to miss Helen's end of the conversation. "Are you at Shepherds now?" A pause. "I understand. We can talk about it tonight," she said, and then, "Just put her on, dear, and I'll tell her myself." It was apparent that Grace came on the line. Helen described the injury to her ankle, making much more of it than she had earlier. "A crutch? Why, yes, it might be just the thing! You and Colin are simply *too kind!*"

I mouthed, "May I speak to Grace?"

Helen nodded. After a moment in which Grace must have been expressing her shock, Helen said, "Yes, we all do, and now Jordan is here, and she'd like a word." She handed me her phone, but not before she told me that Grace and Colin had been calling around and they'd heard that a medical helicopter had transported Mr. Sweeney from the Limerick Regional Hospital to a trauma center in Dublin.

I took the phone. Finn was standing just inside the door, arms folded, so I made it quick. "Grace, I think you should check Mr. Sweeney's things. He has a notepad. I can't say for sure that he wasn't carrying it with him today, but it might be hidden somewhere in his room. It's worth a look."

"A notepad?" Grace said.

"That's the word he used." I said I thought it would be a small notebook that he'd carry in his pocket, one of those with the spirals at the top. "He may have kept a record of his activities since he's been in Thurles. Private investigators do that. Now I have to go. Finn's waiting."

Helen grimaced as she stood. "What in heaven's name do you think Mr. Sweeney's notepad will reveal?"

I didn't know. I just had an eerie feeling that there were still gaps.

Finn let us out at the front door of Shepherds, all except Ian and Molly, who were going on with him to the pub. Doreen darted a wistful look as the van pulled away and said, "I guess he's not a bad sort, Ian Haverty. Seems he does have a conscience."

"I think you can trust him. And trust Molly," I said.

"She doesn't know much about the ways of the world. Sure, I'm mostly to blame for that." Doreen took a long breath that seemed to speak of a greater weariness than today's events had brought on. She said, "I'm going straight to bed."

Charles met Helen with open arms and held her for a long moment. "I was so worried," he said. "Let's get you to the room and look at that troublesome foot." I could imagine Helen might say it was well worth her sprained ankle to get such loving attention from her husband.

Colin and Grace met us, distress in their faces. Grace fussed a little over Helen and gave her a crutch that they had borrowed from Father Tierney. He had once broken his foot, falling from a ladder, and he'd kept the crutch at the church ever since, lending it to anyone who needed it. "The Father was very excited to see me on the church grounds," Colin said. "He seemed to believe I might eventually make it to the confessional." Assuming a more serious tone, he said, "I told him if Bridget got well and came home, he just might see me at mass, if not the confessional."

Alex's steps were heavy on the stairs. "Goodnight, all," he said.

We bid him goodnight. Grace waited until he'd disappeared on the second floor to ask, "Is Alex all right?"

"Exhausted, I expect. He's taking all of this especially hard."

Grace motioned for me to follow her, and we went to the keeping room. There was a glitter in her eyes that answered my question before I asked: "Did you find the notepad?"

"It was between the mattress and springs. A little spiral notepad. Pocket-size, like you said." She went to the bookcase and pulled out a manila folder from between two books. "This probably seems very cloak-and-dagger, but I got to wondering if the Guards might come to Mr. Sweeney's room to investigate. Do you think?"

"There's no reason for the Guards to know about the notepad, but you may be right," I said. "Even in a clear case of attempted suicide, I suppose they'll conduct some kind of investigation."

We sat on the loveseat, and Grace opened up the folder on the low table in front of us. It contained several letter-size pages. "Just in case, I made copies and put the notepad back where I found it. Finished only a few minutes ago, so I haven't had a chance to do much but browse. I know that Mr. Sweeney followed Ian to Shepherds. He mentions Ian's website. There's something about Mr. Sweeney's son—and Ian, I think." She gave me an inquisitive look.

"Ian explained to us," I said. "Tim Sweeney had imagined something between himself and Ian. Mr. Sweeney blamed Ian for his son's death. That's what it was all about, out there on the ledge today."

"It sounds—complicated," Grace said. I agreed. A good word for it—complicated.

She said, "I do want to hear all about it, but let's see what's in these pages. Seems like something that calls for a pot of tea."

Grace went to the kitchen to make tea for us, and I began to read. Each letter-size page contained one of the small pages from the notepad that flipped from the top. Part record of activities and part diary, the entries had started a month earlier when Mr. Sweeney had written: *Went through Tim's things at last. Found writings that I had to destroy. A vulgar story about his literature teacher and verses must be about the same man. Now I understand. Better that his mother died not knowing this about her boy. On her grave, I swear I will make the perverted schoolmaster pay.*

CHAPTER 25

Colin opened the door of the keeping room and stuck his head in. "Any discoveries?"

"We just got started," Grace said. "Come on in."

"Patrick's home," he said, opening the door wide for his son.

Colin joined us for tea. Patrick declined the tea but sat down with us and ate a biscuit. The younger men and women of Ireland did not seem quite the tea-drinkers that their parents were. We put the copies of Mr. Sweeney's notepad aside for a time. Patrick had spent the afternoon getting Bridget settled at the rehab center. He was anxious to report, and his parents were anxious to hear. "Bridget's remembering things, a little at a time," he said. "She's saying the night she went to Dr. Malone's, he had a call from someone, and he was very angry."

"She told me that when I visited her—was it just yesterday? Hard to believe," Grace said. "She remembered that *she* was very angry but didn't remember why."

I didn't add to the conversation. Bridget had told me in confidence why she was furious, that she wanted money from Dr. Malone, Jimmie's father, to take the baby and go away. She'd mentioned that Dr. Malone had been angry with the caller. I waited to see if Patrick knew any more about who the caller might have been or what the doctor had said.

"She says Dr. Malone was shouting, 'No! No more!' and telling whoever it was that he would not be there—he was leaving that very moment, like someone was wanting to come to the of-

fice. Bridget says she's almost certain the doctor said he was going out to Red Stag Crossing and he may have even said her
name."

Colin slapped the table with his palm, making the teacups
and items on the tray rattle.

"Colin! What is it?" Grace said.

"Don't you see? Somebody wanted drugs. Dr. Malone was
providing drugs for Bridget, wasn't he? That's surely the way it
looks, with all those drugs she had in her. So maybe he was
more of a drug dealer than a healer. Sounds like he was trying
to cut somebody off who wanted more. Someone who might
have come back the next morning to try again, and had to commit murder to get what he wanted. Wouldn't that person—the
one on the phone—be a good suspect? Bridget would be in the
clear for sure."

The kind of person he was describing didn't sound like the
kind of murderer who would be logical enough to take the body
out to Red Stag Crossing. Wouldn't he just murder, snatch the
drugs, and flee? Maybe if it was someone who knew about
Bridget, I considered—the only name that came to mind was
Davin Callahan, and I just couldn't see that young man as a
drug addict.

"You have to understand, Dad, that Bridget's memory is
fuzzy," Patrick said. "She has no real concrete details to offer,
just impressions. And even though *we* may believe her—I do, for
a fact—the Guard would have to take her compromised condi-
tion into account. It might sound as if she's making it all up."

"Patrick's right," Grace said. "Also, I think the word would
have gotten around if drugs had been stolen from Dr. Malone's
office. The theory of the drug user has problems."

A moment passed as everyone mulled this over. The only
sounds were the clink of teacups and spoons, and a loud-ticking
clock on the bookshelf.

"The way Bridget's memory is coming back is promising," I said. "She may eventually remember something that *is* concrete—something the Guard can use."

"The good news is that she's doing so much better," Grace said.

"Much-needed good news," Colin said. "After today—much needed."

As if the thought had just occurred to her, Grace said to Patrick, "You heard about Mr. Sweeney at the Cliffs of Moher, didn't you?"

"Dad just told me when I got home. Unbelievable! I suppose I should call Enya." Patrick rubbed his temple, making slow circles, as if the very thought was stressful. Probably the thought of having to be the bearer of such horrible news, I told myself, rather than the thought of having to make any call to his wife. I couldn't help remembering how Enya had flared when I'd started asking questions about Mr. Sweeney.

"Something else I found out when I spoke with Enya's mother about Mr. Sweeney this morning," Patrick said. "I was curious what she might remember about the man. Enya had said they lived on the same street with the Sweeneys until five years ago. She was sixteen when they left."

So Enya was twenty-one now, just a little older than Bridget, several years younger than Patrick. Her age did explain some things about—the phrase that came to mind was *her worldview.*

"Ian Haverty taught Mr. Sweeney's son in ninth grade—a year ago," I calculated out loud, "so five years ago, that would have made him about eleven."

Patrick nodded. "Enya's mam said the same. She thought Tim Sweeney was eleven when they moved away and had no more contact with the Sweeney family. She said Mr. Sweeney was an excellent marksman, and he used to take Tim out to the shooting range with him. He was teaching him to shoot at that young age."

"People do that," Colin said. "Hunters, especially. Boys learn to use hunting rifles early."

"I, for one, am glad you didn't try to teach me to shoot when I was eleven," Patrick said.

"Or any age," Grace said.

Colin looked at me and explained, "I've never had the time to devote to hunting, which makes me a bit of an oddity here in Thurles, but that's fine."

"And it's fine with me that you never introduced me to guns," Patrick said.

"Imagine how it must have affected Mr. Sweeney, when his son shot himself," I said.

"It affected him terribly, according to Enya's mother," Patrick said. "She never heard anything about it when it happened— about a year ago, I think it was—but a neighbor she'd known on the Sweeneys' street called her when Mrs. Sweeney died and filled her in on everything the family had gone through. The boy's suicide, Mrs. Sweeney's kidney disease that she'd battled for a long time, apparently, and one more thing that fits into the equation. Mr. Sweeney spent several weeks in a psychiatric hospital after his son killed himself."

For a minute, all of us seemed to hold a collective breath, taking it all in. This last piece of information *did* fit into the equation. Losing a child was the most horrible thing imaginable, under any circumstances. This case was compounded by suicide as the manner of death and again by the weapon that the boy's father owned and had taught him to use. It was heartbreaking, too, to think of the dying woman, mourning her son's death, and so alone during the time her husband was in the psychiatric hospital, even if friends or relatives had assisted her. Mr. Sweeney returned to their sad life and witnessed his wife's slow decline and, finally, her death. And then he had nothing left but the fire in his belly that insisted, *Someone must pay.*

Colin whispered, "Mother of God," and then he said, "I need to finish some things in the office. Let me know if you find anything else." He nodded at the pages. Probably it was true that he needed to work. It was also a way of wrenching himself from this depressing conversation.

A minute later Patrick stood up to leave as well. Grace asked him about Enya, and he gave a shrug.

"She has to decide what she wants," he said, his eyes turning hard as steel.

"And what do you want, Patrick?"

"I'd like to see her come back, of course," he said, "but not if she's bloody miserable—here—with me."

Grace got up and went to her son. At about five foot two, she did not quite come up to his chin. She reached for his large hands and took them in her own small ones. "Here's a thought, Patrick. Colin and I talked about it at length today. Bridget will get well and come home. I know it will happen. If Enya will come back—after a little time with her parents, sorting things out for herself—the two of you should look for some other place to live in Thurles. You could still help out at Shepherds with the computer work, if your work at the institute allows it, but Little Jimmie will have his mother. Enya won't be bound to us the way she's been." Grace let go of her son's hands. "Think about it, and talk to her. I believe you and Enya could make a go of it if you just didn't live here at Shepherds."

Patrick gave his mother a quick hug. "I'll think about it, and I'll talk to her," he said, and he hurried out.

"Now, let's get back to our work," Grace said.

Knowing that Mr. Sweeney had been in psychiatric care at least once shed a certain light on what we read. Though much of the notepad was simply dates, times, and phrases like *Booked 2 wks at Shepherds B&B, Thurles,* there were passages that read like a therapy journal. From those entries, in particular, it was easy to construe that after his wife's death, Mr. Sweeney had become obsessed with the man he believed had engaged his son in homosexual behavior. He had gone to Ian's website and found photos, so he knew that Ian was an attractive schoolmaster. He mentioned the photo of Ian with several boys, sitting under a tree in what might have been a study group—the photo I had seen. Mr. Sweeney wrote: *Tim, reading one of those damnable verses? His own? Or some other that corrupted his mind? Does I.H. lust after other boys or just Tim?*

From the website, not only had Mr. Sweeney learned that Ian was going to Shepherds on holiday, but he'd read the two stories Ian had posted from his manuscript. In another entry, Mr. Sweeney had referred to the story where the owl came into play: *Man guilty of murder but acquitted. Goes mad with guilt. Three times owl reminds him of his crime. Third time he takes his own life. Interesting that I.H. put up this story. Makes me think I.H. should be reminded of his own guilt. Maybe he would take the out that Tim did.*

Each page that I read, I passed on to Grace. The clock's ticking seemed to grow louder, as I read on, feeling Mr. Sweeney's increasing obsession. After he'd come to Thurles, his entries were often brief: *5-10 12:05 a.m. I.H. walked home from pub, two nights now. Making my plan.* And *5-11 12:40 a.m. Scared him good with hooting owl.*

I took out my phone and accessed the calendar so I could follow the dates. The night Alex and I had arrived in Thurles, we'd gone to the pub and met Ian for the first time. Ian and the Quinn ladies had walked home. About that night, Mr. Sweeney had written: *He knows. He is scared. Women paid no attention to owl, but I.H. did. Don't think he saw me but must find better cover.*

Time to up the ante. Knowing what he had in mind made a chill seep into my bones, but it would be two more nights before he shot Ian. I read the entry written at 10:10 a.m. the next morning. Mr. Sweeney had gone out early to find another site where he could hide and frighten Ian again. The site he described was the turnoff to Red Stag Crossing.

"Grace! We may have something," I said.

She and I began to read together about the morning Dr. Malone was killed.

We brought Colin in, to get his perspective on what we had read. "Is it enough to take to the Guard?" Grace asked. "Even though he didn't *name* anyone."

"The vehicle he described must have been the one the killer used to dispose of the body," I said. Mr. Sweeney had also noted that it was too dark to get the number on the license plate.

"Black late-model SUV. That could be something," Grace said, "even though there may be dozens of black SUVs in Thurles."

"Wasn't Norah Riordan—Malone—driving a black SUV when we saw her, the day we went to the tea house, and she came out of the doctor's office?" I said.

"I think that was Dr. Malone's car," Grace said. Colin agreed that was what the doctor had driven.

"Maybe the murderer used Dr. Malone's SUV to transport the body," I suggested. "That way, if the police examined the tire tracks, they'd only find a connection back to Dr. Malone, not the killer." Colin and Grace both gave me a look that reminded me of what Ian had said, that I watched too many crime shows. It was just a thought, though. As Grace had said, there were probably many black SUVs in Thurles.

"This should be enough to light a fire, get something going

with the investigation." Colin pulled out his phone. "I'll call the Garda station."

"But it's after ten o'clock!" Grace said.

"The station won't be closed. And considering that progress solving the murder has been next to naught, trust me, if anyone's on duty that's worth his wages, he'll want the note-pad." Colin paused before he made the call. "The *notepad*. We'll not say anything about these copies you made. You can say you went into Mr. Sweeney's room to collect his things and clean up, knowing he's not coming back here."

As Colin punched in numbers, Grace said, "Maybe this will make it perfectly clear, once and for all, that Bridget had nothing to do with Dr. Malone's death."

I didn't believe Bridget was in any danger of being accused, but I understood that Grace would continue to worry about her daughter until all the threads were tied up. I thought of the secret Bridget had shared with me about Dr. Malone. One more loose thread.

Colin was pleased that he'd reached Garda Mallory at the station. "Might've been anyone on duty, so this is good luck. Mallory seems like a reasonable sort. He was, anyway, when he dealt with Bridget," Colin said. It took longer than he'd expected for Garda Mallory to arrive, and when he did, he was not alone. Inspector Perone, spiffy in his dress clothes, did not look happy when Colin brought the two men into the keeping room. Colin did not look happy, nor did Garda Mallory, whose expression wavered between sheepish and just plain annoyed.

It was apparent what had happened. Mallory had called his superior, who was not on duty but rather at a fancy function of some kind. Someone, maybe his Sergeant, had demanded that he do so. Perone had been having a good time—from the smell of alcohol and cigars, and a whiff of a nice scent that must have been aftershave or cologne applied at the onset of the evening. Whatever activity was interrupted, he wasn't about to let his underling bring in important evidence in an important homicide—the murder of an important citizen in Thurles, the son-in-law of an even more important citizen in the town.

Colin reminded the men that they'd met me, "our friend from the States," on their previous visit to Shepherds—"that morning you were here about Bridget," he just couldn't resist saying. Grace welcomed them before she went to the kitchen to bring in the tea she had already prepared. She had put away the copies we had finished reading, tucked them in a drawer. I was surprised that the Inspector didn't demand to go to Mr. Sweeney's room right away, but—there was the tea, of course.

"Now what's this evidence you called about?" Perone sat in the comfy chair Colin offered but made no effort to get comfortable. He perched on the edge in what seemed an awkward position, his back straight, hands on his knees, his neck stiff, chin jutted out.

"I know you'll be glad to solve the case on the shooting that injured Ian Haverty—a guest here at Shepherds—and the shooting out at the Curreeny Hedge School," Colin began. "Seamus Sweeney, also a guest here, the man who shot himself today at the Cliffs of Moher, confesses to being the shooter in the notepad we found."

What a shrewd tactic, to begin on this note, a case solved. Perone's posture did not change, but the muscles in his face relaxed a little. "Go on," he said.

"As for Dr. Malone's murder, you'll decide if anything is useful, but Mr. Sweeney was at Red Stag Crossing at 5:15 that morning, so you'll be interested in his account," Colin said.

"Now what was this Sweeney fellow doing out there at 5:15 a.m.?" Perone asked with a trace of skepticism. Had he concluded already that the contents of the notepad were probably not trustworthy? Colin gave a brief answer and promised the notepad would explain everything.

Grace set down the tray. Tea all around. Cream, sugar, spoons clinking on china, the ritual. The air felt a little less tense as we all sipped our tea.

"And how did you come to have this notepad?" Perone asked.

"I found it when I cleaned Mr. Sweeney's room," Grace said, "after we heard about—the tragic thing that happened at the Cliffs. I packed up his belongings—poor man, he didn't have much—and changed the bed, and I found the notepad." Grace was all innocence, a fine act, but I knew the underlying sadness about Mr. Sweeney was sincere.

"Where is it now?" Perone asked.

"I put it back where I found it, under the mattress."

"But you read it?"

"Yes."

"Would have been best if you'd left it where it was, for us to examine."

Colin chimed in. "If you'll pardon, Inspector, my wife wouldn't have known it was anything for the Guard to see if she hadn't read it. Could've been anything. A record of the man's expenses. Could've been something pornographic."

Inspector Perone took a long swallow of tea, and another. And then he finished it off, set his cup on the table, and forced a quick smile.

"I'll need to see the notepad now," he said.

"I'll take you to Mr. Sweeney's room," Colin said.

CHAPTER 26

After Inspector Perone and Garda Mallory had left, Grace and I got out the pages again and pored over Mr. Sweeney's small, tight script. Colin went back to work in his office. The door to the keeping room was open, and we saw Alex come to the kitchen. He acknowledged us, and a minute later he came to the door. Dressed in blue pajamas, he was holding a glass of milk—warm milk, I assumed. "I heard a commotion," he said. "Did someone from the Guard go up to Mr. Sweeney's room?"

"Colin called them," Grace said. "They took Mr. Sweeney's notepad."

I indicated the photo copies on the low table before us. "Grace had the foresight to make a copy of the notepad. I'll fill you in tomorrow." If Alex was having trouble sleeping, he didn't need to get into Mr. Sweeney's notes tonight. I wondered if I'd ever sleep, after delving into the writing that revealed Mr. Sweeney's troubled mind.

Alex accepted my promise and went on to bed. Grace and I kept reading and discussing the significance of certain passages. After Mr. Sweeney heard that Dr. Malone's body had been found at Red Stag Crossing, he knew he'd probably seen the murderer in the black SUV that morning. He wrote: *Might recognize man's face if I saw it again, but can't tell authorities I was there without explaining why. Mission not accomplished yet and I won't jeopardize mission.*

He'd made an entry at 11:50 p.m., the night after he'd shot

Ian, his handwriting more shaky: *Can't get over how my aim failed me. Didn't mean to harm but maybe the clipped wing is not bad. He might be ready if I put pressure.*

"*Put pressure* means he would send the message to Ian's website. 'If you were meant to be dead, you would be,' " I said.

Grace reminded me that Ian had told her and Colin all about it after the shooting at the Hedge School.

"The message accomplished part of what Mr. Sweeney intended. Not only did Ian know for sure that he was the target, but he began to think about the owl in his story and the guilty man. He just didn't go as far with it as Mr. Sweeney thought he would. He didn't connect any of it with Tim Sweeney."

Grace said, "That's what he means by *might be ready*—Ian might be ready to confess that he was involved with Tim Sweeney. Sexually. Perverting him, in Mr. Sweeney's words."

"That's what he wanted all along, an admission of guilt from Ian," I said.

I turned to the last page, the final entry written Friday at 3:17 p.m. after he'd given Alex a ride back to Shepherds from the Cathedral of the Assumption. *Pleasant enough,* he'd said about Alex, *but talks too much.* He wrote about lighting candles for his wife and son and said, *I prayed for forgiveness. Don't think I'll get it, but heaven or hell, I'll be finished.*

"He didn't go the Cliffs of Moher to kill Ian," I said. "He just wanted to hear a confession from Ian before he killed himself." The truth was in the notepad, as Mr. Sweeney had promised: Suicide was the plan all along.

Sunday morning breakfast was a bittersweet time. The guests, except Alex and me, were leaving Shepherds on Sunday, and Mr. Sweeney's absence hung over us with a heaviness of its own.

Helen remarked to Grace, "I thought you'd be at early mass.

I'm sure Mr. Sweeney can use your prayers." Grace said she'd go to the eleven o'clock mass, and she would, indeed, offer prayers for Mr. Sweeney.

"I just didn't think I could possibly leave Colin and Patrick to manage breakfast on their own," she said.

"Right you are! It would have been a disaster!" Colin said, delivering hot soda bread to the buffet.

They didn't mention Enya's absence, and no one asked where she was. Surely they wondered, given that Patrick had returned home.

All the guests made sure we had each other's e-mail addresses. Charles and Helen were already packed, planning to leave right after breakfast. "We will miss all of you *terribly*! Won't we, Charles?" Helen said, and he nodded. I think he was sincere.

"But, Grace and Colin, we may very well see you in just another month!" she added.

Some friends had invited Helen and Charles to stay with them during the Irish Open in County Cork in June. "They have managed to get a *wonderful* house," Helen said.

Charles assisted Helen as she got up from the table. "Always good to see the old chaps from golfing circles," he said. He was not as upbeat as his wife, but he was trying.

"Good to have *contacts*," Helen said, patting his arm. She put her hand on my shoulder and squeezed as she passed. "We'll be fine."

"I have no doubt," I said.

She leaned closer. "I did tell Grace about that—the thing with Lucas Riordan. She was not a bit surprised about the *monstrous* development he's planning."

Charles said, "No more about that, Helen. It's over and done."

"You don't think he'll get the financing he needs?" she asked.

"I have no interest in whether he does or not. For us, it's all over with Lucas." Charles shook the hair out of his eyes.

And then he turned toward those of us still seated in the breakfast room and raised his hand like a departing warrior, bidding us a formal goodbye.

"Goodbye, goodbye, dear friends!" Helen sang out.

Smiles all around at their dramatic exit.

"They did add a flair to our holiday, didn't they now?" Doreen said.

Ian, Molly, and Doreen were making plans to take the train to Dublin. I offered to give them a lift to the train station. Ian said, "If it's not too much trouble, Jordan, it would be a great favor. Colin said he would take us, but the O'Tooles have gone above and beyond in so many ways. I'd rather not ask for one more thing."

"No trouble at all—and you're right about Colin and Grace," I said. "What time?"

They wanted to make the 11:15 train.

Alex shocked me by saying he was going to mass with Grace. "Something I can probably use in my book," he said. Not likely, I thought, but I supposed it was possible.

"I'm about to take this little scamp on a stroll," Colin said, pinching Jimmie's cheek. "We don't get him out in the fresh air enough." The weather was gorgeous, bright sun in a cloudless sky, warm, with low humidity. Perfect day for a stroll. Perfect last day in Thurles.

As Ian and the Quinn ladies loaded their luggage into my car, Colin loaded Little Jimmie into the stroller. Alex and Grace were already outside, dressed for mass. Alex had a sudden splendid idea, that we should meet in town for lunch. "I've wanted to treat you to a meal but you never could get away,"

Alex said to Colin and Grace. "So many obligations at Shepherds."

"Which we still have," Grace said. "There's a lot to do to get ready for new guests this next week. One young couple will be checking in tonight."

"Ah, we can take a little while off for lunch now, don't you think?" Colin said. "The last chance we'll get to spend time with Alex and Jordan."

"Would Patrick join us?" Alex said.

"He might," Grace said, "but we'd have to lock up the B&B! I don't think we've ever done that."

We decided to meet at the Hayes Hotel for their Sunday buffet, which was reported to be extraordinary. Colin said he'd call ahead to be sure we'd have a good table.

"I wish we could go with you!" Doreen said, and I wished it, too. Thinking about the departure of all of our new friends touched me in a way I wouldn't have anticipated.

As it turned out, Patrick wanted to stay at Shepherds. He told Colin it would be a perfect time for him to call Enya and have a long Facetime chat, without any interruptions.

"Facetime, like Skype, but it's an iPhone feature," I clarified for Alex.

He sighed and said, "The wonders of technology."

Ian, the Quinns, and I arrived early at the train station. I parked and said I'd wait and see them off. I didn't need to be at the Hayes Hotel until 12:15. Doreen pressed some bills into Molly's hand, and Molly and Ian went off to purchase tickets.

"They do make a nice couple, I s'pose," Doreen said. Since our trip to the Cliffs of Moher, she'd made a 180-degree turn, and now I wondered if she wasn't going to be a little *too* eager to push a romance between Molly and Ian.

I reminded her that Molly might have other young men in

her life after Ian. "But, yes, they do make a lovely couple," I said.

She gave a dismissive wave. "I'm just hoping this will last long enough for Molly to accept a position in Dublin instead of going off to Sligo. It came to my mind that Ian Haverty would be the best thing in the world to keep her in Dublin. Don't think she'll be wanting to leave him for Sligo, even if she'd leave her mam."

"You're devious, Doreen," I said.

"Just being a mother, looking out for my daughter."

All mothers did not try to orchestrate their adult daughters' lives, but I didn't say so.

Molly and Ian returned with the tickets. Molly was beaming. Ian's smile was a little more guarded, and every now and then, a shadowy look came into his dark eyes. The memory of yesterday's tragedy and the weight of it, I imagined, and maybe of Tim Sweeney.

Even so, in other moments, when he looked into Molly's eyes, I could believe he'd found something in this pretty violinist that would get him through whatever he had to work out in his own mind. Those two might be a force Doreen was underestimating.

The train to Dublin arrived. We said our goodbyes. I promised Ian I would keep up with him—and his book—on his website.

"I can't help but wonder if the farmer that hid the priest from Cromwell's men could have lived in that same cottage in Red Stag Crossing—Magdala's cottage," he said. A light came into his eyes, shining as when I'd first met him, when he'd first told the story. "The priest hole, the gold cup the priest used for the Eucharist—what do you think, Jordan?"

"I'd like to believe it," I said.

"Ah, so would I," he said.

I waited on the platform and waved as the train began to pull away. I watched until it was out of sight.

How sentimental I felt this morning! That squeezing in my chest, like a fist. All the goodbyes.

Back in my car, I had a whim. I checked my phone and found Paul's number. I couldn't just "Reply" to the international call, but I noted all the numbers and punched them in again. I got his voice mail. I *assumed* it was his voice mail, though it was an automated message—in French, naturally. I said it was wonderful to see him on Friday. It's easier to leave a message when you've heard the voice of the person you're calling. I felt awkward, a little foolish, really. Wrapping it up, I said, "I hope you'll call soon. *Au revoir, Paul.*" Now I could add *wistfulness* to those nostalgic feelings constricting my chest.

The buffet at the Hayes Hotel provided a delicious variety—potatoes, of course, but scalloped this time—and the service at our table was exceptional. Everyone seemed to know the O'Tooles. We finished with a pot of tea. We lingered, refilled our teacups, and lingered some more, until Little Jimmie began to whine and reach for Grace, then for Colin—someone to get him out of his high chair. From the high chair to the stroller—the little guy was more compliant than anyone had a right to expect of a toddler who must have just wanted to run around.

"He'll be asleep in no time," Colin said, pushing the stroller out onto the sidewalk.

Grace and Alex were going to ride back with me. We all headed in the direction of the car. When Colin's phone rang, he answered, and then with a big smile said, "Bridget!"

Grace took over the stroller, and we all kept walking until Colin said, "Wait a minute. Let me put you on the speaker so your mother can hear."

Bridget's voice was stronger than I recalled. "It's come back to me, what Dr. Malone said on the phone that night before he was murdered. I remember something like 'He's a good man and he's been nothing but decent to me and I can't believe what I've done!' " He kept saying, 'No more! No more!' and then, 'She doesn't know but what have I to lose? You must stop it now, before it's too late! Get rid of everything!' He was very angry, pacing back and forth." Bridget said it all in a rush, as if she might forget it if she waited, and then she paused. "I think it may be important."

Grace said, "We'll take it from here, love. You're right—it sounds important, but you mustn't worry about it anymore." Bridget said she would call again tomorrow. As Grace and Colin told her goodbye, I noticed that Little Jimmie's eyelids were heavy—nearly closed. He hadn't reacted at all when he'd heard his mother's voice. The very thought tugged at my heart. I only hoped that Bridget would be home soon, ready and able to be Little Jimmie's mother.

Colin put away his phone and took charge of the stroller. As we walked on, a pensive expression etched into his face, the furrows of deep thought in his brow.

"What is it, Colin?" Grace said.

"It's what Bridget said."

"*Get rid of everything.* It does sound like drugs, doesn't it?" Grace said.

"It's *who made that call* that I'm thinking about," Colin said. " '*He's been a good man,*' Dr. Malone said to whoever it was on the phone. '*I can't believe what I've done.*' Maybe he doped up somebody so he couldn't work. So who's he telling that they must stop it?"

My mind had been running along the same track.

"It's not just that I despise the man," Colin said.

Grace's breath caught. "Do you mean—you do!"

"I feel it in my bones. I don't know that he committed

murder, just that he and the doctor were into something bad, in it together." His scowl deepened. "But I know it will take much more to convince that arrogant prick Perone that he should question Lucas Riordan."

CHAPTER 27

Patrick was coming from the kitchen carrying a plate with a sandwich on it and a tall glass of beer when we arrived at Shepherds.

"How did it go with Enya?" Grace asked.

"Time will tell," he said. So much like his father. He headed into the office. Work ethic like his father, too. And his mother. Grace set about her housekeeping chores immediately. Colin came in some time later and put Little Jimmie to bed, and next thing I knew he was trimming the shrubs at the front entrance.

I used the computer in Reception to check on our hotel reservations in Dublin for Monday night, and something possessed me to pull up the Cliffs of Moher website. I was able to find on a map of the cliff paths the point that jutted out, where Ian was forced backward before Mr. Sweeney put a gun to his own head. I wondered if Mr. Sweeney was still alive. The incredible photographs, the wild beauty of the Cliffs of Moher, brought everything back, all too vividly. I closed out the site and went to my room to start packing.

Alex was taking a nap. By the time he knocked on my door, about an hour later, I had made significant progress packing, my mind geared now toward going home.

"We have a little time left," he said, "and there's one more thing I'd like to do."

★　★　★　★　★

"It's quite a walk from here, and the trail is rough," I said when we got out of the car.

"I feel confident that I'm up to it," Alex said. We started on the rocky footpath. Just one week ago I had accompanied Grace through these woodlands to Magdala's cottage. The sunlight danced on the delicate leaves of the alder trees, as it had then. I told Alex the legends of the alders that Grace had told me and explained how the purplish clusters on the alder trees gave the purple tinge to the air.

"A rather magical place, isn't it?" he said. My sentiments exactly. Alex had no trouble keeping up as we made our way along the path. The trail seemed smoother, easier to negotiate than it was the first time I made this trek. Maybe because of the ATVs that had been on it since last Sunday—Davin Callahan's ATV that we used to rescue Bridget and Little Jimmie, and the ATVs that the Guards had used when searching for Magdala.

"Wonder what will happen to Magdala," I said.

"Father Tierney and I talked about that when I had lunch with him," Alex said. "He's already been in touch with the Catholic social services about getting Magdala into a home for the elderly and infirm that the church runs."

I thought—not kindly—that the church might have taken more interest in Magdala when she was simply an old woman living in the woods, before anyone knew of the gold chalice.

"What about her property? The land her cottage is on must be worth a lot," I said.

"We didn't talk about that, but I would imagine it will have to be sold. The proceeds will surely be more than enough to take care of her for the rest of her years."

"Didn't you say the church was going to take care of her? I thought you meant *charity*."

Alex gave a mock scowl. "I didn't realize you were so skeptical of the church, Jordan."

"Says my uncle who went to mass today for the first time in *years*," I said. "I meant to ask: Should I attach some significance to your church attendance this morning?"

"If you mean, am I going to become a more faithful Catholic, probably not. It just felt right today," he said.

I did understand. I wouldn't argue about Father Tierney's motives, where Magdala was concerned. Alex liked him, and probably the priest was sincere. Not my place to judge.

Alex's train of thought apparently led him to Mr. Sweeney. "You said he had a notepad, and the Guards took it." I told Alex all about Mr. Sweeney's ramblings. He had little to say. And then some little creature scurried across our way, into the brush, making Alex jump.

We laughed. I said, "I'm glad you wanted to come out here. Nice way to end our trip."

"It would be such a disappointment to leave Thurles without seeing the place I've heard so much about," he said.

I remarked that he seemed to have more energy these last few days, and he said, "I think you were right about all that medicine, Jordan. I stopped taking it except the pills for blood pressure and high cholesterol, and what do you bet Reuben will take those away when I see him." He gave an exasperated sigh. "I should have trusted my own instincts instead of listening to that young—very *green*—physician."

"It wasn't as bad for you as it was for Bridget, trusting *her* doctor," I said.

Bridget's most recent phone call became the topic of our conversation. "If Colin is right and the caller was the Riordan man," Alex said, "it certainly sounds like the doctor was into drug dealing. *Get rid of everything*—some kind of contraband, no doubt."

"Dr. Malone orchestrated Bridget's dependency on prescription drugs. Sounds like he was doing the same with someone else," I said. "Maybe his own father-in-law." I'd been thinking about Liam Riordan, who had some vague illness—too sick to go to his work at the bank—but he was able to attend the doctor's funeral and had intimated to Colin that he was much improved. Was that because Dr. Malone, who had managed his prescriptions, was dead? Had Liam Riordan realized the medications he was taking were more harmful than helpful?

Alex and I speculated on why Dr. Malone and Lucas would conspire against Liam Riordan. "Lucas may not have wanted his father to *die,* but he wanted him out of the picture," I said. "Liam was a force to be reckoned with. Lucas had this idea for a big resort development and maybe Liam was against it—or maybe he just wouldn't allow some of the methods his son was using to obtain property." *Heavy-handed* was the word Grace had used for Lucas's tactics.

Alex lamented, "But a doctor—it's hard to imagine that a physician, one who has taken an oath to heal, to 'do no harm,' would deliberately prescribe a dangerous mix of drugs for his patients."

I thought—but didn't say—that Dr. Malone felt he was backed into a corner with Bridget, because she wanted him to be a father to Little Jimmie. I said, "Maybe he was backed into a corner with Liam. I wonder if Lucas threatened him somehow. If he didn't go along with drugging Liam, maybe—I don't know." And then it came to me and seemed so simple. Lucas could have known about Jimmie, and that was what he held over the doctor's head. But I couldn't say it because I had promised Bridget I wouldn't tell *anyone* who Jimmie's father was. I said, "It might have been an accident—a fight. Simple as that. Lucas has a temper. Maybe he just lost it and then had to cover up somehow, so he brought the body out here, hoping to implicate Bridget. She'd gone to see him, and the doctor told

Norah—on the phone—that Bridget was hysterical."

"Or Dr. Malone could have turned the tables on Lucas and said he was going to confess what they'd been doing to the elder Riordan," Alex said, "and Lucas wouldn't have it."

We agreed it was too bad we had to leave Thurles before any of our theories were proven or disproven. Nothing would be resolved for a while. There was that little thing called evidence.

Then all at once, as if we had turned a page in a storybook, we came upon the cottage.

"There it is," I said, and I realized in the same breath that someone was at the woodpile. I touched Alex's arm, and we stopped walking.

The man had heard us. Something about his stance made me think he might run. Instead, he called out in a harsh voice, "Who are you?"

I whispered to Alex, "It's Lucas Riordan."

"Who are you?" he called again, and he came toward us, taking long strides. In a swift movement, he put something in the pocket of his jacket. Something he may have taken from the woodpile. I'd seen a flash from whatever was in his hand in that instant when he turned toward us.

"Tourists." Quick thinking, on Alex's part. He kept walking, showing no alarm, and I followed, hoping we could keep up the ruse. I didn't know exactly what Riordan was doing out here, but he had to be up to no good. Alex and I had just come to a conclusion that Lucas Riordan was a murderer.

"Mind if we take some photographs of this cottage? Do you know how old it is? What an amazing find!" Alex said as we met Lucas Riordan near the alder tree where Magdala had smoked a cigarette. We stood just a few feet from each other.

Maybe Alex had overdone it just a bit. Riordan was scrutinizing us, his dark brows pulled together. "Private property," he said, and then, as if ordering a dog, "Go on now. Be off with you!"

"Let's go," I said. We had a way out and we should take it.

"Just one photo?" Alex said. Maybe it wasn't all pretense with Alex. He seemed mesmerized by the cottage. Didn't he realize the danger that Lucas Riordan posed?

"Come *on.*" I gave an insistent tug at his sleeve.

"I've seen you at the pub," Riordan said, and then, in a flash of recognition, his curious gaze turned into something sinister. He pointed at me. "*You.* You were at Shepherds."

I'd thought he might not remember, as I had simply faded into the background that day he and Colin had exchanged words in Reception, and he'd warned Colin to keep away from his father.

"That's where we're staying," I said, trying for an innocent tone, though I probably was no better at pretense than Alex was.

"Friends of Colin O'Toole, you are."

"Guests at the B&B," I said.

"Not much goes unnoticed in this town." Riordan's chuckle was more bitter than jovial. "I heard all about how O'Toole's good friend, an architect from the States, discovered the priest hole where the girl was hiding with her baby. Her bastard child."

I felt myself wince. He was talking about his brother-in-law's child. Surely he knew that. I was even more certain now that he blackmailed the doctor, found out about Jimmie and threatened to tell Norah Riordan. Wouldn't he have some feeling for the child? Probably not. If I was any judge of character, Lucas was a narcissist, incapable of love—or anything resembling affection.

"That's why we're here. I wanted to see the priest hole," Alex said. As it was the absolute truth, I hoped Riordan would assume we had no other motives. But he had a cagey look that I didn't trust. We just needed to *go.*

"Maybe you ought to see it then." Riordan took another step toward us. His voice, never friendly, was more menacing as he said, "How much do you know?"

There was the moment of decision that might mean *every-thing*. Fear began to course through my body. Should I keep feigning innocence, hoping Lucas might let us slink away? The glint in his eyes said not likely. Put up a fight? Not wise. Even as I wondered whether he had a weapon, he slipped his hand into the pocket of his jacket.

Instinct made me take a step backward. Riordan lunged and grabbed my arm.

Alex made a move toward him, shouting, "Take your hands off her!" but in that instant, Riordan was brandishing a blade—a scalpel. I didn't know *how* I knew it was a surgical scalpel, but I did. And I knew just as well that it was from the doctor's office, the weapon he had used to stab James Malone. Lucas had taken it from the woodpile. Why was it in the woodpile?

He jerked me toward him and twisted my arm behind my back.

"How much do you know?" he repeated, his mouth next to my ear, his hot breath on my cheek, the cold tip of the scalpel on my neck.

"About what?"

I knew the time for pretending was over. Maybe I was just buying time. But no one was coming to rescue us. Colin and Grace knew where we were, but it would be a long time before they'd worry about us.

"Don't be such a bitch." Riordan jerked my bent arm upward, and I yelped.

Alex flinched, as if he could feel my pain, but he remained remarkably calm. "Whatever we know, you can be sure Colin and Grace know it as well. They have information for the Guard. Your best bet is to flee if you can—before the authorities catch up with you. No reason to harm us. We're not the ones you should be afraid of."

"Nice speech, old man. You think I don't know about the *information*—that daft man's notepad."

"*New* information," Alex said with a trace of smugness. "About the call you made to Dr. Malone the night before you killed him."

I couldn't see Lucas's face, but from Alex's expression, I guessed that he'd struck a nerve. But was that the right move or a very dangerous one? My mind was spinning as I tried to work out what we ought to do. In the end, with a scalpel at my neck, I didn't have many choices. Nor did Alex. He wouldn't do anything to risk my life. Not on purpose. But standing up to Lucas Riordan wasn't working.

"Let's go see that priest hole," Lucas said.

The door was unlocked, as it had been all along. When Ian and I had been to the cottage, I was glad the Guards hadn't padlocked it; now I was wishing they had.

Lucas had the upper hand here, with me in tow, my arm twisted behind me and a scalpel that he seemed ready and willing to use. Given my situation, Alex followed instructions without resistance. And so we found ourselves inside the cottage, in the room where the priest hole could be accessed. I looked up into the corner where I knew the panel could be removed. Alex's gaze followed mine. The panel was inconspicuous, but I had told him where it was, above the sleeping loft. Lucas knew where it was, too, for he'd directed us to the room without any hesitation, and now he said, "Bloody good hiding place." Someone had given him details about the priest hole. Someone had told him about the notepad.

"You wanted to see the priest hole, old man, so go on up that ladder. It's in the corner," Lucas said.

"I don't see anything," Alex said.

Lucas thought about it. He jerked at my arm. "Tell him. You're the one who found it." He gave a twist that made me howl. "Tell him!"

"For God's sake, man!" Alex said. "That's not necessary. We're following your orders."

"Because you have no other choice," Lucas said. As a further reminder, he touched the scalpel to my cheek. "Tell him how to get in."

He was right. I had no choice. Alex climbed the ladder, taking time and care as could be expected of a man his age. He began to sound the boards. "Enough stalling!" Lucas said. "Every minute you stall, she gets a mark on her face," and he made a tiny scrape on my cheek. It was just a sting, but I knew there was blood. I swiped at it with my free hand and wiped my fingers on my pants.

Alex was focused on his task. He didn't seem to know what Lucas had done. "I'm doing the best I can!" he said. "It's been concealed for centuries. It's not easy to find."

"Tell him what to do," Lucas said, putting pressure on the arm behind my back.

I tried to remember what I'd done, how I was able to detect the particular board that was movable. Maybe two inches from the side wall, I instructed. Looked like trim.

Alex finally said, "All right, all right. Here it is." Another minute and he had the panel off. He sat back and wiped his brow.

"Good work, old man. Now you just stay put. We're coming up."

Lucas forced me up the ladder in front of him.

All of us in the loft—I thought it might collapse, and that might be good luck for Alex and me, but it didn't happen. The loft was solid.

Lucas examined the panel. The priests who had hidden in the secret chamber had no way of getting out on their own. Someone on the outside had to remove the panel. Lucas smiled—a maniacal smile, I thought. And he ordered Alex to climb into the hole.

Alex didn't obey immediately. "You will not get away with this," he said.

Lucas demanded our car keys, and I took the keys from the pocket of my jacket.

"I don't think you're a cold-blooded murderer," I said. "You never killed anyone before Dr. Malone, did you? I'll bet you didn't intend to kill him."

"Shut up!" To Alex, "Get into the damn hole!"

Alex climbed in. My blood ran cold when he looked down— and back at me.

I hesitated. "Don't do this, please," I said. One last appeal.

A moment after Alex had disappeared into the hole, Lucas shoved me through the opening and gave me another push. I landed on Alex. The light that came from the opening went out. Everything was black.

CHAPTER 28

I cried out in pain. I was sure my wrist was broken.

I had fallen on Alex with an *ooof!* He said he was all right and asked if I was hurt. I lied and said no. In this pitch dark hole, he couldn't see the pain etched in my face.

We scrambled, as much as it was possible to move, until I was able to steady myself. We had just enough space for both of us to stand upright. The stench was reminiscent of the worst restrooms in service stations on the back roads of Georgia, before interstate travel took over. But most terrifying of all was the absolute darkness. A cloying darkness, a suffocating blackness.

I spent a minute just getting my breath.

"We told Colin and Grace where we were going," Alex said. "They'll find us."

"Didn't Lucas think of that?" I said.

"He wasn't thinking clearly," Alex said.

"He didn't take my phone." I added. I unzipped an inside pocket of my jacket and retrieved the phone, punching buttons. Colin hadn't been able to get service on his phone until he was on the path, some distance from the cottage. Ian got service in the yard. We were in a black hole. I hadn't had great expectations. But nothing lit up. Was the battery was gone, too?

"Someone will find us," Alex said, his voice too consoling. It made me think *he* didn't believe it, that he was placating me, as if I were still a little girl.

I rubbed my wrist, trying to focus on our situation, our chances. What had Lucas hoped to gain by putting us here? Didn't it occur to him that we would have told someone where we were going? Was he just buying time? He had our car keys. I hadn't seen *his* car, so he must have walked from town. He planned to take ours, wherever he was going. If Colin and Grace came looking for us, they'd expect to see our car parked at the head of the trail. If they didn't see it, would they just go away? Lucas might leave the car somewhere else to throw off anyone trying to find us. I was sure someone would eventually come to the cottage, but it might be a long time. Too long. How long could we survive in here? Priests had survived in these secret hiding places for several days, but—I began to conjure up all the problems a long detention would create, and I refused to let my mind go there.

Alex and I stood shoulder to shoulder. We might be able to sit, maybe one of us at a time. Lying down would be impossible, even for one person and certainly not for two. Eventually, standing would become excruciatingly tiring.

"He could have killed us," I said.

"You said you didn't think he was a cold-blooded murderer. You're probably right."

"Maybe he just wanted to get away, and he had to be sure we were confined for a while."

"Not too long, we hope," Alex said.

My uncle's patience was admirable, but I wasn't wired to just wait and hope. I groped for the rungs of the ladder, to climb back up. Crying out when I moved my wrist, I finally had to tell Alex that I thought it was broken.

"Which one? And why did you say you weren't hurt?" he said.

"Left—better than my right—and I—don't know why. We can't do anything about it."

"You can keep it immobile. What are you trying to do?" He was scolding now, more like Alex. *That* was reassuring.

"Hoping against hope that I can loosen the panel," I said. I had to proceed slowly up the ladder. I finally reached the top and pounded as hard as I could, but it was no use. The board was secure. And climbing was not a good thing for my wrist. The pain was more intense when I came back down.

"You have a watch, don't you?" I said after a moment. I hadn't worn a watch in a while, since I'd come to depend on my phone for the time.

"Not one with a luminous dial," he said.

"I wonder how long we've been in here."

"Maybe half an hour. We'll be all right, Jordan. Come now, settle down."

Sometime later, I said. "I'm glad I'm not alone, Alex. That would be—unbearable."

"Me, too," he said.

"But if you weren't in here with me, you'd be looking for me," I said.

"Someone is looking for us—or will be, soon," he said.

It was the darkest dark I'd ever known. A sucking blackness that made it hard to breathe. Silence made it worse, so I talked.

"Not that Lucas Riordan would shed a tear if we didn't make it out of this place, but stabbing someone with a scalpel is something else," I said. "He didn't have it in him to do that."

"Shall we give him a medal?" Alex said.

"No, Alex, he's a *horrible* man who deserves to be locked up, but—I was just thinking about Dr. Malone's murder," I said. "Suppose Lucas just lost his temper, lost control, and grabbed what was handy, the scalpel—and before he knew it, his brother-in-law was dead. He did some fast thinking and realized Bridget would make a good suspect. Maybe he didn't think it all through, but he left the body out here to put the Guards on the wrong track."

"Yes," Alex said without much expression. I had advanced that theory earlier, but now that I'd seen Lucas with the scalpel, I could go farther with it.

"He hid the scalpel in the woodpile, thinking it would further implicate Bridget," I said.

"*Oh.*" Alex sounded more interested now.

"But when the officers came to question Bridget, they didn't find the scalpel. I heard Colin's account, and he didn't mention that they did a search. Sounded like they never really considered Bridget a suspect. Maybe because she was so frail," I said.

"Maybe because the doctor's car was not parked at the head of the trail, as it would've been if Bridget had stabbed him when he brought her out here the night before," Alex added.

"And then, later, the coroner said time of death was early morning. Magdala did provide an alibi for Bridget, whatever that was worth," I said. "So here's the new puzzler, Alex. Why did Lucas come out here today and take the scalpel from the woodpile?"

"He took it from the woodpile?"

"Didn't you see him do it?"

"No." Alex sighed. "I didn't put all of this together about the scalpel. My concern was simply that he didn't use it on you." I thought I detected a smile in his voice.

"I suppose he was going to get rid of it now, since it hadn't served his purpose."

"Implicating Bridget," Alex clarified.

"Yes. But why now? It has to be because of Mr. Sweeney's notepad."

"He did mention the notepad when he was ranting to us," Alex said. "But didn't you say Mr. Sweeney just got a look at the SUV? Maybe the driver's face, too, but it's not likely he'll be able to make an identification now." Alex paused and I could sense the wave of sadness. "Mr. Sweeney didn't write anything about seeing someone hide a scalpel in the woodpile, did he?"

"No, but Lucas might have thought he did."

We were quiet for a moment.

I was thinking that Lucas couldn't have known about the notepad until late last night—very late—after Colin gave it to Inspector Perone. I had not liked the Inspector, but the notion that he'd given information to Lucas was hard to accept. An inspector, tipping off a murderer? As improbable as a doctor getting his patients addicted to drugs.

"All he had to tell Lucas was, *There's an eyewitness.* Before he'd read through the notepad, when all he knew was what Colin had told him."

"All *who* had to tell Lucas?" Alex asked.

The sound and vibration from my zippered pocket jolted me. I dug for my phone. Incredibly, a row of numbers lit up, and I answered with a breathless "Hello!"

"Hello, Jordan, I am so glad you called. Only now did I—"

"Paul! Oh, Paul!"

"Are you all right, Jordan?"

Alex broke in. "Tell him to call the Guard. Hurry."

I stammered. "Call the Guard in Thurles. Alex and I are stuck in a priest hole. Lucas Riordan took our car. Paul? Are you there, Paul?"

I took the phone away from my ear. The screen had gone black. Alex had thought ahead. The phone had gone dead after a few seconds. I might've just hung onto Paul's voice. It had felt like a lifeline.

"I don't know if he got any of it," I said.

I slid down the wall and sat there on the nasty floor, balled up. Nothing to do but wait.

★   ★   ★   ★   ★

Time was hard to measure in that dark hole. It seemed longer than it probably was when Alex said, "Paul Broussard, I presume."

"Yes," I said. Alex was better at playing the waiting game than I was. After a minute, I said, "And yes, I had lunch with Paul in Dublin on Friday. You knew, didn't you?"

"I did not *know* anything," he said.

If Paul had lost the connection before he heard what I was saying, I wondered if he might call Shepherds. In Dublin I had told him the name of the B&B, and he could get the telephone number from their website. He had asked if I was all right. He would be curious. Wouldn't he?

More silence. "Are you thirsty, Alex? What I'd give for a glass of iced tea."

"Thanks for the reminder."

Time dragged on.

And then, the sounds from above brought me to my feet. The noise of the panel being removed. A voice. The Guard? But I couldn't shake the fear that if Lucas was back, he had come to kill us. I grabbed Alex's arm and stifled a groan. I had forgotten about my wrist.

The board came off, letting in a square of light. "Mrs. Mayfair? Mr. Carlyle?" A concerned voice. A face peering in. Not Lucas.

Water had never tasted so good. I drank a whole bottle in a few gulps, and a female Guard handed me another. I recognized her; she was the small woman who had helped to get Magdala out of the priest hole. She swung her thumb toward the back of the cottage and said, "There's a toilet back there in the edge of the bushes if you're needing one. It's not much, but it'll do." She'd spoken to me, it seemed, but both Alex and I answered that we could wait.

The Guards were kind. One of them examined my wrist and said, "Don't think it's a fracture, but looks like a bad sprain. You'll be needing to go to the A&E." He gave me a cloth to wipe my cheek. I'd forgotten that Lucas had nicked it. A little blood, a little soreness, but it could have been much worse. When I told the Guard that Lucas had used a scalpel, which was probably the murder weapon, he said, "You'll be wanting to tell Inspector Perone everything."

Inspector Perone. I didn't know what to think.

We went outside and stood in a patch of green under the alder tree, sipping on our water while the Inspector gave orders to other Guards. When he came over to us, leaving his people to check out the cottage and grounds, his first words were not to ask how we were. Maybe he determined by looking at us that we were all right. He said, "Seems you have some impressive contacts, Mrs. Mayfair."

"So Paul *did* hear what I was saying."

"Apparently he heard enough."

"I'm amazed we connected at all," I said. The service, the battery—it made no sense.

The female Guard who was standing by spoke up. "Maybe it was magic. I'm told the old woman, Magdala, was a believer in fairies and leprechauns, fanciful things like that."

"I would call it a miracle," Alex said.

There was actually a trace of warmth in Inspector Perone's smile. "You may be right, sir. Come now. We'll get you to the A&E."

He directed us to one of the two ATVs that had transported the Guards, and when we had squeezed into the seat, Inspector Perone himself slipped into the driver's position. We zipped along the rough path and came to the parked cars in no time.

Besides the four Guards back at the cottage, two others waited here. Quite an afternoon for the Thurles Guards.

Alex and I got into the back seat of Perone's car, a non-descript sedan. As he transported us to the emergency room, he asked what had happened back there, and we told him. Alex and I both supplied factual information, and I ventured some of my opinions about Lucas Riordan and his motives. Alex gave me one of those looks that said I was overstepping.

"Whether or not you arrest Lucas for murder, he has now stolen a car. That's a significant crime," I said.

"Yes, 'tis that," Perone said.

A little farther on, he said, "It was Garda Mallory."

I caught my breath. Perone may have realized that I'd suspected him as the leak. He turned his head just enough to cut his eyes at me. "I was surprised myself."

I said to Alex, who hadn't met Mallory, "Garda Mallory was one of the officers who interviewed Bridget. Colin liked him. He was with the Inspector at Shepherds last night."

"I won't excuse what he did, and he'll pay for it," Perone said, "but I think he just let himself be taken in by Lucas Riordan."

"What did he do, exactly?" Alex said. "I don't understand."

"Just kept Lucas informed of the investigation," Perone said. "Told him facts we hadn't made public, things we didn't want released."

"He wasn't suspicious of Lucas?" I asked.

"Y'know, the Riordans are a prominent family in Thurles." Perone echoed what Helen Prescott had said over and over. "When they ask for something, it's hard for some to say no."

"So Garda Mallory was just trying to impress Lucas?" I said.

"Something like that. I'm thinking Lucas rang up Mallory and asked for a favor. Mallory went to school with Norah Riordan—Norah Malone. Not that they would have been friends or anything like that." Perone's chuckle was sarcastic. "So Lucas says, 'My sister is distraught. Can't you tell us anything?' Might've started that way. We'll get to the bottom of it."

Alex was nodding but with an expression that said he was still trying to figure it out. "So Garda Mallory didn't *know* Lucas was the murderer?"

"I don't think he knew," Perone said.

"But he leaked something about Mr. Sweeney's notepad that made Lucas think the Guard was on to him," I speculated.

"I might have implied to Garda Mallory that the notepad revealed more than it did," Perone said. "No one at the station has read it but me."

"You suspected Mallory all along?" I asked.

"His Sergeant heard him on the phone a couple of times. Mallory has been known to talk too much, other times. Lack of boundaries, you know."

Colin had liked the man for that very reason, when the information Mallory gave was favorable to Bridget.

Inspector Perone got immediate medical attention for us at the A&E. Alex was "fine as old wine," in his words. Seems his blood pressure was a little high, but the pretty nurse who was taking care of him exclaimed, "Sure, why *wouldn't* it be!" Everyone by now seemed to know what had happened to us.

Inspector Perone, who must have been making calls, came by our exam cubicles before he departed. The privacy curtains were pulled between us, as a matter of protocol, but we were both fully dressed, and the Inspector was able to stand back from our exam tables and talk to both of us. He said Colin was on his way to take us to Shepherds. He had no news about our car but promised he would update us as soon as he knew anything.

"We're supposed to go to Dublin tomorrow and fly home Tuesday," I told Perone. For the first time, going home was not a sorrowful thought.

"One thing at a time," he said. "Finish up here, and get some rest. You'll make your flight."

Alex thanked him for rescuing us.

"Glad we could do it," he said. He gave me a meaningful look. "Be sure to thank the fellow in Paris."

I had already taken care of that. On our way to the emergency room, I had texted: *All OK. You saved my life again.*

Chapter 29

Scrubbing all reminders of the priest hole from my body was my first priority. Grace, who never missed a beat, insisted on running a load of laundry with the filthy clothes Alex and I had been wearing. I wondered if I'd ever wear those clothes again without feeling I was smothering.

Colin said Grace would have soup and bread on the table when we were clean and refreshed.

"Going above and beyond for us—again," I said.

"Ah, but you'll tell us everything that happened, play by play. That's part of the bargain," he said. His eyes were twinkling with the knowledge that the Guard was onto Lucas Riordan, that Lucas would be getting what he was due.

Later that night, over a supper of tasty potato soup and warm, crusty bread, we gave our account of the afternoon's events to Grace, Colin, and Patrick. A call came for Colin from Inspector Perone while we were having chocolate ice cream all around. When Colin returned to the table, he said, "The Inspector wants to interview Bridget tomorrow afternoon."

"He's going to Dublin, to the rehab center?" Grace said.

"Yes. I told him it would be fine, but I wanted a family member there, and he was agreeable. So I was wondering, Patrick, do you think Enya might be willing to help us out?"

Patrick's eyes widened, and I was sure I detected a spark of pleasure. "Enya? You'd want her to do that?"

"Why not? She's family, and she has no obligations there in

Dublin to take up her day, not that I know about."

"I think Bridget would like having Enya with her," Grace said.

Patrick pursed his lips and nodded, giving it some thought. "I'll ring her up and see what she says." He took one last bite of ice cream and left the table.

Colin winked, and Grace gave him an approving smile.

"The Inspector wants you to come to the station in the morning," Colin told Alex and me. "I said I'd have you there at nine o'clock. That's good, isn't it?"

We said yes. "I don't know what else we can tell him," I said.

"It's protocol," Alex said. "We'll need to give an official statement."

"I suppose they haven't found Lucas Riordan," I said.

"Nothing yet, but they'll get him."

"What are we going to do about our car?"

"That was another thing. Inspector Perone says he'll call the rental company and take care of things there, and he'll drive you to Dublin himself."

"Very thorough, isn't he?" Alex said.

"Not a bad sort." Colin took a big bite of ice cream.

After we had one last memorable Irish breakfast, Colin dropped us at the Garda station in Thurles, a modern facility, not too different from what one might expect in the States. We met in Inspector Perone's office, which I imagined was a courtesy. I was sure there were less comfortable interview rooms, but we were not being grilled. We simply went over the things we'd already told the Inspector on the way to the A&E. Protocol, as Alex had put it.

"Your car has been located," the Inspector said at the end of the interview, "but we can't get it back to you yet, of course, so I hope you don't mind making the trip to Dublin with me."

"You found Lucas?" I said.

"In Rosslare. He'd made arrangements to take the ferry to Cherbourg. Not surprising that he'd head for France. It's easy to disappear on the continent if you're trying to get lost." The Inspector was very matter of fact about it. All in a day's work. He stood up. "Thank you for coming in. Now I'll have someone drop you back at Shepherds. And if it's suitable with you, I'd like to leave for Dublin shortly after lunch. I think Colin has made arrangements for me to see his daughter at four o'clock."

Back to Shepherds to finish packing and say goodbye.

Grace was adamant that we needed to have a substantial lunch before we left. In the end, we agreed to a small salad, cheese, and bread—and tea. Grace made the best tea.

Several other guests were arriving that afternoon. The couple who had come in last night were Asian honeymooners from London—"not especially young," Grace said. "Around forty, I'd guess." They'd gathered brochures about sites in the area, and they seemed to have done a lot of research in advance. "As soon as I put out breakfast, they wrapped up some toast and jam, filled thermos bottles with hot tea, and went on their way," she said. "They were heading to the Cliffs of Moher."

A long moment passed before Alex spoke. "I hope you'll have some peace, with this new bunch of guests. Heaven knows you didn't get it with our group."

And then Colin came to tell us that Inspector Perone was waiting. He said, "I hate to see you leave us, but I think you must go before you do something awful to harm yourselves. Does your travel book require that you endanger your lives over and over, Alex?" He was right, that the longer we stayed, the more trouble we seemed to attract. Nevertheless, it was hard to go.

The Inspector was patient as we said our long, affectionate goodbyes and made promises to never ever lose touch again.

Inspector Perone drove fast on the M8. I missed the emerald countryside, the sheep and meadows and rock walls that we'd passed on side roads to Shepherds nearly two weeks ago, but this trip to Dublin was not for sightseeing.

Unlike our short drive to the A&E, when Alex and I both rode in the back seat, this time the Inspector indicated that I should take the passenger's seat. He wanted to know if my wrist was painful. He asked us how long our flight would be and said he'd never been to the States but he and his wife had considered a trip to New York to celebrate their twenty-fifth wedding anniversary. Inspector Perone was quite a different fellow in this setting.

Different also was his willingness to talk about the murder case. Once he was over his initial reticence with us, he must have decided he didn't have to be so closed-mouthed, since we'd be leaving Ireland in less than twenty-four hours and surely nothing he'd tell us would come back to haunt him.

"Lucas abandoned your car at a lodge in Killnick, not far from Rosslare Harbour," he said. "Once the car was located, it wasn't any grand piece of detective work to figure out that Lucas was laying low in Rosslare until time for the ferry to depart. He's in custody in Rosslare." Perone gave a chuckle. "I would've taken Lucas to be more clever than that, but then I suppose he's a novice when it comes to the arrangements hardened criminals make all the time."

"Not a cold-blooded murderer." Alex repeated my words.

"I expect not, but one thing's for sure. Lucas Riordan was not the model citizen people believed he was. Anyone who would harm his own father with drugs! Dr. Malone, too, who was supposed to be such a fine man." The Inspector's voice grew more contemptuous with each word, his dark eyebrows pulling together in an angry scowl.

My theory about how Lucas and the doctor were drugging Liam Riordan was not far from what Inspector Perone now knew to be the truth. Norah Malone had supplied the missing details.

"I had a long chat with Mrs. Malone last night. She'd come to the point people often get to, where they have to tell everything," Perone said. She'd wondered for some time why Dr. Malone's regimen for treating her father's vague illness was only making him worse, but she hadn't suspected that her brother had anything to do with it. She finally had it out with Dr. Malone—on the phone, the night Bridget came to his door—and that was when he told her Lucas was behind the scheme. Bottom line: Lucas didn't want Liam Riordan back in the bank.

"I've yet to understand how Lucas could have forced the doctor to commit malpractice, but we'll get to the bottom of it," Perone said.

So Norah Malone hadn't exactly told *everything* she knew. She hadn't revealed that Dr. Malone had a child, Little Jimmie, Bridget's child, which must have been what Lucas held over the doctor's head.

She hadn't confronted Lucas. The Inspector explained that her brother had always been the dominant one. " 'The Alpha dog,' she called him," Perone said. "The doctor was dead, their father's health was improving—she didn't want any of it to come out."

"Did she suspect Lucas had killed her husband?" I asked.

"She said no." The Inspector gave a twitch of his shoulders, as if to convey his belief that she might have had an inkling. "She said not until yesterday, when Lucas lost his bearings. Up until then, we had nothing on him."

"But you suspected him?" I said.

"What we knew was that the murder occurred in the doctor's office, and the weapon was a scalpel. No evidence of forced entry. No junkie breaking in or anything like that. The doctor had come downstairs and let someone into his office very early in the morning. Time of death was before five a.m. We had to ask who he might have admitted at that hour—and why. Likely it was someone he knew very well. His family, naturally, were persons of interest."

A light rain had started to fall. The Inspector slowed down, but he was still driving much faster than I would've considered safe.

Alex, who had been quiet in the back seat, spoke up. "You said you didn't really have anything on Lucas until he—what was it you said? Lost his bearings yesterday?"

"After Garda Mallory informed him that someone had been at Red Stag Crossing the morning of Dr. Malone's death and had seen the killer. The man who kept the notepad."

"Seamus Sweeney," Alex said.

"Mallory probably did us a favor, as it turns out, though at his own expense, I'm afraid."

The Inspector put it all together for us at last. Lucas received that call from Mallory late Saturday night. He must have spent a tormented night, fearing the Guards would be coming for him, trying to work out a plan. The next morning while Norah was at Mass, he went to the bank and withdrew sufficient funds for a long trip. By the time Norah returned from Mass, he was feeling some relief. The Guards hadn't shown up at the Riordan house, but he believed it was just a matter of time, since he'd been told there was an eyewitness. He made a full confession to Norah, told how he'd used Dr. Malone to harm their father—and he told her what happened that early morning in Dr. Malone's office. He begged her forgiveness and asked her to give him time to get away from Thurles. "It was the first time she'd ever seen Lucas contrite, like that, apparently," the Inspector said. One thing Lucas decided to take care of became his undoing. He had hidden the scalpel in the woodpile at Magdala's cottage, and he wanted to get rid of it.

"He'd planned to go straight to the train station from Red Stag Crossing. It wasn't a bad plan. I had no reason to look for him at that point, so he could go to Dublin and then fly to anywhere in the world. But a couple of Americans upset his plan," the Inspector said.

"We saw him with the scalpel," I said. "And he panicked."

"Norah Malone told you all of this last night?" Alex said.

"Most of it. You completed the story with what happened out at the cottage."

"You believe her?" Alex asked.

He nodded slowly. "I don't think she had anything to do with the murder or that she participated in the scheme to dope her father," he said.

As unpleasant as she'd been to Grace that day in front of the office, I couldn't help feeling sorry for her, for the husband who cheated on her and the rotten brother she had.

"There is one thing, though," the Inspector said, "that we'll need to sort out. Lucas told Norah that he went to Dr. Malone's office that early morning because the doctor had called *him*. Dr. Malone had said he was finished supplying the drugs for Liam, but when he called late in the night, Lucas thought he'd changed his mind. The doctor said he must come to the office while it was still dark. So Lucas did as he was asked, and when he went inside the office, which was unlocked, Dr. Malone tried to kill him. Lucas was the stronger man."

"What?" I cried.

"You're saying Lucas told his sister he killed her husband in self-defense," Alex said.

"That's what she said." The Inspector took a deep breath. "We'll get to the bottom of it."

"I don't know what to believe about the murder," I said, when Alex and I were seated in the hotel dining room that night.

"It's not our problem to solve," Alex said.

"Do you think Dr. Malone *really* tried to kill Lucas Riordan, or was that story just a way Lucas had of gaining his sister's sympathy?"

"Really, Jordan, it doesn't matter what I think. Are you drinking wine, or are you still on painkillers?"

"Both," I said.

"And you were the one who lectured me about mixing my medications!" Alex said.

"You feel better now, don't you?"

"Actually, I do," he said.

Alex and I both ordered one of the specials, monkfish with saffron sauce, which came with a small salad and creamed potatoes. Over our salads we talked about Liam Riordan and how hard it would surely be for him, learning that his own son had been responsible for his illness. According to the Inspector, who had results from the pill bottles Norah Malone had given him, Liam was taking massive doses of Zoloft, an antidepressant, along with the prescriptions he was already taking for his heart. For a man who had already had one heart attack, the results could have been fatal.

One by one, the guests at Shepherds figured into our conversation.

"I'll definitely send Ian an e-mail about—yesterday," I said. I couldn't bring myself to say the words that described being confined in the priest hole for what was only a couple of hours but had seemed like so much longer.

"You might mention the shamrocks to him," Alex said.

292

"The shamrocks?"

"Didn't you notice? Under the tree, the patch of shamrocks. I noticed it when I was drinking water, after the Guards had come. I remembered Ian's story. The daughter ran from the house when Cromwell's men killed her father, and they shot her as well. Where she bled and died, a shamrock patch grew."

I remembered. "I will tell Ian," I said.

We finished another delightful Irish meal, and Alex and I were both ready to turn in early. I said, "I promised Paul Broussard I'd call tonight, when I had some time to talk. He deserves a full account. We've only been texting."

"You've forgiven him, then?" Alex said. "For standing you up in Atlanta?"

"I suppose I have to forgive him," I said, "since he saved our lives."

CHAPTER 30

The July heat in Savannah was oppressive. Even at six o'clock in the evening, the temperature was ninety-two, with a sweltering sixty-seven percent humidity. Sometimes, just out of curiosity, I checked the weather app on my phone to see what it was like in Thurles. Today the temperature there was seventy degrees. I thought about Ireland often, these weeks since I'd been home.

Tonight I was thinking about Provence, too, as I would be driving to Atlanta for Alex's book signing tomorrow. He was launching the first of his travel guides, the product of our trip to Provence last year, in an independent bookstore owned by one of his oldest friends. The tiny venue would be bursting at the seams, no doubt. Alex had many friends and many more acquaintances. He had not said so, exactly, but I had the sense that the little bookstore *needed* this lavish event—it would be lavish, with champagne and catering along a Provencal theme—and Alex's loyalty to his friends was unfailing.

I warmed a plate of pasta from earlier in the week, tossed a small salad, and poured a tall glass of iced tea. It was Catherine's night to volunteer at the free clinic. Julie was going out with friends after work. Yes, Julie had a job! At a bike shop. Not what she'd hoped for, with her degree from Cornell, but it provided a regular paycheck. I took my dinner to the sunroom and settled at my desk. The sunroom was an addition across the back of my century-old house on Abercorn. Huge white oaks draped with

Spanish moss shaded the backyard. *Shade* didn't mean *cool*, not on an evening like this, summer in full swing. My backyard was best enjoyed from behind a wall of glass. Flame azaleas, crape myrtle, hydrangea, wisteria, and bougainvillea—the native plants flourished in the Savannah climate. They did look a little thirsty tonight, though.

Winston stretched out under the desk. I kicked off my shoes and ran my foot along his back. I turned on the computer and let it go through its gyrations as I checked my iPhone for texts. Nothing recent. I was feeling a little low—*lonely*, I supposed. Why, I couldn't say. Being alone was nothing new to me. Maybe it was just post-vacation letdown, like the blues you get after Christmas, although my vacation, those extraordinary two weeks in Ireland, had ended more than a month ago.

The phone startled me with its jingle, and Drew's number appeared. I was smiling when I answered. Drew said, "You sound cheery!" I couldn't tell him what I was thinking, that I must have been feeling *really* blue if a call from my brother lifted my spirits.

"You win," he said a minute later. "I've decided to go with you."

"Oh."

"That's all you have to say? Oh?"

"I'm glad, and—most important—Alex will be glad. It would've hurt his feelings if you didn't show up at his book signing."

"Alex isn't like that, Jordie," Drew said. "But I've switched some things around, so I can go. What time do you want to leave? Your car or mine?"

"I suppose Walter Sutton cancelled sailing on Hilton Head?"

"Happens he did have to cancel tomorrow, but he's still counting on meeting you Saturday night," Drew went on. "Alligator Soul all right with you? I'll make reservations."

I sighed noisily for his benefit. "Sure." It was business. We still hoped to get some work from Walter Sutton.

"You know he wants to pin you down about flying up to Ohio before they start filming the documentary."

Something knotted in my stomach.

"I can't understand why you're not more excited about going up there," Drew said. "I think it's way cool that he invited us. Not everybody gets a chance to go inside a hidden room that was a stop on the Underground Railroad."

"I know." Maybe someday I would tell my brother how Alex and I were stuffed into the priest hole, but the time had not presented itself. Going into the secret chamber in an Ohio farmhouse, with people all around, wouldn't be anything like the black hole in Magdala's cottage—or not anything like it was in the mid-1800s when lives were at stake, to be sure—but the thought of a confined space still spooked me. I realized my breathing was shallow. Drew hadn't paid attention, though. I took a cleansing breath. "Let's talk about it Saturday night."

"Good. Now what about tomorrow?"

We finalized our plans. I would drive to Atlanta. If Drew was supposed to come by for me, chances were he'd be dreadfully late and we would fight all the way there.

He was reminding me of something work-related that I didn't want to hear when I pulled up my e-mail. "See you tomorrow, Drew," I said, and rang off. Sisters can do that to brothers.

There was an e-mail from Grace.

Jabbing some greens with my fork, I began to read. It was a lengthy e-mail, reminding me of the kind of letters people used to write—newsy and full of personality.

Mr. Sweeney had lived. He'd gone to the National Rehabilitation Hospital in Dublin, a facility specializing in treatment of brain injuries. Apparently he had a sister who was seeing to his needs. Colin had met her when he had visited Mr. Sweeney, and she had told him that her brother was always difficult and they'd never been close, but now he was easy to love. She seemed most attentive. Colin reported that "he doesn't say a word, but he smiles and nods, and though it wouldn't be right to say he's happy in that state, he does not seem in any way troubled or uncomfortable." I could hear Colin, his lilting words. Grace had added: "Very strange, the way things turn out, isn't it?"

Helen and Charles had spent a night at Shepherds on their way to the Irish Open in Cork. Grace said they continued their bickering but Charles generally seemed more affectionate. Helen had confided to Grace that one of their investments had taken off in a surprising way, and it looked like Charles might not have to go to work after all. How glad they were that he didn't get mixed up in a scheme with Lucas Riordan!

Ian had e-mailed Grace and Colin, thanking them for their kindness, and had mentioned that Molly was accepting a position as a music teacher at a heritage school in Dublin. "Where the children learn the Irish language and culture," Grace wrote, "as in the performance you saw of schoolchildren from Thurles." I had kept up with Ian's website myself, and we had become Facebook friends, so I also knew that he and Molly had been on holiday together to a music festival in Wicklow. Somewhat surprising to me that he continued to put his private life "out there" on social media, after the experience with Mr. Sweeney.

My stomach suddenly felt unsettled as I read, "Lucas Riordan is awaiting trial for manslaughter, and the case is still much debated in Thurles." Lucas Riordan. I felt a chill, remembering the foul, suffocating priest hole. I pushed aside my plate and kept reading. The general feeling in town, Grace wrote, was that there was nothing to Lucas's self-defense story. So *that*—what Inspector Perone had told us on the way to Dublin—had come out. Secrets were plentiful in Thurles, but so was gossip, I thought with a smile. Though the whole town knew about the way Liam Riordan was drugged, it had not caused a backlash against Dr. Malone, who had done everything for his patients from delivering their babies to holding the hands of their dying elders. "People don't forget those things, and they don't know that Dr. Malone had a dark side to him," Grace said. Most residents of Thurles hoped Lucas would be convicted, but they worried that the case might be too circumstantial.

The bright side was that Liam Riordan was healthy again and back to running the bank, and he had been generous, working with Grace and Colin to meet their debt burden. "Shepherds is having our best season ever, booked solid most of the time," Grace said.

Enya was back. She and Patrick were still living at Shepherds, but the prospect of finding their own place had done wonders for Enya's frame of mind. She seemed to thoroughly enjoy looking at rental properties. Rentals were not in great supply in Thurles, and Enya was very selective, looking for the perfect one, but "as long as she's not discouraged, we are all happy," Grace wrote. Even Patrick commented that Enya was in no particular hurry to leave Shepherds.

And the very best news of all—Bridget had finished her treatment. She was home.

"She told us everything, Jordan, and I thank you from the bottom of my heart for letting her confide in you at that confusing time," Grace said. "Colin and I did speculate about James Malone when Bridget got pregnant. As time went on, the doctor handled it all in such a way that we felt sure he knew who the man was but was keeping Bridget's secret, being a friend to her. He was very manipulative—and we never imagined the terrible thing he was doing with prescription drugs. But what matters now is that Bridget is doing so well, and you should see her and Jimmie together."

Grace ended with an apology that it had taken so long for her to e-mail. "Do you Skype or Facetime?" she asked. "Wouldn't that be fun to do sometime?"

"Definitely!" I said out loud as I closed the message.

Winston was delighted when we went outside to water my plants. Evening was the payoff after a blistering Savannah day. As rosy twilight melted into a soft darkness and lightning bugs begin to flicker, a hint of a breeze began to move the perfumed air across my skin. I leashed Winston and we took a short walk around the neighborhood. Earlier than usual, I was yawning. "Won't make it through the news tonight," I told Winston, back in my bedroom. I closed the overnight bag I'd packed for Atlanta. Thinking about Alex's big event, about his travel books, our trip to Provence, our trip to Ireland, I suddenly wanted to hear my uncle's voice. I decided to call. He always stayed up past eleven to get the headline news.

I told him what Grace had reported—most of it. Bridget's secret was not generally known, and it was not my place to tell. No doubt Alex was glad to know that Colin had seen Mr. Sweeney, but he didn't say much, just "Poor man," prompting me to move on to a brighter topic. I directed the conversation to his book signing.

"My living room is full of flowers," he said. He'd received deliveries from his publisher, his agent, and friends who were not able to attend, even my daughter Claire from Santa Fe. Good for her! "And a most exquisite basket I could hardly lift that featured lavender and sunflowers, along with a bottle of a fine Bordeaux," Alex said. "It must have been the most challenging order the little flower shop here in Buckhead had ever received. The woman who delivered the basket went on and on about the Frenchman's explicit instructions."

"Nice." I tried not to sound too smug. I didn't say who had given the Frenchman Alex's address or recommended the little flower shop in Buckhead.

"Paul Broussard is an exceptional man, Jordan," Alex said. "I'm sorry I didn't see that in the beginning. And when the call from him saved our lives—I can't quite get over that."

I let him go on a bit longer and then said it was getting late. "We'll talk tomorrow," I said. "Just one more question. Where are we going next?"

"Ah, I've been thinking about that. But it's getting late. We'll talk tomorrow," Alex said.

Now I was wide awake.

ABOUT THE AUTHOR

Phyllis Gobbell is the author of *Pursuit in Provence*—the first Jordan Mayfair mystery—and co-author of two true-crime books based on high-profile murders in Nashville, Tennessee: *An Unfinished Canvas* with Michael Glasgow (Berkley, 2007) and *Season of Darkness* with Douglas Jones (Berkley, 2010). She was interviewed on *Discovery ID*'s "Deadly Sins," discussing the murder case in *An Unfinished Canvas*. Her narrative, "Lost Innocence," was published in the anthology *Masters of True Crime* (Prometheus, 2012). She has received awards in both fiction and nonfiction, including Tennessee's Individual Artist Literary Award and a nomination for the Pushcart Prize for short fiction. An associate professor of English at Nashville State Community College, she teaches writing and literature.